ONLY GOD CAN
SEPARATE US

ONLY GOD CAN SEPARATE US

THIS BOOK IS PART THREE OF A
TETRALOGY SERIES. IT IS THE
CONTINUATION OF " I'LL CONVINCE
HIM OF MY INNOCENCE" PART ONE &
TWO BY HEMCHAND SINGH

HEMCHAND SINGH

Copyright © 2017 Hemchand Singh
Published by Hemchand Singh

Designed by Vince Pannullo
Printed in the United States of America by RJ Communications.

ISBN: 978-0-9909343-3-2
EPUB: 978-0-9909343-4-9

CHAPTER ONE

FOURTEEN MONTHS LATER

IT was a pleasant Monday morning at work in the office. Prastan sat in his chair with both hands folded at the back of his head as he gazed at the ceiling into nothingness.

Mark whispered at Jannet, "What's the matter with Prastan? He seemed to be in a different world."

Jannet replied, "I don't know, but I wish I knew what's bothering him," and decided to pay more attention at her husband.

Joe, who always had the weird sense of humor, asked, "Jannet, what's the matter with Prastan? Have you slept in another room last night?"

Jannet whispered at Joe, "Shut up, Joe. It seemed worse than that; it seemed like something is bothering him."

Joe asked, "Did you give him a hard time?" and he pressed his hands against his mouth not to reveal his smile.

Jannet said, "Watch your mouth, watch your mouth. Everything was fine last night. He never did this before; perhaps, he's thinking of something. So don't look at me." She gently approached Prastan from behind with her arms wrapped around his neck and then whispered in his ear, "What's the matter, Prastan? I have never seen you like this before. Is everything okay with you?"

He replied, "I am okay, Jannet. But—"

Jannet asked, "But what?" she demanded an answer while trying to cheer him up by rubbing his head.

Mark and Joe went and stood beside them. Prastan looked upon them and said, "What is the matter with all of you? Why are your faces filled with sadness?"

Mark and Joe replied in one voice, "Because your problem is our problem."

Prastan said, "Okay, I know. Now, tell me something that I don't know."

Jannet said, "How about you tell us something that we don't know."

Prastan replied, "Okay, have you realized it's been over a year since we had any contact with Charles, Angie, Mike, Peter, Paul, and Rick? It obvious, we have forgotten them completely and turned our back on them, consumed by our businesses; our thoughts have gone blank on them, as if we have forgotton our past journey in this life."

Jannet said, "Don't say that, Prastan. We will never forget our past."

Mark added, "Prastan, we will never forget our past, though, it seems like we have forgotten it."

Joe added, "Why don't we visit them sometime, Prastan?"

Jannet supported, "Joe is right, Prastan. We should give them a surprise visit someday."

Mark replied, "Great suggestion, Jannet. We should spend a day or two with them. What do you think, Prastan? Say something."

Jannet urged, "Yes, Prastan, let's go spend a week with them."

Prastan replied, "Okay, we are going next week and we will spend the entire week with them." Shortly after, Prastan called Frankie and George at the office. He said, "Have a seat, gentlemen."

Frankie asked, "Did something wrong, Prastan?" George asked as well, "Did something wrong, Prastan? We have never been called to the office before."

Prastan said, "Nothing wrong, gentlemen. George, next week I want you to manage the entire farm. And make sure you keep all your records up to date."

George, without any question replied, "Okay Prastan, I'll do my best; you may trust me and count on me."

Prastan said, "I already did that when I bought this company." He then turned at Frankie and said, "Frankie, next week you will be in this office all by yourself, and make sure you keep all your records up to date, okay?"

Frankie replied, "Trust me, Prastan."

Prastan said, "I did that a long time ago, Frankie."

Frankie and George were in wonderland when Jannet broke the peculiar, "We are going on a week of vacation, guys."

Prastan said, "That's it, guys. You may go now."

Prastan picked the phone and called Mike. Mike wasn't around. Angie picked up the phone. "Hello, hello."

Prastan asked, "Angie, is that you?"

Angie said, "Hi, Prastan, yes, it's me, it's really me." Prastan put the phone on speaker so that everyone could hear the conversation.

Prastan asked, "How is everyone? Give them our regards."

Angie said, "I will, Prastan. We over here really thought that you guys forgot us. It's been almost a year now."

Prastan said, "That true, but we always remembered you guys. How is Charles doing?"

Angie did not answer the question. She hesitated for a little while and was crying on the phone.

Jannet said, "Hi Angie, It's me, Jannet."

Angie said, "Hi Jannet, it's so nice hearing from you after so long."

Jannet said, "I know, girl. So how is everything?"

Angie said, "Not too good. When problems hit, they hit from all directions at the same time."

Jannet asked, "What are you saying, Angie? What sort of problems you guys having over there? Don't tell me those bullies again."

Angie said, "We have never seen those bullies again. But our problem over here is worse than that."

Prastan asked, "What problem you guys having,

Angie? Stop crying and talk to me. Tell me what's going on."

Angie said, "Our biggest problem over here is Charles became very sick six months after we got married. He was unable to do his business and within six months we lost everything.

Our house is currently in foreclosure because all the money we had, we spent it on doctors to restore his health. So I have no choice to work with daddy in his restaurant." Jannet said, "Oh my God. We are so sorry to hear this," and placed both of her hands on her mouth.

Prastan asked, "How is Charles doing now?"

Angie answered, "He's getting better. But he cannot work; he's too shaky."

Prastan said, "I am so sorry to hear this. Where is Mike?"

Angie answered, "Daddy went to buy liquor and beer for the restaurant."

Prastan asked, "How are the boys Peter, Paul, and Rick doing?"

Angie replied, "I haven't seen them for almost a month now. They are facing some financial hardship as well."

Prastan asked, "And what would that be, Angie?"

Angie replied, "They have problems with their boat, I guess it's leaking. They need a new boat, I assume, and they don't have the money to buy a boat. We aren't in a position to help them. I'm so sorry."

Jannet said, "Oh my God. I am so sorry to hear all of this."

Prastan said, "Maybe that the reason why they didn't visit us. Angie, we are very sorry to hear of those problems that you guys having over there. Give everyone our sympathy and regards. Mark, Joe, Jannet, and I are coming over Monday. We will spend a whole week with you guys. Tell your dad that we will stay at his place. You think that that will be okay to stay by your dad for a week?"

Angie said, "Sure, he'll be so glad. I am so glad that you guys are coming over. Everyone will be happy but, how will you cross over?"

Prastan said, "Don't worry. I will take care of that. We want to see you, Charles, and all the boys Monday at your dad's restaurant."

The week went by very busy and profitable. Early on Monday morning Prastan, Jannet, Mark, and Joe went to Allgreen's beach. The beach is not a stranger to them anymore. At the horizon across the river, the sun commenced its journey towards the sky slowly leaving the earth beneath. The sun's reflection reflected across the surface of the water like a streak of flame. Jannet recalled her past and momentarily remembered Prastan's poetry and smiled inwardly in appreciation.

Joe looked at Mark and smiled.

Mark said, "Why are you smiling at me? Do I look like a girl to you? Never mind, share it with me." Prastan and Jannet were listening to their conversations and decided to pay more attention to what is going on. As they headed their way towards the boating dock, Jannet asked, "How far is the dock, Prastan? It seems like we'll never get there."

Prastan replied, "It's less than a mile from here. Don't tell me you just started and have already given up on me."

Joe added, "Come on Jannet. You did this before, and you can do it again."

Jannet said, "Who said I am giving up on you guys? I can handle it, I am a tough girl. I am not lazy."

Mark said, "Bet, you are." Hearing this Prastan smiled.

As the wind swept slowly across the river, it damped softly and gently upon their faces. Birds flew above, whistling and swaying with the wind. The sun climbed slowly. The morning became brighter and brighter.

Mark asked, "Joe, why were you smiling at me?"

Jannet said, "There goes it again, Prastan."

Prastan whispered, "Shu!"

Joe said, "Smiling at you. Even if you were a girl I wouldn't smiled at you."

Mark asked, "Why not?"

Joe replied, "Because you are not that good looking like me."

Jannet said, "There it goes." Prastan glanced at her and placed his right finger on his lips.

Mark said, "You said I am not good looking. When that customer came in last week, she was admiring me and not you. Why? Why? Say something; I bet you can't because, she found me more handsome and attractive than you."

Jannet said, "Oh my God, please give me fate with them."

Joe said, "I was smiling because I remembered when Jannet and I were looking for Prastan. She said, I am so tired, my feet hurt. She sat and didn't want to get up. I had to pull her up."

Prastan whispered, "Is that true, Jannet? You had just said that you are a tough girl."

Jannet answered, "It's true, but that doesn't mean that I am not a tough girl; I am tough."

Prastan held her around her arms and said, "You are a tough girl."

Within ten minutes they reached the boating dock. While Mark, Joe, and Jannet stood on the beach admiring the morning, Prastan went in the dock office and made all arrangements to cross the river.

The boat's captain said, "Okay Prastan, time to rock the boat and slide away." This was his usual billboard slogan.

Prastan said, "You're very funny, captain."

The captain said, "Everyone says the same thing."

Prastan came out the office door and shouted, "Come on guys let's go."

Mark said, "That was fast."

Joe said, "You know him better."

Jannet said, "That's him. That's my man, he talk his way out very fast. God only knows how he did that."

They went in the boat. This boat was quite unlike the fishing boat. The captain was at the front at the steering wheel. The center of the boat had three rows of seats, each row capable of seating four passengers. Joe occupied the front seat all by himself. Mark occupied the middle seat while Jannet and Prastan occupied the rear seat. With the roaring of the engine the captain could hardly overhear passengers' conversations.

Mark asked, "How much he charged to cross us over Prastan?"

Joe asked, "What did you say, Mark?"

Mark replied. "I said nothing to you, so don't you worry. I only asked Prastan how much this crossing cost us."

Prastan said, "Two hundred bucks, Mark."

Joe shouted, "What did Prastan said, Mark? How much"

Mark said, "Two hundred bucks."

Joe said, "That's too much. Jannet and I paid one hundred fifty bucks. Wait, I am not hear everything. May I come and sit near you?"

Mark said, "No, stay your butt just there. You are too inquisitive, too nosy. You want to know everything. Besides, you rushed for the front seat, so stay your butt just there."

Jannet and Prastan started to laugh.

Jannet said, "Isn't that too much, Prastan?"

Joe asked, "What did you say, Jannet? What did Jannet say, Mark?"

Mark said, "Oh my God, you're making me sick now. Come sit your butt here. I am not an interpreter." Joe was awaiting that opportunity, and without any hesitation he immediately jumped over and sat beside Mark.

Joe asked, "What did you say, Jannet?"

Jannet said, "I told Prastan, two hundred bucks is too much."

Joe said, "Now I can hear everything. Yes, Prastan, two hundred bucks is too much."

Prastan said, "You guys paid one hundred fifty bucks for two of you. That is seventy five bucks for each person. I paid two hundred bucks for four persons. That is fifty bucks per person."

Joe said, "You see what I mean, Jannet. He's good, he's smart. Your husband is very smart, Jannet."

Jannet said, "I know, I know."

Prastan saluted with his right hand and said, "Oh thank you guys so much for the compliment."

Jannet said, "Although this river is a memory for me, for some reason, I enjoyed crossing it."

Joe said, "I know why."

Jannet asked, "Why, Joe?"

Joe answered, "Do you remember two guys named

Chuck and Vick?" Of course, he was relating to Jannet and himself.

Jannet said, "Yes, I do."

Joe said, "Once you remember, this river will always be a memory to you."

Prastan said, "What should I say, it's a memory for me also." This he said while he hugged Jannet.

The captain turned around and noticed Prastan hugging her. He asked, "Is she scared? We should be there in the next five minutes. Hold on, pretty girl." He hesitated for a few seconds. "You truly deserved it." They finally reached the shore.

The captain said, "Prastan, if you need me, call me at this number."

Prastan said, "Thank you very much, Captain. If you don't hear from me, that doesn't mean that I forgot you."

The captain said, "Thanks, Prastan. Now you guys take good care of each other."

Not too far away from where they disembarked, dozens of boats parked on a lot were marked for sale. Prastan looked at the boat.

Jannet said, "It isn't a bad idea what you have in your mind, Prastan. Wonder what price they are selling for?"

Prastan asked, "How do you read my mind, Jannet?"

Jannet replied, "Because I am your wife. Did I answer your question?"

Prastan said, "Absolutely Jannet, you really did."

Joe asked, "Why did the captain say, 'Hold on pretty girl'? You truly deserved it."

Mark said, "Stupid, he meant that Jannet is a very pretty girl and Prastan is a very handsome guy, so they deserve each other, as simple as that. Is that so hard for you to get?"

Prastan said, "It cost us nothing to find out the price, Jannet. Let's go and check it out."

Joe said, "Look at this boat. This is exactly like the one the boys have."

Jannet said, "Not bad for $900.00 bucks. Oh, look over here at this one, for $1,200.00 bucks; you cannot go wrong. This is the perfect boat for Peter, Paul, and Rick; they will be glad to have a boat like this. What do you think, Joe?"

Joe replied, "I think that they will go crazy if they have a boat like this. What do you think, Mark?"

Mark said, "Who wouldn't go crazy for a boat like this?"

Jannet said, "Hey, Prastan, what do you think?"

Prastan replied, "I know, let's buy it for them."

Jannet smiled at Prastan and asked, "How did you read my mind?"

Prastan replied, "Because I am your husband. Did I answer your question?"

Jannet, Mark and Joe at the same time in one voice said, "Absolutely, Prastan. You really did."

Prastan said, "Really, I want all of you to be very

honest with me. Do you guys think that they will like this boat?"

Everyone at the same time in one voice, replied, " Definitely."

Jannet emphasized strongly, "This boat is a modernized boat, well equipped, not like the junky boat they have right now. Oh my God, I should not have said that."

Inwardly, Prastan knew that the boat was a very nice boat. Jannet also knew that Prastan knew that the boat was a nice boat. And she also knew that Prastan was trying to have everyone's opinion.

Prastan announced, "Okay, let's do it."

They were the first customers of the day. The sales agent noticed that they seemed very interested.

He asked politely, "You guys looking for something special? What are you guys looking for, a sport boat or a fishing boat?"

Prastan answered, "We are planning to buy a fishing boat, maybe, in the next week or two, but right now we are shopping around for the best deal in town."

He hesitated for a little while and then continued, "This little town has many boats dealership"

The sale's agent said, "That's true, but if you like something here. I'll do my best for you. I will guarantee you that I will beat any other dealership price in town."

Joe said, "Really?"

The agent said, "You bet."

Jannet said, "Sound promising."

Prastan asked, "Mister, is this the best price for this boat—$1,200.00?"

The agent replied, "For a boat like this, you cannot go wrong. Yes, this is the best price."

Prastan said, "Hey Mark, the first place we went that boat is exactly like this one and they were asking for $1,000.00 bucks." He turned around, gazing for a little while and then asked, "Mister, when was this boat built?" He pulled one on him.

The agent had no clue when the boat was built.

He honestly replied, "As a matter of fact, I really don't know, but it costs me nothing to check it out for you."

Prastan answered, "Oh, don't even bother." This he said pretending as if he's no longer interested and he made a slight attempt to walk away.

The agent noticed that Prastan was not interested in the boat any more. He thought maybe because of the price and had decided to reduce the price. He said, "Sir, if you are interested, I can give you for $1,100.00."

Jannet, Mark and Joe smiled inwardly, but they knew Prastan would try to beat the price as low as possible, so they kept their mouths shut.

Prastan asked, "You guys do financing here?"

The agent replied, "If you're going to buy it, I can work out a financing plan for you."

Prastan asked, "Assuming I buy it cash. Will it be the same price?"

The agent answered, "Well, that is the bottom price, I don't think I can go any lower than this."

Prastan said, "I'll give you $1,000.00 cash. Here is my business card. If you are interesting in making a deal, call me at this number," and once again pretended as if he was going to walk away from the deal. He raised his head looked at the direction of the nearby boat's dealership. He was trying to impress the agent that his next move from here was to the next dealership to shop.

The agent quickly got the message from Prastan and decided to accept the $1,000.00 dollars before the boat sat there forever.

The agent said, "Okay, since you guys are the first customers of the day, I wouldn't let you guys down. I will accept the $1,000.00 but cash only."

Prastan said, "Thank you. Could we do the paper work now?"

The agent replied, "Sure, why not." They went inside the office. "Since we truly never took the opportunity to introduce ourselves outside, let us do it now. You're Prastan because I heard this pretty young woman called you Prastan."

Prastan said, "That's me." They shook hands.

Agent said, "I'm Tommy, but they called me Tom. Please have a seat and make yourself comfortable."

Prastan then introduced him to Jannet. "This pretty

woman, as you have just mentioned, is my beloved wife, Jannet. And my two best friends are Mark and Joe."

Tom said, "Since you're the first purchaser for the day and you're paying cash. I wouldn't charge you any tax. The tax is on the house."

Jannet said, "Oh thank you so much," while counting the money.

Prastan said, "There is one little problem here, Tom."

Tom asked, "What is it, Prastan?"

Prastan answered "You see, I am buying this boat not for myself, but for three of my good friends."

Tom asked, "So, what you want me to do for you?"

Prastan replied, "I want the title to be in their names."

Tom said, "Oh that's no problem. We do all the paper work now and when your friends come to pick up their boat, I will put their names in the title."

Prastan said, "Sounds good, but, let this be a surprise for Rick, Peter, and Paul."

Jannet added, "I have an idea."

Tom said, "Share it with us."

Jannet said, "How about if we rent a car from you for an hour or two. We'll go get them and then we'll let them return your rental car."

Tom said, "Sounds good, when they return my car, I'll give them the surprise."

Prastan called Mike and once again Angie picked up the phone "Is this you Angie?"

Angie replied, "Hi Prastan. It's me. How are you?"

Prastan said, "I am fine. Are the boys there—Peter, Paul, and Rick?"

Angie answered, "Oh yes, they got here about an hour ago. Where you guys at?"

Prastan said, "Tell them we should be there in less than an hour."

Angie said, "Okay, oh, we can't wait to see you all."

Prastan said, "Okay, see you then, bye."

In less than an hour they reached at the restaurant. Prastan parked the car across the street in front of the restaurant. When they came out of the car, they were welcomed with lots of kisses and hugging from Angie, Mike, Peter, Paul, and Rick.

Mike said, "Come, let's go inside. You guys must be tired and hungry."

Angie hugged Jannet and said, "Let's go, girl; you looked the same; you haven't changed a bit."

Prastan said, "Hey guys," he said turning at Peter, Paul, and Rick. "Could you guys do me a favor?"

They replied in one voice, "Sure Prastan, Why not? What is it?"

Prastan said, "Could you guys drop off this rental car at this address for me."

Peter said, "Sure, Prastan. I don't know why you rented a car. We should have picked you guys up."

Prastan said, "I know, but then, what the heck."

Rick said, "Okay, we should be back by the time you guys finished your breakfast."

Jannet said, "Take your time and do what you guys have to do."

Prastan said, "We have a whole week to spend with each other, so take your time."

Paul drove the rental car. Peter and Rick followed behind in Peter's car. In less than an hour they reached the place where they were going.

Paul questioned himself inwardly. *This is a boat dealer. Why did they rent a car from a boat dealer?*

Rick said, "I never knew boat dealers rented cars."

Peter parked his car on the street. He and Rick came out and were admiring boats. Paul drove the rental car in the parking lot. The agent came out. "This was fast." He received his car from Paul. "My name is Tom. And yours?"

Paul replied, "I am Paul."

Tom asked, "Those two gentlemen came with you?"

Paul answered, "Yes."

Rick said, "Wow! Look at this boat, Peter."

Peter said, "Wow! Rick." The both stand admiring the boat. They fell in love with the boat. Tom and Paul went near them.

Tom said, "You guys looking at a real baby here. This is the best boat on this lot, well equipped. It has everything. The most luxury fishing boat you could ever find in Town."

Paul said, "Wow! Look at this baby."

The phone rang in the office. Tom said, "Excuse me guys. I have to get the phone."

Peter said, "Something is bothering me."

Paul asked, "What is it, Peter?"

Peter said, "Why did Jannet say take your time and do what you guys have to do? Did you hear her say that, Rick?"

Rick said, "Yes, but right now I am not worrying about that. Maybe she meant let us take our time. Right now I am worrying about this baby."

Paul said, "How could we afford to buy a boat like this. Forget your dream; let's go. Prastan must be waiting for us."

Peter and Rick in one voice said, "That's true." this they said while heading out to the road. Tom shouted, "Hey guys, come over here."

They went in the office. "Have a seat and, may I ask, who is Rick?"

Rick said, "That is me, sir."

Tom said, "And you must be, Peter." He pointed at Peter.

Peter said, "I am Peter."

Tom smiled, "What a friend you guys have."

Rick asked, "What are you talking about, sir?"

Tom said, "You guys sign here."

Peter asked, "Sign what?"

Tom said, "You guys will really love that boat, I know."

Paul said, "Yes, we really do but we cannot afford to buy one like that."

Tom said, "I know, now, tell me something that I don't know. He's a real friend."

Peter, Paul, and Rick in one voice said, "We don't understand, sir."

Tom said, "Your friend Prastan bought that boat for you guys. He paid cash for it. He told me he's buying this boat for his three friends Peter, Paul, and Rick.

This is a gift for you guys from Prastan."

Peter, Paul, and Rick were astonished. They now recalled why Jannet used that statement, "You guys take your time and do what you have to do." They were so happy. They took the boat at the boating dock. Peter said, "Next week when Prastan gone we will start our fishing business again."

Mike asked, "What took those guys so long? It's like almost two hours now. As soon as they return we will go and see, Charles."

Prastan asked, "So, how he's doing?"

Mike said, "He cannot work anymore. It's a long story, Prastan."

Prastan said, "I know. Angie told us everything."

Angie and Jannet went in the room. Angie started to cry. Jannet felt sorry for her and inwardly promised herself to help her get back on her feet. She dried the tears on her face and said, "Don't cry Angie; we are here for you. That is the reason why we came here. We didn't come here on a vacation. We came here to help you." They hugged each other.

Two hours later Rick, Peter, and Paul arrived.

Mike asked, "What took you guys so long? You guys looked extremely happy."

Together in one voice, "Of course, we are happy," and they hugged Prastan.

Rick said,, "Prastan bought us a boat, a beautiful boat." laughing and smiling.

Jannet and Angie came out of the room and participated with them.

Angie said, "I have to see that boat. Is it that beautiful?"

Jannet said, "Believe me, Angie, it is."

Mike said "As we have said before. We are like one little family."

Prastan said, "I am so sorry for Charles. He is such a nice guy. Is he that shaky, Angie?"

Angie said, "He got better but two weeks ago when he learned that our house was in foreclose, he became depressed. It seemed like he took it too hard on himself, and his physical situation became worse since then."

Jannet said, "So he actually stressed out."

Angie said, "Absolutely."

Prastan said, "Probably, that is why he became depressed. So at one point he had fully recovered from his sickness. The only problem he's facing right now is his stress."

Angie said, "I see no other problem with him, Prastan."

Jannet asked, "What happened with his business?"

Angie said, "His business demolished few weeks after he fell sick, but I don't think that the business depressed him. He could always find a new and decent job whenever he became healthy again. I think that the house is what stressed him out."

Prastan asked, "How much the house actually worth right now?"

Angie said, "With the market value now, maybe, fifteen thousand."

Prastan asked, "And how much you guys actually owe on it?"

Angie said, "A lot of money, Prastan."

Jannet asked, "And roughly how much would that be?"

Mike said, "I saw the final notice, twenty one thousand seven hundred."

Angie said, "He refinanced the property and pulled out some cash. He invested the money."

Prastan glanced at Jannet, Mark and Joe glanced at Prastan and Jannet. Their eyes met.

Peter said, "We wish we can help out a little. But unfortunately, we are broke. God bless Prastan and Jannet, they bought us a boat. Next week we will start fishing again."

Mike said, "The little money that I have I cannot

handle it. Business is not like before. Besides, what difference will four to five thousand make?"

Prastan looked at Jannet, Mark, and Joe. Jannet knew exactly what Prastan had in his mind, likewise, Mark and Joe.

Jannet smiled and said, "Do it, Prastan."

Mark and Joe said, "Yes, Prastan, do it."

Prastan said, "Okay, no problem; I will definitely do it."

Angie asked, "Do what, Prastan? What are you guys talking about?"

Mike was also anxious to know what they were talking about. He asked, "Do what, Prastan?"

Jannet said, "He's going to pay off the mortgage for you guys."

Angie was shocked hearing such words from Jannet, "What? Pay off our mortgage?"

Mark and Joe said, "You heard her right. Prastan is going to pay off your mortgage today."

Jannet said, "And we don't need the money back."

Mike asked, "You have all that money, Prastan?"

Joe said, "You bet."

Mark said, "See what he own in Allgreen."

Peter, Paul, and Rick asked, "Really?"

Prastan mentioned, "As Mike just said, we are one little family now, we must help each other." He then asked for an excuse and went a few feet away from them.

He called his bank manager Jim Curtis at the bank in Allgreen. "Hello Jim. This is Prastan here."

Jim said, "Hello Prastan, how are you, man? I hadn't heard from you for a while now. Is everything okay? How is business? I can see it here in your account. You are doing well, Prastan, I mean your business is doing good; keep up the good work."

Prastan said, "Thank you, Jim." As they were talking with each other, he did not realize that their conversation was overheard by everyone.

Jim asked, "So how may I help you this morning, Prastan?"

Prastan said, "If I give you a mortgage company name and the account number could you pay off that loan for me?"

Jim said, "Sure Prastan why not?"

Prastan said, "Hold on a second, Jim. Let me gather some information."

Jim said, "Sure."

Prastan turned at Angie. He said, "Could you remember your bank name and your loan number?"

Angie said, "Yes. Welfar, and the loan number NO73."

Prastan said, "That is my bank too. Hey Jim, this is the bank name and loan number."

Jim said, "I will do this transaction right now for you, Prastan."

Prastan said, "Thank you, Jim."

Jim asked, "Are you bailing out someone?"

Prastan said, "Yeah."

Jim said, "Must be a very close one. Do you have a fax number where you at. By the way only God knows where you are at."

Prastan asked, "Do you have a fax number here, Angie?"

Angie replied, "Yes, we do."

Prastan gave Jim the fax number, he then asked "What's this for?"

Jim replied, "I'll I fax you over this payment transaction. And the bank will also fax you a payment satisfaction letter."

Prastan asked, "And how long will this take?"

Jim said, "Well, it is the same bank. You should get it in less than an hour."

Prastan said, "Thank you, Jim."

Jim said, "Well, it's all done; you're good to go."

Prastan replied, "Thank you so much, Jim."

Jim said, "No problem, man. So when we are going to catch up and have a few beers?"

Prastan answered, "Not this weekend, the following weekend I'll pick you up and we'll have some beers at my place. Is that okay?"

Jim said, "Sound good to me. Okay, see you then."

Prastan said, "You take care, man, until."

Prastan returned to everyone. He said, "Well, it's done. Congratulations, Angie."

Jannet said, "Congratulation, girl. No more mortgages, no more stress. Just work, eat, and live a simple life."

Peter, Paul, and Rick said, "Wow! God bless Prastan and Jannet. You guys have bought us a beautiful boat so that we can make our living. You guys have paid off Charles and Angie's mortgage. We are so proud of you,guys, we don't have enough words to thank you guys."

In the middle of talking, a car's tires screeched in front of the restaurant. A minute later Charles walked in very slowly. "Hello, guys." This he said hugging everyone. "Nice seeing each other again after so long."

Mike said, "Thank you so much Prastan and Jannet. God bless you guys," and he went to the bar for beers. Meanwhile, the boys gathered two tables together. They sat around the table, Prastan, Mark, and Joe drinking beers. And as usual Mike and the rest of the boys were drinking liquor. Charles didn't drink because of his sickness but couldn't avoid it; he took a glass of champagne with Jannet and Angie. Everyone raised their glasses. Mike said, "This is for Prastan and Jannet. May God shower blessing on them. They are very good persons. They are a godsend, cheers."

Charles asked, "So when will you guys try to get a boat? I know it's very tough on you guys but you guys have to work. I am so sorry I cannot help you guys. Right now we need help ourselves. Our house is going into foreclose."

The phone rang. Angie said, "That's a fax coming." She rushed at the fax machine. She grabbed the first page. She said, "This is for you, Prastan."

Prastan said, "Jannet, will you please get that for me?"

Jannet said, "Sure." She went by the fax machine and collected the paper from Angie.

Angie said, "Here comes, another fax. This is for us from our bank."

Charles asked, "Our bank?"

Tears of joy flowing down, Angie's cheeks. She held the satisfaction letter in her hand.

Charles asked, "Our bank? I thought they were going to let us stay in the house at least for a few more months." He placed his drink on the table and his face suddenly became sad and pale. Everyone had noticed him and felt very sorry for his emotions but inwardly happy for them since they knew that when he learned what Prastan and Jannet had done for them he'd be very happy and his sad emotions would suddenly disappear.

Peter decided to answer Charles question and said, "Prastan bought us a beautiful boat. When they leave, we will start fishing again."

Charles said, "Really. Oh that is so nice of you, Prastan." This he said tapping Prastan on his left shoulder

since he sat beside him. Jannet and Angie walked slowly
to the table.

Jannet asked, "So when will all of you guys pay us a
visit in Allgreen?"

Charles said, "I wish we could visit you guys tomorrow,
but we are in a messy situation with our house right now.
And as a matter of fact, financially, we are totally broke
over here. It's a very good thing that you bought these
guys a boat, Prastan."

Rick added, "And he doesn't even want back the
money."

Paul added, "He's such a nice guy."

Charles said, "How nice of you, Prastan." He then
asked "What did the bank say, Angie? How long more we
can stay in the house?"

Angie drying her tears with a slightly smile in her
face. She said, "Forever." This she said and she gave him
the letter. Without looking at the letter, he asked "Forever.
What do you mean, forever?" He then read the letter "Is
this a miracle? Am I going crazy? Our house was paid in
full. Am I dreaming?"

Angie said, "No, you're not."

Charles said, "Then someone explain this miracle to
me."

Angie explained, "Jannet and Prastan paid off for our
house. Last week when I spoke with them I explained
everything to them. That is the reason why they came
here."

Charles said, "Our house paid off. Oh thank you so much, Prastan." He stood upright, along with Prastan, and they hugged each other once again. Charles then hugged Jannet, "Oh my sweet sister. A minute ago we were seeing ourselves on the street." They then released themselves.

Jannet said, "No more streets. Now, I think you guys need a good vacation. I mean all of you guys here need a good vacation. And after the vacation, then you guys can think of work."

Rick said, "That's true Sounds good."

Jannet and Prastan in one voice, "And we have good news for you, Charles and Angie."

Angie and Charles in one voice "What is it?"

Prastan said, "We don't need the money back."

Angie and Charles said, "What?" they were shocked.

Jannet said, "You heard him right."

Charles and Angie said, "Oh thank you guys so much. We cannot repay you guys."

Jannet said, "So, you guys ready for this vacation?"

By now they were on their second round of drinks.

Joe said, "You guys wouldn't believe this."

Everyone turned looking at him, waiting to hear what he had to say. "Prastan and Jannet gave us their house."

Mike said, "What?" he hesitated for a while and then continued, "So where you guys living, Prastan, with your in-laws?"

Mark said, "No, they bought a mansion."

Angie asked, "Really Jannet, really. You guys bought a mansion."

Jannet replied, "It's really beautiful, girl. So my question once again, are you guys ready for this vacation?" This she said trying to change the topic.

Prastan announced, "Well, I think all our missions have been accomplished successfully. What do you think, Jannet?"

Jannet said, "As a matter of fact, yes. We came here with an intention to get things done. And as you have just said, our mission has been accomplished successfully. Let us all say thank God for everything. He knows what the best is for everyone. One thing we must never forget that he is out there looking over us, and we should always believe in him."

Mike added, "That's true, Jannet."

Prastan asked, "So what you have in mind to do, Charles, I mean whenever you feel better."

Charles answered, "I feel better and relief already, Prastan. Thanks to you guys. My only problem right now, I am very shaky and I cannot guarantee whether I can do any strenuous jobs at this point."

Mark said, "May I suggest something if you guys don't mind."

Jannet said, "Feel free Mark. Any little suggestion that can help will be considered useful at this moment."

Mark said, "Start a small business at the shopping mall."

Mike added, "It's a very good suggestion, Mark, but right now in this town business isn't doing so well. That maybe a little risky; besides, that may also require some cash to get started."

Charles said, "You know what? Let us all go by our house and spend some time there."

Prastan agreed. He said, "No problem."

Mike said, "I will close the restaurant early and join you guys later."

Prastan said, "Very well."

Moments later they all went over at Charles's house.

Jannet said, "It's a beautiful house, Angie."

Angie replied, "Oh, thank you Jannet." This she said while trying to clear off a bundle of bills laid on the table that has been piled up, apparently, for some time. Jannet glanced at Prastan, Mark, and Joe and shook her head. They felt sorry for Charles and Angie inwardly. She opened her purse and then glanced at Prastan in a sad face. Prastan nodded his head, giving her okay. Joe and Mark smiled at each other. She gave Angie five hundred dollars and said to her, "Clear out this mess on this table top, Angie."

Angie said, "You guys have done more than enough for us, Jannet."

Prastan said, "Take it, Angie."

She took the money, and her tears flowed down her cheeks.

Charles said, "God has sent you in this world to help." He tapped Prastan on his shoulder. Jannet counted another five hundred dollars and gave it to Peter, Paul, and Rick. She said, "You guys take this money and make a jump start back into your fishing business. And yes, another thing guys. We don't need back this money."

Everyone in one voice, "You guys are angels. You guys descended directly from heaven."

Jannet said, "Hey, Prastan, I suppose we don't need to spend the entire week considering the fact that we have already accomplished our mission in one day."

Mark said, "That true, Jannet."

Jannet said, "Tomorrow morning we can drive around town sightseeing and then leave around noon."

Prastan said, "I have no problem with that."

Charles said, "I have a suggestion. Why don't you guys spend the night here and tomorrow we show you guys around and—" He then hesitated.

Angie asked, "And what?"

Charles said, "And, we can go and spend the rest of the week with them in Allgreen, since they are on a week of vacation. Jannet is quite right, we need to get out of here and open our thoughts and minds. Since we have no mortgage to pay and our casual bills will be paid off, I feel like my miserable life is leaving my body. I feel happy, Angie. Can we go with them tomorrow?"

Angie said, "I'll be glad to."

Prastan said, "I have a strong feeling, Charles, after

your vacation with us in Allgreen, you will be fully recovered."

Jannet supported, "I believed so myself. Prastan may have a genuine point. What do you think, Joe? Hey Mark, what do you think?"

Mark and Joe in one voice replied, "That's true."

Peter, Paul, and Rick asked, "Can we go with you guys also?"

Prastan said, " That will be fun."

Jannet said, "We will have a lot of fun, guys. Oh, I am so happy." and she grabbed Angie with both hands around her neck. She then continued, "I have to make a call. I have to make a call."

Prastan asked, "Call to whom?"

Jannet replied, "I have to call mom."

Prastan said, "I got it."

Jannet called her mom, "Hi, Mom."

Mom answered, "Jannet, is that you?"

Jannet said, "Yes, mom."

Mom asked, "Where you at? Are you still at work or home?"

Jannet said, "We are not at home or at work, Mom."

Mom asked, "Then where the hell are you?"

Jannet replied, "We are across the river. We had urgent business to take care of. Now that we have got everything accomplished we are coming home tomorrow.

We are leaving here at noon and should be there by

3:00 P.M. Ask Dad to arrange a mini bus and pick us up at Allgreen beach. We have some friends coming with us, and they will spend the rest of the week with us."

Mom said, "No problem, dear. You may count on that. But you didn't tell me anything."

Jannet said, "Sorry, Mom. I love you and I love Dad, too."

Peter said, "Let's go, Paul, let's go, Rick."

Rick question, "Where to?"

Peter said, "Home."

Joe asked "Home. Why?"

Peter replied, "Because we have to pack up things. Have you forgotten we are going on vacation too."

Joe said, "Oh, I see."

Charles said, "When you guys finish packing your bags, you guys come back and we all are going to spend the night here. At least, we will have some fun together."

Peter, Paul, and Rick replied in one voice, "Okay, we'll be back as soon as we can." This they said and walked out the door one after another.

Jannet looked at Charles, then glanced at Angie, and asked, "Did you observe what I observed, Angie?"

Angie shook her head and said, "It seemed like he's getting better."

Jannet said, "I know, girl. He had stressed out. He will recover very soon, girl, believe me."

Peter, Paul, and Rick returned with their shoulder bags. It just began to dust when they rang the doorbell.

Charles went and unlocked the door and said, "About

time you guys showed up. I thought you guys changed your minds."

Rick said, "Changed what minds? We're not going to miss this out."

Peter asked, "Is Mike here?"

Angie asked, "Who are you asking for Peter, my dad?"

Peter replied, "Yes, I thought he's here."

Angie asked while she was curling Jannet's hair, "What made you think that way?"

Peter replied, "We drove by the restaurant and we noticed that the restaurant was closed. So we thought probably he was over here."

A few minutes later there was a knock on the door. Angie went and answered the door "Hi Dad, we were just talking about you."

Mike said, "Really. Does that mean I will live long?"

Angie said, "Oh come on, Dad, you're not into that superstitious belief."

Mike said, "Just kidding."

Angie asked, "What you have in your bag, Dad?"

Mike said, "A bottle of liquor and some beers."

Angie said, "Dad, you must keep an eye on the house. Tomorrow we are leaving on a week of vacation with Jannet and Prastan."

Mike said, "That is very good. I wish I could go with you all myself, but someone has to be at home at least. Besides, who will run the restaurant for a week?"

Angie took the bag from him. She placed the liquor and few beers on the table, and she put the rest of the beers in the refrigerator. Charles fetched some glasses. Mike was observing all of Charles's movement. He whispered in Jannet's ear "I can see some improvement in him."

Jannet said, "I'm not a doctor, but I can tell you this, he's getting there. It's an indication of getting better."

Angie said, "Jannet, you guys are right; we really need a vacation. I am so sorry that you guys cannot spend more time with us here."

Prastan said, "Some other time, Angie. But right now, let us work on him. He needs to improve very fast. The faster he gets better, the better you guys future will be."

Mike said, "That's true, that's true." nodding his head.

After a few drinks Peter hugged Prastan, "You're a good person, Prastan. We owe you big time, my dear beloved friend. Thanks to you and Jannet, we will be on our feet again."

Jannet said, "If someone needs help and you're in a position to help that person without causing you any harm or loss and you deliberately turn your back away from that person, it's a sin."

Angie said, "Wow! Where did you learn that from?"

Jannet raised her head and looked at Prastan, "From him. I have learned so many things from him."

Joe and Mark added, "We have learned many things from him as well."

Mike said, "I wish everyone would have been like you guys."

Prastan said, "Mike, if you want to help a person, don't feed him the fish; teach him how to cast the net."

Mike tapped Prastan on his shoulder, "Keep up the good work, son the more good you can do in this world, the more prosperous in life you'll be."

Prastan said, "God sent all of us in this beautiful world. He give us two books, one book to record all the money and wealth that we have achieved and the other book to record all the good and evil things we have done. He said, go, work, and build yourselves, enjoy yourselves, I have nothing against that, but when you're returning home to me, leave the book with the wealth; leave that with someone else. Bring me the other book."

Everyone looked at Prastan and nodded their heads because they were having a very nice time. They had learned some good things from Prastan.

Jannet said, "Well, as Mike always say that we became one little family now. We should try and co-operate with each other, help each other, and look out for each other."

Everyone clapped their hands at Jannet's speech.

It was almost midnight when Prastan suggested that they should have some rest since tomorrow they would have only few hours of sightseeing, and besides, they had to leave at noon.

Everyone agreed with Prastan's suggestion and finally called the night over.

Tuesday morning Angie and Charles woke up very early trying to make a head start with breakfast and necessary arrangement for the sightseeing. But they were surprised to see that Prastan and Jannet were already in the kitchen preparing breakfast for everyone.

Jannet said, "Hi Angie, Hello, Charles; good morning."

They replied "Good morning Jannet, good morning, Prastan."

Jannet said, "I made breakfast for everyone, pancakes and eggs. I hope it tastes good."

Angie said, "Oh Jannet, you shouldn't have taken the trouble. I'm supposed to prepare breakfast for you guys."

Jannet said, "I feel at home girl, so give me a break."

Joe sniffed on the sofa.

Mark said, "What the matter with you Joe. Do you have an allergy?"

Joe said, "No. What made you think that I have an allergy?"

Mark said, "Because, I heard you sniffing."

Joe said, "I smell food. I smell eggs. Damn, I feel hungry." He stood up "Jannet, is that you in the kitchen? I'm hungry."

Mark said, "Quiet, fool. People are still sleeping."

Joe said, "But I'm hungry."

Mark said, "Since I knew you, you've always hungry. Especially, when you smell food. Why don't you get married?"

Jannet glanced at Prastan, Angie, and Charles, "Oh boy. There goes it again."

Angie said, "Are they serious?"

Jannet said, "That is the everyday story with them. Pretend that you did not hear anything."

Charles looked at Prastan.

Prastan said, "That's an everyday thing for them, Charles."

The rest of the guys woke up, but they pretended that they were still a sleep. They wanted to know whether these two guys are serious.

Joe said, "Why should I get married?"

Mark said, "Because she will prepare breakfast, lunch, and dinner for you."

Joe said, "I'm hungry and I am going to the kitchen to get something to eat. If you don't eat, you die, and when you die, you don't eat."

Everyone smiled and laughed silently at their conversation.

Peter whispered, "I only hope that they are not serious."

Joe went in the kitchen and was astonished to see that Prastan, Charles, and Angie were busy helping Jannet with the breakfast, "Hey, hey, good morning guys."

Smiling at him everyone in one voice said,, "Good morning, Joe."

Joe grabbed two plates. Angie glanced at Jannet.

Jannet said, "Shu! Just look on."

He put pancakes and eggs in both plates and returned to the sofa, "Oh, it tastes good. I'll get some coffee." He returned in the kitchen, grabbed two cups of coffee, and returned to the sofa. Both sat beside each other eating.

Mark said, "Tastes good."

Joe said "If it smells good, it tastes good."

Mark said, "Shut up, fool, and eat. Have some respect for your food."

Peter whispered, "These guys are something else. They don't mean a bit of what they say to each other."

Jannet looked at Charles and Angie, "You see what I mean. Just like that they can pick a fight with each other. But they don't mean it. Sometimes, I have to yell at them."

A few minutes later, Mike said, "Wake up, guys. It's a busy day for you all."

Paul said, "We already did, Mike."

Rick said, "Mark and Joe are fun. But you know what? I like them. I wish I could be like them."

Mike said, "I must leave now. I have so many things to do. You guys have a nice time sightseeing and have fun in Allgreen. I'll see you guys later."

Jannet said, "Mike, you cannot leave like that, I had prepared breakfast, eat something before you leave."

Mike said, "If you insist, Jannet, then definitely, I'll eat something."

Jannet said, "Thank you." This she said while she gave him a cup of coffee and a plate with pancakes and eggs. She continued, "We don't know when we will see each other again."

Hearing this Mike said, "You're right. You never know what life may be tomorrow. I changed my plan."

Angie asked, "And what is that, Dad?"

Mike said, "I'll go with you guys sightseeing, and I will give you guys a ride to the boat dock. As a matter of fact, I'll be there to pick up you guys upon return."

Charles and Angie in one voice exclaimed, "Oh, thank you so much, Dad."

After breakfast they went sightseeing. They drove around in town. They stopped at a few places here and there to go shopping. Prastan bought two beautiful watches. He gave Jannet one and the other to Angie.

Angie said "Thank you, Prastan," she said smiling.

Jannet bought a beautiful dress for Angie.

Angie said, "Oh thank you so much, Jannet," she said and gave her a tight hug.

Prastan bought watches for all the guys "This is for remembrance guys." He emphasized.

After that they drove around the village area for a little while, they returned home.

Jannet said, "The village area is really beautiful. It reminded me of Allgreen. Isn't it beautiful, Prastan?"

Prastan said, "Yeah, yeah."

Jannet asked, "Where is your thought, Prastan? And what you have up your sleeve?"

Prastan asked, "What are you talking about, Jannet?"

Jannet said, "I'm your wife. I knew when you're up to something."

Mark and Joe said, "Yeah, yeah, spit it out, Prastan spit it out."

Prastan said, "I like that water fountain I saw in front of the shopping mall. It will look nice in front of our house."

Jannet said, "You're right. Why didn't I think of that?"

Joe said, "Because you're too busy shopping."

Jannet responded, "Oh shut up, Joe, and give me a break. Girls love to shop."

Joe said, "I didn't know that girls love to shop."

Mark asked, "Know what?"

Joe said, "That girls love to shop."

Mark said, "When you get married then you'll know, fool."

Joe said, "Get married. Which girl will marry me?"

Jannet and Angie, "Oh don't say that, Joe," They felt sorry for him.

Jannet said, "Even the birds have a pair, Joe. She's out there somewhere. Beside, you good looking so don't degrade yourself."

Joe said, "You know what, Prastan. I know a place in Allgreen. It has all kind of water fountains. I'll take you there tomorrow."

After a moment Mike gave them a ride to the boating dock.

Peter, Paul, and Rick took the opportunity to introduce their boat to Charles, Angie and Mike. "This is our baby Prastan bought us."

Charles said, "Wow, she looks good."

Angie said, "I like the shape and color of this boat."

Mike said, "She must be very fast."

Peter said, "This baby will put us across in an hour time."

Paul said, "Look at the engine, Mike. It is new and it has twice the horse power than the engine we had before. Beside, this is not wood boat, it is fiber glass."

Angie said, "I knew that every boat actually has a name."

Paul said, "Oh yeah. We'll name our boat *Prasjan*—princess of the river."

Mike said, "Its sounds good. But what is *Prasjan*?"

Peter and Rick said "We named our boat after Prastan and Jannet. *Prasjan* is a short name for Prastan and Jannet."

Prastan said, "Oh, you shouldn't have named it after us."

Peter said, "Its call remembrance. We will always remember you guys."

Angie said, "Oh, that's so sweet."

Mike said, "Okay, when should I pick you guys up?"

Prastan said, "This question I cannot answer."

Peter said, "We will start fishing on Monday morning. We will need some rest over the weekend. Let me see. Pick us up Saturday morning let's say 11:00 A.M." This he said looking at his new watch.

Mike said, "Okay, but, I want to see you guys take off."

Everyone went in the boat. Rick turned the engine on.

Mike said, "Wait a minute. Is this a key-start engine? Wow!"

Charles said, "You got that right."

Rick turned the boat around. They waved hands, and then the boat speed into the deep heading towards Allgreen shore.

Mike said, "Wow! That's a boat."

When the boat speeding across the river. Angie held Charles tightly since it's her very first time riding in a boat.

Jannet stood beside Prastan admiring and enjoying the beauty of the scene, sea birds flying overhead whistling, and swaying with the wind looking down for fish. Her hair swaying as she tried to part it gently with her hands backward. Prastan looked at Jannet and smiled.

Jannet asked, "What's the matter, Prastan? Why are you smiling at me?"

Prastan said, "Oh, you have looked so beautiful, Jannet." She smiled blushingly.

Angie added, "She doesn't look beautiful. She is beautiful."

Joe added, "Jannet is beautiful like the ocean."

Mark said, "Shut up fool and sit down. Don't try to remind us of something that we all know. Make sure you find that water fountain tomorrow."

Jannet said, "Oh, stop it guys. Have you seen what I meant, Angie."

Joe said, "Oh boy, I remembered the first time when we met. Do you remember, Jannet?"

Jannet started to laugh, "Yes, I did. I'll never forget that day when you fell down from the tree top."

Mark said, "That was his fault. I told the fool to hold on and close his eyes. But no, he's too nosy and intended to take a peek to see what's going on, and there he goes aahhhh."

Rick said, "It seems like you guys grew up together and have a lot of fun together."

Angie asked, "Why did he yell 'aahhhh'?"

Jannet laughed covered her mouth with both hands, "He fell down from the tree top. I was so scared, then, I felt sorry for him. Tonight I'll give you guys the details on this one."

Everyone was laughing and having fun, not realizing that they were approaching Allgreen's shore until Prastan said to Rick, "Head over there. That's our boating dock."

Rick slowed the engine and went slowly into the dock.

The dock captain said, "Welcome aboard, Prastan. I see some new faces with you."

Prastan said, "Hi, Tom, how are you?" Prastan shook

his hand and palmed it with a hundred bucks. "Keep this boat for me until Saturday."

Tony said, "Count on that, Prastan. So, they will be staying with you for the entire week."

Prastan replied, "They surely will," he said while he turned around looking at them.

Tony said, "I sure am glad to go over there some day with you and hang out a little."

Prastan said, "Why not? Next time I go, I'll give you a buss."

Tony said, "I'll be looking forward for that day, Prastan. You guys have fun. See you guys Saturday."

They went to the beach.

Prastan said, "Welcome to Allgreen, guys."

Jannet held Angie and said, "You've finally made it to Allgreen, girl. We will surely have some fun together."

They roamed on the beach shore waiting for their ride.

Angie said, "It's a beautiful beach, Jannet."

Joe said, "Here comes our ride."

Mark asked, "Where?"

Joe said, "Look over there."

Mark asked, "Where, where?

Joe said, "Look over there." He pointed his hand at the direction.

Mark said, "That a rock, you fool. That's the rock

on which Prastan used to sit on, and that is the rock he mentioned in his poem."

Joe said, "You are right; I have confused myself."

Mark said, "That isn't something new."

Jannet said, "There goes it again," she said while she glanced at Angie. By now everyone understood their behavior and smiled inwardly in appreciation of how they were getting along with each other without meaning a damn thing.

Charles said, "Look over there, a bus is coming."

Jannet said, "That must be our ride." A few minutes later the bus arrived.

Jannet said, "Hi dad," she said and gave him a big hug.

Prastan said "Hi dad." This he said and they shook hands.

James said, "Well, nice seeing some new faces. Will someone take the opportunity and introduce me, please?" This he said while he glanced at his son-in-law, Prastan.

Prastan said, "Sure, Dad. This is Peter, Paul, and Rick. They are the one with the boat."

James said, "Oh, I see," nodding his head.

Jannet said, "Dad, and this is Charles and his loving wife, Angie."

James said "I see." He shook everyone hand and then he requested everyone to get inside the bus. "Let's go," he urged.

Jannet said, "I thought mom is going to come also, Dad."

James replied, "She's so excited. She's baking fruit-cakes for our guests. By the way, she said, when she finished baking, she will call for a ride."

Jannet said, "No problem, Dad."

On their way home, Joe directed the driver to stop the bus at his home first. When the bus stopped, Joe just ran in, opened the door, went inside the house and dropped off his bag.

Angie asked, "Is this the house you gave to them, Jannet?"

Jannet said, "Yes."

Joe ran out and back to the bus "Let's go, driver." At the same time Jannet and Prastan were looking forward to seeing a reaction on Charles's face since he knew the house. Charles did remember the house and also the mistake he had made. But as he could recall, Jannet mentioned to him that that mistake was meant to happen. And it was meant to happen by God so that she could change his life around.

Charles looked at them, "Thank God my life is now changed." Prastan and Jannet understood exactly what Charles meant.

Prastan said, "Life goes around in a circle, Charles. You won't be in one situation forever. You know what I mean, just forget the past and keep going with your life. Just think about the future."

Charles understood clearly, "I know. You're right."

Quite unlike the rest of them, they thought Charles was mentioning his sickness, so they said, "Yes, Charles, forget completely about the past and concentrate on your future."

A few minutes later they reached Prastan's neighborhood. The bus moved slowly on the street. Everyone in one voice said, "Wow! Look at this neighborhood. Look at the huge mansions."

Peter said, "Only rich people must be living in this neighborhood."

Rick said, "Look at the landscaping at the front yard, so unique, so beautiful with flowers and plants, well designed."

Angie shouted, "Wow! Look at that house over there. That's a beauty." This she said pointed her hand in front towards the house as the bus moved slowly.

Paul said, "That's a beautiful house. That's a mansion. I wish I could say I know the people living there."

Mark said, "That one you may have right, Paul." Before Paul could ask, "What do you mean, Mark?" the bus slowly drove in the driveway.

Angie said, "Admiring the house from outside is more than enough sightseeing. We can get in trouble driving in people's driveway."

Peter and Rick agreed, "That's true, driver. Back out, back out."

Charles added, "Make it fast before someone sees us."

Jannet clapped Angie on her shoulder, "Don't worry, girl; you wouldn't get into trouble. It's our house."

Angie said, "Excuse me, Jannet, Am I hearing right? You said it's your house."

Jannet said, "You heard me, girl. You heard me right."

The bus stopped. Everyone came out admiring the house from outside.

Peter asked, "Is this your house, Prastan?"

Prastan said, "Yes Peter. Welcome guys, welcome to our home.

Charles, Rick, and Paul shook their heads, "You have got a mansion, Prastan."

Jannet opened the door. They went inside the house.

Angie said "Oh my God, it's so huge and so beautiful. It seems like I am daydreaming." This she said while trying to catch Charles's attention.

The phone rang. Jannet picked it up, "Hi, Mom."

Mom said, "Hi dear. You want to send a ride for me?"

Jannet replied, "I am sending Joe and Mark. Dad is coming too. Hey Mark, take the car. You and Joe go and pick up mom. I think dad is going too. On your way back, you guys drop in at the corner store and pick up enough beers and liquor." This she said and threw him the car's key. She then walked them through house and around. "Angie, this room is for you and Charles. Peter, this is your room, Paul, this is your room, and Rick, this is your room. Mom and dad will spend the night here; they will have that room and Mark and Joe will have that room."

Angie asked, "How many rooms does this house have, Jannet?"

Jannet said, "Seven bedrooms and four baths."

Rick said, "Wow Seven bedrooms."

They went outside.

Angie said "Oh my God, look at this pool. It's so beautiful." They all sat back in chairs around the pool, enjoying the blue water.

Jannet looked at Prastan and said "Prastan, we will buy Chinese food today."

Prastan said, "No problem, Jannet." She picked up the phone and called her mom, "Hi, Mom."

Mom asked, "What's up, dear?"

Jannet said, "When you guys come, ask Mark to pick up Chinese food. He'll know what to do."

Mom replied, "Okay, dear."

Angie said, "Jannet, it seemed like Mark and Joe understand you guys so well."

Jannet said, "As Rick said, we guys grew up together."

Prastan asked, "Would you guys like to take a swim?"

Charles answered, "Why not? We are on vacation, guys." Shortly after they all found themselves in the pool swimming. Charles swam across the pool, back and forth.

Prastan mentioned, "You're doing fine, Charles. You see what I mean? You need a good vacation. By the end of your vacation, I think that you will be perfect, I mean absolutely perfect." This he said and he turned around and looked at Angie. He then continued "Hey, what do you think, Angie?"

Angie swam, trying to hold her breath, "I can see that, I can see that."

Peter said, "Oh boy, I feel so nice." This he said and he dived down.

Paul said, "Peter, you're diving like a fish."

Rick added, "What do you expect from a fisherman?"

Jannet stood splashing water on her face with both hands laughing, "You guys are something else."

Mark, Joe, and James reached James's house. While Deecia packing her fruit cakes, James went in the shower and freshened up. A few minutes later they are on their way. They stopped at their usual corner store and picked up beer and liquor. Then they drove to the restaurant and picked up food.

When Mark reached home, Jannet took the opportunity and introduced her mom to them. They drank and had lots of fun together.

Charles said, "Oh boy, I feel so happy. I have to take a vacation more often."

Angie said, "He's getting there, Jannet."

Jannet said, "It's only the first day, girl, and you can see the changes in him." When the place started to get dark they went inside the house.

Angie said, "Okay Jannet, now give us the story about Joe, I mean the tree story."

Jannet said, "I can't."

Rick asked, "Why not, Jannet?"

Jannet blushed, "Because mom and dad are here." This she said and looked at them.

Mom said, "Don't be ashamed or scared, dear, go ahead, say what you have to say."

Charles said, "Oh come on, sister, let's hear about the tree. Share the fun with us."

Joe said, "You don't have to, Jannet." Prastan and Mark laughed.

Mark said, "Why not, Joe? Go ahead, Jannet." Everyone leaned back looking at Jannet.

Mark said, "Let me begin first."

Everyone in one voice declared, "Go ahead, Mark."

Joe threatened, "I'm warning you, Mark, I'm warning you."

Jannet said, "Okay."

Joe said, "You don't have to, Jannet."

Everyone in one voice asked, Why not, Joe?"

Jannet's mom said "This sound like fun."

Mark began, "Joe and I made plans to cook at Allgreen's Park. We said to ourselves that when we finished all the preparation at the park, we'll call Prastan and give him a big surprise. Joe and I had no knowledge that Prastan was on a date with Jannet at the same park at the same time. Suddenly, we heard a voice. The voice sounded like, Prastan, and of course, it was Prastan. We then questioned ourselves why he was this early, so we climbed up a tree and hid ourselves from him. We saw he kept looking around as if he was looking for someone, so we decided to pay him more attention. Joe then called my attention to her: 'Look, look an angel appeared from heaven.' I said, 'Wait a minute I saw her somewhere.' Joe asked me, 'Where in heaven?' I said, 'No, I saw her at the office, she is working at the office.' Prastan and Jannet then headed towards the same tree. We heard Jannet say to Prastan, 'Promise me that you will never love another girl besides me'."

Jannet defended herself, "That isn't true."

Jannet's mom said, "If Mark said so, it's so. And what did Prastan say?"

Joe said, "I promise you from the bottom of my heart."

Prastan defended himself, "That's a lie."

Charles said, "I believed them," nodding his head.

Peter, Paul, and Rick all said,"We think you guys should accept the fact."

Mr. and Mrs. James said "That is something you guys should have proud of. As everyone said you guys are match made in heaven."

Angie said, "Yeah, yeah, let's hear it."

Prastan and Jannet, "Okay it's true," they replied, blushing.

Mark continued, "Joe called my attention. You heard that. I said 'Shu, close your eyes and hold on.' He then said, 'What are you going to do?' I said, 'Don't be a wise guy, I'll do the same.' Joe peeped and he caught me with my eyes wide open. I had no excuse to defend myself so I asked him once again to close his eyes and be quiet. Prastan said, 'Jannet I love you, I cannot live without you.' Joe smiled with his eyes closed shaking his head, inwardly having a point to tease Prastan at work. His stupidity caused his hands to slip, and he was unable to control himself. Jannet, you may go from there."

Angie insisted, "Yes Jannet, let's hear it."

Jannet said, "Prastan and I sat on the ground when suddenly I heard, 'Aahhhhh.' From on top of the tree, Joe fell down just beside me. I was scared to death, and I jumped up and grabbed onto Prastan's waist tightly. I heard another voice from top of the tree, saying, 'You're stupid .I told you to be careful.' I then recalled that voice. I said, ' Mark, is that you?' Prastan said, 'Joe, you swine, why you have done this to me?' I then realized that they were friends so I asked, 'Are you hurt, Joe?' From then on we are very close to each other and cannot stay without each other. They are my husband's best friends and also they are my brothers."

Everyone in one voice said, Ohhh, isn't that so sweet."

Charles said, "Jannet, don't forget I am your brother also."

Hearing this they all laughed together and had another drink.

They prolonged their celebration until midnight when, finally, they decided to get some sleep.

Early Tuesday morning just before sunrise Jannet and Prastan woke up from bed. They considered themselves to be the first to get up but were astonished to see everyone already up and relaxing by the pool.

Everyone in one voice at them, "Good morning Prastan, good morning Jannet."

Deecia said, "Sweetheart," of course referring to Jannet's "It's a long story."

She continued, "I could recall one day you came in very happy, blushing, laughing, and smiling. I glanced at you from the corner of my eyes. I asked you, 'Where were you, dear? where have you been, dear?' You replied, 'I went and visited a friend, Mom.' Was that the same incident you guys were referring to, last night?"

Jannet blushed again, "Yes, Mom. I recalled all those events and couldn't control myself laughing." This she said lied to her mom. That was the week after the events when she had a date with Prastan at Allgreen's Park and finally ended up at Prastan's house.

After a healthy breakfast, Joe reminded Prastan about that water fountain that he had mentioned.

Prastan said, "Well, let's go and have a look at the water fountain, guys."

Jannet said, "We are nine of us, Prastan. We need another vehicle."

Prastan nodded his head. While he was nodding his head, Mr. Martin pulled in the driveway.

Prastan said, "We'll take Mr. Martin's car."

Martin said, "Hello, Prastan; Hello, Jannet; hello everyone. What's going on here? You guys have a party and I wasn't invited, so many new faces." Prastan then introduced him to everyone, not forgetting to mention that he was a very good man and that he was the boss for all of them before.

Peter said, "So you guys have a new boss now."

Martin said, "He's the boss now. He bought over my company. He's the new boss and owner now."

Prastan asked, "Could I borrow your car for a little while?"

Martin said, "Prastan, you don't have to ask me. Take it. I love you guys much, I can even give you my heart." This he said rubbing his chest.

Joe said, "Okay, okay Mr. Martin leave the heart where it is; right now we need the car."

Mr. and Mrs. James came out and said, "Well hello, Martin."

Martin replied, "Hello James; hello Deecia."

Deecia asked, "What brought you this early?"

Martin replied, "You really want to know? Okay, I'll tell you." He then turned at Jannet, "What do you have in the kitchen for breakfast?"

Everyone laughed.

Jannet said, "Mom will take care of you."

Deecia said, "Let's go inside; there is a lot of food to eat."

Mark, Joe, Peter, Paul, and Rick went in Prastan's car and Prastan, Jannet, Charles and Angie went in Mr. Martin's car. Prastan pulled out and Mark followed him. Prastan headed straight to the auto dealer.

Joe said, "He's supposed to follow us. Where he's going?"

Mark answered, "You're stupid. How long since you've known him? He's going to buy a car right now."

Paul asked, "Did he mention that to you?"

Mark said, "No. But we know him very well."

Joe, "You're right. I am stupid."

Mark said, "Please don't say you are stupid. You're more than stupid."

Rick said, "You guys are fun, I mean really fun. It's been pleasure to be with you guys, fun, fun, fun, all the time."

Peter said, "You guys are very good friends. Now we've became friends, too. Tell us something more about, Prastan, something that we don't know about him."

Mark said, "He was very poor. He grew up as an orphan all by himself, looked over by good neighbors. Then, Mr. Martin hired him. Jannet was a secretary working for Mr. Martin. The very first time Prastan and Jannet met they fell madly in love with each other."

Joe added, "Mark, don't forget to mention that they are still madly in love."

Mark said, "Shut up fool." He then continued. "He's a very honest and kindhearted person. He was then appointed manager."

Joe added, "Before he became manager we had a little problem with the supervisor."

Peter asked, "What problem?"

Joe said, "One day the supervisor went to the office and he saw Jannet. He fell in love with her.

Mark continued, "And when he realized that Jannet loved, Prastan. He started to give us a hard time on the job."

Peter said, "Really? Why didn't you guys kicked his ass?"

Mark said, "You bet, Joe really did kicked his ass."

Rick said, "If we were in your shoes, we would have kicked his ass as well."

Joe said, "Well, of course, he asked Prastan and Jannet for forgiveness. Now he's a changed person."

Mark said, "And would you believed this, when Prastan bought over the company from Mr. Martin he appointed him as the company manager. Right now he's running the entire show at the farm."

Paul said, "Wow sounds dramatic."

Peter asked, "So what work you guys doing?"

Mark said, "We are working in the office beside them."

Rick asked, "So what position do you guys have in his company?"

Joe said, "Well, let me see. I really don't know. Our job is to sit beside them. But, at the same time we don't take orders from anyone beside them. We mostly can tell the manager and supervisor what to do."

Paul said, "So they actually pay you guys to be near them."

Mark said, "So to speak"

Peter said, "You know what? They love you guys more than anything in this wide world. And, I think that no one can take that away from them."

Angie recapped to Jannet, "So you guys owned your own company. You gave Mark and Joe your house. You bought a boat for Rick, Peter, and Paul. You have bailed us out, plus, you guys gave those guys $500.00 and gave us $500.00. You guys owned a mansion outright. You guys are really doing well. God blessed you both."

Charles said to Angie, "I wish I could be like Prastan."

Angie asked, "In what way you want to be like Prastan?"

Charles said, "Well, what I mean, I want to be a good person and wish I could help people too just like, Prastan."

Angie said, "Well, at one time in your life you were

in a position to help but instead you helped people in different ways."

Charles asked, "And what is that supposed to mean?"

Angie said, "Well, I hate to remind you of your past, because, I want you to forget about it and just concentrate on what you have just said."

Charles said, "I promised you, Angie and I want to keep to my promise, so I am working strongly on that."

Jannet said, "You see, my husband grew up very poor. I have a feeling he was inspired by God to help. The more good you can do in this world I think it's better for you in the long term. God is showing you the way how you can help yourself and when you help yourself he's happy. Look at this, Angie. Charles, I considered my own brother. As we all learned, he was doing very well in life at one time. But since he fell sick, things have changed. That does not mean that God doesn't love him. God loves all of us, even if we are sinners. We are his children. He has created all of us. And if he created all of us, we are supposed to live like brothers and sisters. God will never do wrong things to hurt you. He loves you too much to do something like that. What he's doing is, he's testing your faith, your reliance, your loyalty. Don't let him down; count on him. Believe me, he's out there looking at us. What I am trying to say here is, don't give up on hope and on life. Even if your body is in a crocodile's mouth and only your head alone is showing, don't give up. Please, don't give up. Don't let him and yourself down. It's not fair to either of you. One day, one day, you guys will surely get back on your feet. But understand this: God will not lift your feet for you. He will inspire what to do or how to do it, or he will inspire someone to lead you to the path to success and righteousness. I am not praising my husband, Prastan but if he deserves a compliment I will definitely make sure I give it to him. The same love we have for Mark and Joe is the same love we have for you all. The same way God is inspiring us to help them is the same way we have a feeling that he wants us to help you guys. Let me point it out this way. If you're in a boat in the middle in the ocean, you fill a glass of water from the left side of the boat and then fill another glass of water from the right side of the boat. Look at both glasses—it is the same water you're looking at. When you guys return home we will call you guys often to find out how you guys are doing, what you guys are doing, or what you guys want to do."

Prastan said, "Wow! Is that you, Jannet? Where did you get all this from?"

Jannet answered with a smile, "From you, from my loving husband."

Charles and Angie in one voice affirmed, "We agree with every word you have said, Jannet."

Prastan drove his car into the car's dealer parking lot. "Let's go guys." They came out of the car and stood looking around. Mark pulled in and parked just beside Prastan's car.

Joe asked, "What are we looking for, Jannet?"

Mark turned and looked at him, "For a car, stupid. If we are looking for a cow we'd be at a cattle ranch."

Peter said, "These guys are fun." This he said smiling.

Jannet glanced at Angie and shook her head, "I am tired with them but at the same time I am having fun all day long." She then turned at them "Would you guys stop it and start look for a good car."

The sales agent said, "Hello Prastan. How are you? How may I help you today?"

They shook hands. He then continued "Are you looking for something special?"

Prastan said, "Oh yeah," he then turned around. "Look for something good, guys; it must have a third- row seat and it must be an SUV."

Jannet said, "This look good, Prastan."

Joe and Mark inspected the vehicle, "How much for this vehicle?"

The agent answered, "You're looking at $5,000.00, guys." He then looked at Prastan and said, "For you Prastan, I'll give you for what it cost me because I know you'll buy it cash, I'll give it to you for $4,000.00. I expect a shipment of cars today, and I will need some cash."

Jannet said, "You have just got yourself a deal, Mister; prepare the paperwork."

The agent was astonished, "Are you sure, Jannet?" He looked at Prastan.

Prastan said smiling, "Don't look at me; if she said you have yourself a deal, then, believe her. She's the boss"

The agent said, "Oh thank you very much, Jannet"

They went in the office and did the paperwork. After that they decided to follow Joe to purchase the water fountain. They now switched cars. Mark drove Martin's car. Joe drove Prastan's car, and Prastan and crew rode in the SUV. They drove almost fifteen minutes to the fountain's yard. When they reached there, the owner knew Prastan. He had recently bought some flower plants from Sunshine Farm. "Hello, Prastan; nice seeing you. How may I help you today?"

Prastan did not recognize him, but from his statement he knew that this guy met him before somewhere. He said, "Hey, nice seeing you too." He shook his hand. He then continued, "I want to look at some water fountains. Is this all you have?"

The gentleman smiled and he said, "No, follow me over here." He then turned to Jannet, "Hi, Jannet; hello, Mark; hello, Joe."

Mark, Joe, and Jannet in one voice said, "Hello, how are you? Nice seeing you."

Jannet inwardly tried to recall where they had met. She whispered,"Oh boy."

The gentleman pointed out at the fountains. They are varied in sizes and shapes. "What size are you looking for, Prastan?"

Prastan said, "I am looking for something tall and of course beautiful to place at the front yard of my house."

The gentleman mentioned, "Well, from what you describe to me, I think I have something like that, but that is for shopping malls, golf courses, or places like Sea World. It's huge."

Jannet asked, "May I have a look at it?"

The gentleman said, "Sure, Jannet. You guys follow me."

Jannet covered her mouth with both hands, "Oh, this is so beautiful. What is the price for this?"

Gentleman said, "This one is for three hundred bucks. I could have given you this for two hundred fifty bucks since I knew you guys."

Jannet said, "Okay, we'll take it. It's so beautiful. We will place this fountain in front of the window; when I sit in the chair I will admire it."

However, the gentleman said, "I'm sorry Jannet, this one has already sold."

Jannet said, "Oh no." she was disappointed and she walked towards the SUV.

Mark and Joe looked at the gentleman and shook their heads, "She was disappointed."

The gentleman felt sorry for her. He said, "Jannet, how can you walk away from the fountain you really love."

She turned around, ran, and grabbed Prastan, "Yes,

yes." She then turned around at him, "But you have said it was sold."

The gentleman answered, "Not anymore, Jannet. I want to see my sister happy. Take it for two hundred fifty bucks. I will make an excuse to the people to whom I had sold it to. By the way, when you want it to be delivered?"

Jannet said, "Today will be fine, if you don't mind."

The gentleman said, "It will be delivered between 3:00 and 4:00 P.M."

Prastan said, "Thank you so much; I'll see you later."

When Martin had finished his breakfast, they went outside at the front of the house and were admiring the beauty of the house.

Martin stamped his foot on the ground. He continued, "Jannet should put a nice water fountain on this spot, straight this window. Oh, the first time I met Prastan, I saw potential in him. He's handsome, talented, ambitious, hardworking, and most important of all, he's smart. We must never look at a person and judge a person because of his or her poverty. If I had a daughter I could have taken him for my son-in- law, I so much love this kid. When I looked at Jannet sitting beside me I saw a perfect match. Look what they have achieved. They have accomplished wealth within a few years that I haven't accomplished in my lifetime."

James said, "That's true. They are doing pretty good. As you have said they were made for each other."

Shortly after, they drove in the driveway in the SUV.

Martin said, "Well, I can see you have good choice. How much did you pay for it?"

Jannet said, "Four thousand bucks."

Martin said, "For an SUV like this, it's worth every penny. So what you're going to do with this car that you have?"

Prastan and Jannet looked at each other, "We'll give it to Joe and Mark."

Joe said, "Yes, yes."

Mark said, "Shut up fool."

Charles and Angie said, "There it goes again."

Peter, Paul, and Rick , said, "We have gotten accustomed to it."

Mark said, "Yes, Jannet, you keep on smiling."

Jannet continued smiling, "What Mark?"

Mark said, "That mean, 'We have to go and open the office.' And you and Prastan will take your time and come later."

Joe said, "Oh yeah. I never thought of that."

Mark said, "Shut up fool, you never thought of anything in your entire life."

Everyone started to laugh.

Martin nodding his head, he said, "I'm getting too old for this. I need some rest. I must go now. I'll come back sometime next week." This he said and he shook everyone hands. Then he walked slowly to his car. He then turned and looked at the new faces "You guys are living like brothers and sisters and let it be that way." He then turned at Mark, "Hey Mark, how does my car ride? Smooth, right"

Mark replied, "Yes sir, very smooth, sir. Like it never been used before."

Martin said, "TLC boy, tender love and caring." Everyone laughed.

Jannet said, "Sir."

Martin said, "Yes dear." He turned around once again.

Jannet said, "We have bought a huge and beautiful water fountain to put at the front of the house. It will be delivered may be in one or two hours' time. With your experience, do you want to help me find a spot for it before you leave?" Hearing such words Martin changed his mind about going home. He went and stood on the exact spot where he had suggested to put a water fountain. And with a smile on his face he asked, "Do you have in mind a spot for it?"

She replied, "Yes, sir, I do, but I don't know whether it will look good there."

Martin asked, "And where is that spot?"

She said, "Exactly on the same spot where you standing."

Martin turned at Mr. and Mrs. James, "You see what I mean. Smart people think alike. Tell her what I said earlier. Well, this time I am surely going. I need some rest. This old man is getting older day after day. I'll be back next week." This he said and went in his car and drove slowly away honking his horn at them.

Jannet said, "I can't understand." And she turned at Angie.

Deecia asked, "Understand what, dear?"

Jannet said, "My old man said he's getting older day after day. I asked him to help me find a spot for the water fountain and, he did not bother with me. Do you think he's mad at me?"

Angie said, "That old man loved you guys too much to be mad with you. But why you think he's mad at you?"

Jannet said, "Maybe he wanted to go home and we took too long with his car."

Deecia said, "Don't confuse dear. As Angie has just mentioned, he loves you guys too much to be mad at you."

Jannet said, "But then?" and she turned at Prastan.

Prastan said, "If Mr. Martin is getting grumpy, I understand that he's old, but not my young wife."

Jannet said, "I'm not grumpy, Mr. Prastan." This she said and chased Prastan around the yard to give him a friendly punch. Prastan ran among Peter, Paul, and Rick.

Deecia continued, "When you guys left this morning, Mr. Martin suggested that you should buy a water fountain and put it on the same spot."

Jannet said, "Really, Mom?"

Charles said, "You heard what the man said to your mom and dad that smart people think alike."

Jannet said, "Oh, I love my old man."

James said, "Oh thank you, dear." Smiling, he fully acknowledged that she was referring to Mr. Martin. Everyone laughed.

Jannet said, "Not you, Dad. I was referring to Mr. Martin."

James said, "I know sweet heart, I know."

She then added, "And I love you too, Dad. You're my life." Everyone smiled.

Prastan teased her once again smiling and laughing, "I thought you have said I'm your life." Once again everyone laughed.

Jannet blushed, "I'll punch you." This she said pointing at him.

Deecia said, "Let's go inside. I have prepared lunch. Let us eat while the food is still hot."

They went in the house.

Angie said, "You may have to get a maid, Jannet. This house is too huge."

Deecia added, "You've got that one right, Angie."

Prastan said, "Okay guys, let us have something to drink before we eat."

Mark and Joe fetched beers and James fetched liquor while Prastan fetched glasses. Deecia helped with a pitcher of ice. Everyone stuck to their regular choice and of course, Jannet and Angie shared a bottle of beer, as usual. The first round went very fast. On the second round, there were more talking and laughing, and the drinking was going very slowly. Charles decided to share a joke with everyone. Everyone now braced back looking at him. He said, "This old lady."

Prastan butted in, "Are you referring to Jannet or Angie?" Everyone laughed almost on top of their voices. Jannet showed him a punch and shook her head at him.

Angie said, "Stop it, Prastan. We aren't old."

Charles continued, "Now, I have forgotton the joke." They noticed that Charles was improving rapidly from his sickness. Mr. and Mrs. James were excited for them.

Jannet mentioned, "Your husband is coming back, Angie."

Angie replied, "I can see that, girl"

After the second drink they ate their lunch and were relaxing. The doorbell rang. Jannet peeped through the window, "There is our water fountain, guys." They all went outside and helped unload it from the flatbed truck.

Jannet gave the delivery guys a tip and thanked them for showing up earlier than they were scheduled.

Peter, Paul Rick, Mark, and Joe then placed the fountain exactly where Jannet wanted it to be. She then went inside. She sat on the sofa and looked through the window "This is beautiful. This is exactly what I wanted." She then called everyone inside to have a look.

They decided to continue their drinking and to make their vacation a wonderful one. They made jokes and laughed among themselves. Jannet picked up the phone and called Frankie.

Frankie said, "Hello Jannet. Nice hearing from you. I really glad that you have called. When you guys coming back?"

Everyone stopped talking and looked at Jannet.

Jannet replied, "We are coming home tonight. Why, is something wrong?" Everyone could hear the other side of the conversation.

Frankie said, "No, everything is going good. We are very busy. We are selling like crazy. I have a long list of orders from customers. This is something I cannot handle; only you or Prastan can handle it."

Jannet gave the phone to Prastan.

Prastan said, "Hello, Frankie."

Frankie replied, "Hello, Prastan; nice hearing from you. As Jannet said, we are coming home tonight. We have some guests coming with us and they will be leaving Saturday. We are coming tomorrow at the office. I will take care of all the orders and Mark and Joe will be in the office. How is George doing at the farm?"

Frankie said, "He's doing fine. But we have a lot of work there."

Jannet butted in, "Okay Frankie, Mark and Joe will be in the office tomorrow. Show them where you left off and you can then return to the farm."

Frankie said, "Okay."

Mark looked at Joe.

Joe said, "What? Why are you looking at me? Haven't you seen me before?"

Mark said, "Shut up, fool, and go slow with the beer. We have to work in the morning."

Joe said, "So what?"

Mark said, "So, so. I don't want you to get drunk and then I have to do all the work at the office by myself."

Joe replied, "Look who's talking. I don't want you to get drunk and I have to do all the work all by myself." He repeated Mark's words, teasing him.

Jannet said, "Okay guys, tomorrow morning is far away. I am sorry it had to be this way. You guys could still have a few more drinks."

Prastan added, "Remember one thing guys, Frankie knows field work not the office work. We will visit you guys at the office on and off. And you guys can close earlier and join us."

Mark said, "If we are busy, we will not close early. Your business is our happiness."

Joe added, "Without you guys." and he bent his head.

Jannet said, "Oh come on, Joe."

Joe continued, "Without you guys, we are nobody."

Mark said, "Shut up, fool, with them we are somebody."

Joe objected, "I said without them."

Mark said, "Oh."

Joe said, "We're going to leave early tonight."

Jannet asked, "Why? You guys have your room. You guys can spend the week with us."

On Wednesday morning Jannet and her mom woke up very early and prepared breakfast. Mark and Joe had their breakfast and then went to the office. They had taken over the work from Frankie and subsequently discharged him from office duty. Frankie then returned to his respective job as manager.

Angie and Charles slowly went in the kitchen, "Good morning, Jannet. Good morning, Mrs. James."

They replied, "Good morning."

Jannet asked, "Ready for some breakfast, guys?"

Charles said, "Oh yeah. I'm hungry." This he said while rubbing his stomach. Angie looked at Jannet and smiled, then, she shook her head "He's getting there."

The rest of the guys came in the kitchen a few minutes later. And as usual they greeted each other with hello and good morning. Finally, Prastan and James walked in.

Prastan said, "Okay guys, after breakfast I will show you our office and business."

Peter said, "Jannet, this breakfast is really delicious."

Paul and Rick added, "You're a very good cook, Jannet."

Jannet said, "I think I will share a part of that compliment with my mom. She did most of the cooking."

James said, "You looked very sharp this morning, Charles."

Angie added, "Is it Allgreen? Probably he needs to live in Allgreen."

Charles answered, "Indeed, I feel much better, Mr. James, and you're right, Jannet; this vacation makes me feel good."

James said, "Prastan, before you guys go, would you please give us a ride home? I have a closet to fix. By the way, how about you guys spend some time this evening by my place?"

Prastan looked at them, "Say it, guys."

Charles, without any hesitation said, "No problem. What do you think guys?" This he turned around and asked everyone.

Everyone in one voice responded, "Sure, why not?"

Jannet said, "Okay, Dad, whenever you guys ready, I'll give you guys a ride home."

James said, "We are sure ready, sweetheart."

Jannet said, "Okay, then let's go. I won't take long, guys. Would you like to accompany me, Angie?"

Angie replied, "I'll be glad to."

When they reached there, Jannet took the opportunity to show Angie around the house. She emphasized, "This was my room Angie. Oh I miss my room."

Her mom glanced at her and smiled. She whispered to Angie, "Lie."

Jannet overheard and said, "That's not true, Mom. I really miss my room."

Mom added, "Whatever, dear."

Angie said, "It's a beautiful house, Mrs. James."

Mrs. James answered, "Oh thank you, dear."

Jannet had suggested to her mom not to cook. She had promised to buy the food.

Mom said, "Okay dear, no problem."

Jannet said, "Dad, you don't have to worry, I will also buy the beer and liquor."

Her dad replied, "If you so desire, sweetheart, your old man has no problem with that. At least you have saved me some money and time."

Angie said, "Oh, my sister can afford it."

Mrs. James said, "God blessed them both."

Jannet said, "As many people said that we were made for each other and our match was made in heaven."

James added, "I have said so myself, dear."

Jannet said, "Okay, we must leave now. See you guys this evening. Let's go, Angie."

On their way home Jannet asked, "So what do you think of Allgreen so far?"

Angie replied, "It's really beautiful, Jannet."

Jannet asked again, "So what business you think Charles has in mind to do when he returns home?"

Angie answered, "Maybe sell insurance. I really don't know. When we settle down, we'll think about it. You guys gave us a restart in life, and we cannot let you guys down. We definitely have to do something."

Jannet said, "As I said, don't give up. You guys must work together."

Angie said, "You're a very lucky girl, Jannet."

Jannet said, "Oh thank you, Angie." and inwardly, *Em. Why did she say that?* she question herself.

A few minutes later they reached home. All the guys were at the front yard admiring Allgreen and at the same time they were admiring the early morning weather, the clear blue sky and a few stray clouds floating over their heads.

Peter mentioned almost seriously that, "Allgreen is a really beautiful place. I wish to live in a place like this."

Angie came along and supported Peter's statement, "I myself wish to live in a place like this. It's a really beautiful place."

Rick, Peter and Paul went in the SUV and sat in the third-row rear seat. Charles and Angie sat in the second row seat. Jannet was at the wheel, and Prastan sat on the front passenger seat.

Jannet had both hands on the wheel. She looked at Prastan and asked, "Well?"

Prastan said, "Well, let me think. We are going to the office first and make sure that Mark and Joe have everything under control."

Jannet asked, "Then?"

Prastan replied, "They will close the office for an hour and follow us to the farm."

Jannet again for the third time she asked, "And?"

Prastan answered, "We will show them around, and after that we'll go to a restaurant and have lunch."

Jannet said, "Sound really good to me."

Rick said, "That's what you call planning."

Paul added, "Well, that's the way it should be. A husband and wife must put two and two together, and make a decision together." He then hesitated for a few seconds. "Damn, I'm becoming like Prastan now." Everyone laughed.

Angie asked, "What do you mean, Paul, put two and two together?"

Instead of Paul, Charles answered her, "A slogan like that means both parties must think about something and decide on one thing."

Angie asked, "Could you give me an example?"

Charles answered, "Sure, why not. Have you heard what Prastan and Jannet have just said?"

Angie replied, "Of course."

Charles said, "Well that is an example."

Angie said, "Oh, now I understand what Paul meant by putting two and two together."

Moments later they reached the office. The office was very busy. Customers were in line waiting their turn. Most of the customers knew Prastan and Jannet. They greeted them with "Good morning, Prastan; good morning, Jannet."

Prastan and Jannet smiled at them and in one voice they said, "Hello guys, good morning." This they said waving their hands at them. They went in the office. Prastan asked, "How is everything, guys?" referring to Mark and Joe, of course. Jannet was busy taking care with the customers, and moments later they had everything under control.

Joe said, "Thank God you guys came or else we should have backed up."

Angie said, "It's a beautiful office you have here, Jannet."

Jannet smiled at her, "Oh thank you, Angie."

Rick, Peter and Paul, "Nice office, it's beautiful"

Charles asked, "Are you guys busy like this all the time?"

Mark answered him smiling, "Every day is the same, busy, busy,.."

Joe gave Jannet the report, "Here's the report sheet for Monday and Tuesday. And, by the way, Frankie gave me this money."

Jannet asked, "Did you count it? Is everything balanced up?"

Mark added, "Yes, Jannet. Everything is okay."

Jannet said, "Prastan, I have $6,000.00 here. In which account you want me to deposit it?"

Prastan said, "Deposit $2,000.00 in the saving;

$3,000.00 in the payroll account and $1,000.00 in the regular checking account."

Jannet said, "Okay." She then gave Mark the money and said, "Go to the bank and deposit this cash."

Joe asked, "You guys want to take a ride with us?" he asked, referring to Peter, Paul, and Rick.

"Sure. Why not," they replied and then walked out of the door.

Joe then turned back, "Hey Prastan."

Prastan said, "What?"

Joe said, "Could I?" before he could complete his question Prastan said, "Oh no. never, you have your own."

Charles asked, "How come you read him so fast?"

Jannet laughed, "We could even read their minds. How you treated people and showed them love. That is the same way people treated you and show you the same love and kindness."

Mark and Joe sat in the front seat. Peter, Paul, and Rick sat in the rear seat. Mark was driving the car.

Peter mentioned, "This car is running very good. You know what guys? Prastan is a very nice guy. He's a very kindhearted person."

Joe mentioned, "Before he got married to Jannet, he suffered a lot in life. Maybe God smiled on him."

Rick added, "I believed you. And you know something? Probably Jannet brought him good luck too. I heard many older people said that."

Paul asked, "Older people said, what?"

Rick replied, "That when you got married. Sometimes getting married brought you good luck and sometimes bad luck."

Peter added, "And it seemed like his business is doing very good."

Mark said, "Oh yeah, he's smart and he knew how to manage the business."

Paul mentioned, "God blessed him. He's so kind-hearted; he bought us a boat and gave us $500.00 bucks. Where will you find a person like him?"

Rick added, "Not in this modern world."

They reached the bank. They went in.

Mark said, "Hello, Jim."

Jim smiled, "Hello, Mark; hello, Joe. And who are these guys?"

Mark said, "They are with us."

Jim said, "Hello guys. So how may I help you, Mark?"

Mark said, "We need to deposit this money for Prastan."

Jim asked, "How he's doing? Tell him I said hello and tell Jannet hello for me as well. Tell Prastan to give me a call. Come, don't join the line; follow me." Within five minutes they finished their business and were soon on their way back to the office.

Peter asked, "Who's that guy?"

Joe answered, "He's the bank manager."

Rick added, "It seems like Prastan is a very popular guy in Allgreen."

Mark said, "You bet. And everyone in Allgreen is talking good about him. Through them we became known as well."

Paul said, "I can see that."

Rick mentioned, "Kindhearted. When you're kind-hearted and nice, people must talk good thing about you."

Once again customers came in the office. The office was crowded. Customers had formed a line, awaiting their turn to order whatever they wanted to purchase.

Jannet asked, "Angie, do you want to help me out until Mark and Joe return?"

Angie said, "Sure, why not, Jannet? Just tell me what you want me to do."

Jannet said, "Write down the order for me please and make sure you get their names, address and phone number. Then you give the order to Prastan."

Angie said, "Okay, Jannet."

Charles asked, "If you guys want me to do something, I am willing to help out."

Prastan said, "You're on vacation, Charles. Have you forgotten?"

Charles said, "I know but at the same time I can still help you guys do something."

Jannet said, "Okay my dear brother, you can work with Angie."

Charles said, "Thank you, my loving sister." This he said and he smiled.

Shortly after, Mark and the rest of the guys arrived. Prastan gave Joe a list. "Call Frankie and make sure he gets all this order ready for customers pick up."

Joe said, "Okay."

Mark said, "Hey Prastan, before I forget, Jim said to tell you guys hello and he wants you to call him whenever you have time."

Prastan replied, "Oh thank you, Mark."

Jannet said, "As soon as we finish with these customers we will close for lunch. But as Prastan said, we will visit the farm first and then go for lunch. And just a reminder, guys, mom and dad invited us tonight."

After a little while they closed the office for lunch. And as usual Prastan, Jannet, Charles, and Angie drove in the SUV and Mark and the rest of the guys went with the car. When they reached the farm some of the customers were there picking up and some were already gone. Prastan and Jannet then took the opportunity to introduce their guests to the manager, supervisor, and the rest of the employees. Then they took a tour around the farm. After that they went to a restaurant. They placed their order and while waiting for the food, they cooled off with a cold beer. After lunch Mark and Joe returned to the office while the rest went in the SUV. When they reached home they laid themselves on the sofa, taking a rest for the upcoming night event.

Jannet then called Mark and Joe and reminded them to close the office early.

It was late in the evening and everyone is getting dressed to go over by Jannet's mom. Jannet called the restaurant, "Hello, I would like to place an order."

The receptionist asked, "What is your name?"

Jannet answered, "My name is, Jannet."

The receptionist asked, "Is this the Jannet who owns Sunshine Farm?"

Jannet answered, "Yes, I am."

The receptionist said, "Oh, hi Jannet, I remember you. Okay, what are you ordering tonight?"

Jannet said, "I need eleven large chicken fried rice."

The receptionist asked, "Would you like me to deliver it, Jannet?"

Jannet said, "Yes, but not at my home. I would like you to deliver it by my parents. Let me give you the address."

The receptionist mentioned, "Don't worry, I remembered the address. Before you got married to Prastan I used to deliver food for you when you were living there."

Jannet added, "You have good memory. Thank you."

By now everyone was ready. And as usual, Prastan, Jannet, Charles and Angie were in the SUV. Mark, Joe, and the rest of the guys were in the car. Prastan drove out. Mark followed him behind. Prastan stopped at the corner store. Mark stopped behind the SUV. All the guys went in the store.

The cashier said, "Hello Prastan" She smiled at him.

Prastan said, "Hi how are you? Nice seeing you again."

Rick mentioned, "I can't believe this. Everyone in Allgreen knows this man. Anywhere you go, anywhere you turn, someone know him."

Prastan said, "Pick whatever you want, guys. Whatever you feel like drinking tonight."

Mark looked at Joe.

Joe said, "What? Haven't you seen me before?"

Mark said, "Remember, we have to work tomorrow." Within ten minutes they picked up their liquor and beer and were soon on their way. When they reached there it was getting dark. Mark parked behind the SUV. Jannet and Charles came out of the SUV from the other side of the door. Prastan and Angie came out from the driver side. Prastan was trying to close the door with his right hand. Angie was trying to reach Jannet when her right fingers lingered in Prastan's left fingers for a second.

Joe said, "Oh no."

Mark asked, "Oh no what?"

Joe said, "I saw Angie hold Prastan's fingers. Haven't you seen that?"

Rick added, "I saw that crystal clear."

Peter said, "I saw it."

Paul mentioned, "I haven't seen it. But she is wrong

to do that knowing that he's married and is living a decent life. Wonder if Prastan fell for it?"

Joe said, "No way. He loves Jannet too much. He will never cheat on her."

Rick said, "I cannot believe she's still after him."

Peter said, "Haven't you seen Prastan walked away from her. But let's assume that she's still after him. We cannot let this happen. If Jannet finds out our friendship will over."

Prastan knew that it happened accidentally, and it remained unspoken. Angie was quite worried about it and wondered what Prastan must have thought of her. Inasmuch as she loved Prastan before she got married to Charles and she still loved him.

She was trying not to let this overcome her emotions. Considering the fact of what Prastan and Jannet had done for them and that she's now a married woman and considering their friendly relationship, she doesn't want to place a red ribbon between them. She always considered Jannet to be the lucky girl at the same time as she considered herself to be lucky too by having Jannet as her friend.

Mark said, "Guys, guys. Let's not accuse her. Probably it accidentally happened and we're arriving at a conclusion to degrade her. We don't know if it was deliberately happened or, as I said it, if it happened accidentally, even if she still loves him. And who would you blame not to fall for a guy like him. If I were a girl, I would have fallen for him myself. She will try to avoid a situation like this, considering all that they have done for them and their friendship. She knew that if she did not let bygone be bygone and Jannet should find out about it, their relationship would be dissolved. I think she knew this. And she will rather swallow that emotion than to destroy the way they are living right now.

Peter mentioned, "I agree with you, Mark. Guys, we all knew that she was madly in love with him. And whether or not she still loves him as Mark had just said, she will swallow that emotion. She's also a smart girl, and she knows if she continues with it and it happen to be exposed, she will destroy the speedy recovery of Charles and also their friendship for good."

Paul added, "I love the way we are living. I don't want to lose this friendship."

Joe asked, "What should we do?"

Mark said, "There is nothing we can do. We cannot accuse her; we have no solid grounds on her. As I said probably she is innocent. But, there is something we can do."

Peter asked, "What?"

Mark said, "We can praise our friendship. We can elaborate how nice we are living and how we should try not to destroy this relationship."

Joe asked, "If we're going to repeat this, what point are we getting at?"

Mark answered, "In the event she is still after him, she will try to forget it and swallow that emotion."

Everyone laughed and gave a low clapping of hands among themselves.

Mr. and Mrs. James were at the front door welcoming them as they entering the house.

Deecia said, "You have ordered so much food, dear."

Jannet mentioned, "You are worrying too much, Mom. I would rather have too much food than too little. Come this way, Angie. We will hang out at this corner."

Prastan said, "Guys aren't biting."

Angie replied, "Sometimes they do." This she said smiling.

Prastan said, "Put the liquor over there on that table, guys. Joe, you can put the beers in the refrigerator."

Deecia said, "I want you all to make yourselves comfortable and feel at home. You guys are living very nicely among yourselves."

Charles and Prastan sat in one sofa. Mark, Peter, and Paul sat in another sofa. Joe and Rick also sat in a sofa. Jannet and Angie stood beside each other at a corner. Mr. and Mrs. James were busy trying to make everyone happy.

James said, "Well, you guys can call me the bartender tonight."

Jannet said, "Okay, Dad; no problem." She hesitated for a little while.

"But Mr. Bartender, where is your bartender's hat?"

Everyone laughed. James went in his room and put on a beautiful hat and immediately returned, "Well, how do I look?" This he said and bowed, "May I take your order, please?"

Charles laughed, and laughed and kept laughing, "Yes, Mr. Bartender, one drink for me."

Everyone looked at Charles; they felt very happy that he was recovering rapidly from his sickness. Jannet emptied a bottle of beer in Angie's glass and a bottle in hers. "Aren't you going to take a drink, Mom?"

Mom said, "In a get-together like this, you bet." She also took a beer.

Joe went to the refrigerator and brought three beers. He gave Prastan a beer, Mark a beer, and Of course took one for himself. Mr. Bartender gave Peter, Paul, Rick, and Charles a drink of whisky and of course he took a tall one for himself. "This bartender is getting old. After this drink he'll retire and enjoy the rest of his retirement drinking. So from now on you guys may help yourselves."

Mark looked at Joe.

Joe said, "What? Why are you looking at me?"

Mark said, "Nothing. I didn't say a word." This he said and glanced at Joe's beer.

They were on their third drink and everyone was feeling good, making jokes, laughing, and being merry among themselves. Angie, Jannet, and Mrs. James eventually moved closer to the guys. Angie got drunk, and she felt courageous. "I'm so happy." This she said and hugged,

Jannet, "I love you Jannet. You're my sister, you're everything to me. We cannot forget all the good things that you guys have done for us. Thanks, thanks a lot, sister. We're living so nice ever since we have met. How did we meet again?" This she asked nodding her head trying to answer her own question by repeating "How did we meet? Where did we meet?"

Charles held her in his arms as they faced each other, "Have you forgotten what I told you, sweetheart? Prastan is a very handsome and attractive guy. Jannet always kept her eyes on him. One day Prastan worked late and when he came home Jannet was mad and picked a stupid fight with him. Prastan got angry and walked out of the house." Hearing this everyone took a deep breath. He then continued, "Rick found him that job at your Dad's restaurant and that's the way we met."

Angie said, "Oh yes, yes. I remember now you told me that." She then turned and looked at everyone. "I want to say something if you guys permit me to."

Joe said, "Go ahead be our guest; say what you have to say. Don't keep it in; spit it out."

Peter added, "Don't be scared, Angie. Say it."

Angie turned and hugged Jannet, "Oh Jannet. Please don't mad at me. And please forgive me."

Inwardly Jannet said,, *Don't say you have flirted with my man. I'll kill you.*

Everyone was astonished over her statement and

leaned back looking at her waiting to hear what sort of bad news she had to contribute at this joyful moment.

Charles inwardly said, *Oh Angie, please don't degrade me and yourself.*

CHAPTER TWO

JANNET said, "You don't need to tell us now, Angie. You could tell us some other time."

Angie said, "Oh Jannet, please don't feel that I'm drunk. I've got this inside of me, and I want to say it. I was waiting for an opportunity like this to say it."

Mrs. James inwardly muttered, *Oh Lord, let it not be that she flirted with Prastan. Jannet may not be able to take it.*

The rest of the guys were speechless and couldn't take their eyes off of her.

James urged, "Get over it, Angie. Probably, you will feel better."

Angie said, "Charles, you and I loved each other for a long time. I mean long before we met Prastan and Jannet. Please say that you'll forgive me. And Jannet please say that you'll forgive me also."

Joe and Mark said in one voice, "This sounds very bad," quietly nodding their heads.

Jannet urged, "Speak it, Angie. No one will hurt you." This she said and she braced back for the worse to come from her.

Charles also braced back for the worse. He began to have a negative feeling about her sleeping with Prastan, "Say it, Angie. If you didn't kill anyone, no one will hurt you. Everyone made mistake sometime in life. Look how many mistake I made in this beautiful life that God has given me."

Jannet added, "No one is perfect in this life, Angie. A man is liable to make a mistake; everyone has made a mistake in this life; only God doesn't make mistakes. Tell us what is bothering you." And then she continued silently, *If you flirted or slept with my man I'll kill you.*

Angie said, "Let me begin with you Charles."

Charles bent his down and said inwardly, *Oh boy.*

Joe said, "Wait, let me get a beer before you start." Mark who was very cautious in drinking because they had to work, said, "Get me a beer, Joe."

Charles insisted, "Let us all get a drink." Everyone now expected to hear bad news from Angie.

Angie said, "Charles, you and I loved each other almost five years before we met Prastan and Jannet. Though, I knew that you have many girlfriends out there, I still love you, and I love you much from the inside of my heart. When my dad hired Prastan to work with us, Prastan was so handsome and cute I got carried away. Please forgive me everyone. I did not know. Let me emphasize, please, I did not know that Prastan was married. I'd never asked him, nor did he tell me that he was married. All that I had noticed in his face was that he seemed very worried. Charles let me be honest with you. I said to myself that if Prastan loves me, I'll dump you. But he didn't love me. He didn't even look at me. Every time I tried to say something to him, he walked away. A few times I held his hand and he shook it off. I tried to show him in many ways that I loved him, but he just ignored me." She then turned at Jannet, "Jannet, You have a very honest man, a man who loves you so dearly. Any girl can get carried away with him. Oh Jannet, please forgive me and don't mad at me." She then bent her head.

Mrs. James placed her hands on her chest "Oh boy."

Charles said, "Let's take a drink for this, guys." And after a moment of silence he continued, "Angie, if you had dumped me I shouldn't have blamed you, my reputation was bad, and I admit it without any objection."

Jannet took a deep breath, "I don't have to forgive you, Angie. You haven't done anything wrong based on what you've said. And from my point of view, any young girl would have done the same as you. Even I would have done the same if I was in your shoes, considering the fact that you knew at the time that the person with whom you're madly in love with had many girls out there. I'm a young girl too and I know exactly how you had felt at the moment of that situation. And correct me if I am wrong. You had probably felt that if you got married to Charles maybe he would not change his way of life after marriage and that your marriage would be jeopardized, or maybe it wouldn't lost for long. Inasmuch as you loved him so dearly, you probably were thinking of another solution. And that is, if you could find a single guy who has no girl, maybe you wouldn't have to worry about marriage corruption and domestic dispute. And as you mentioned earlier that you did not knew that Prastan was married. I personally wouldn't blame you for that and as a matter of fact, in my opinion, I feel that no one should have blamed you for that if they put themselves in your shoes."

Angie said, "Oh Jannet, thank you so much for understanding me. This was eating me inside. And now that I have spit it out, I felt so relieved," she said as she hugged her.

Mrs. James said, "I don't blame you, Angie. I have a daughter too. And I am a woman too. I would have done the same."

Angie released Jannet and stood firm with her head slightly bent forward. Charles then embraced her against his chest. "As Jannet has said, you have done nothing wrong. And I would say the same; you have done nothing wrong. Look how many mistake I had made in my life. And I was forgiven. So I don't have to forgive you, sweetheart. Probably if I were a girl and if I were in your shoes probably I would have done the same."

James said, "That is so sweet of you to think that way, Charles. And I feel that no one should hold any hate or grudge against her. I have a daughter too. Parents who have children have different feelings. You guys may not understand this. You may be married and still not have this feeling. But, as I said,, when you have children it's a different feelings. And one day in your life you guys will remember this."

Joe said, "Jannet, when will you guys have this feeling? And Charles, when will you guys have this feeling?" Hearing this from Joe, Jannet and Angie laughed blushingly.

Mark said, "Shut up, fool, why don't you get married and then ask yourself that same question."

Rick glanced at Peter and Paul, "These guys are fun. When we leave, we'll miss this fun."

Joe said, "I will have this feeling when I get married someday." Everyone laughed. He then continued, "But who will marry me?"

Jannet and Angie in one voice said, "Oh don't say that, Joe. That day will definitely come one day."

Prastan said, "Nothing happens before its time, Joe. That day will surely come one day."

Joe answered "That will be a miracle."

Mrs. James added, "God has created pairs for everyone, even for the birds in the air. God will show his miracles in a mysterious ways. Don't ever forget that."

Jannet said, "I think we should go now. It's getting late, and Mark and Joe have to work in the morning."

Angie said, "Yeah, let's go; I'm feeling sleepy."

Jannet drove the SUV, and Mark drove the car. It was just a little over midnight when they reached home.

Everyone was happy and tired at the same time. They went to bed and soon fell asleep.

The next morning Jannet and Prastan woke up early before dawn and prepared breakfast. Mark and Joe woke up and went in the kitchen.

Jannet and Prastan said, "Good morning Joe, good morning Mark."

Mark and Joe said, "Good morning"

Prastan said, "Short sleep, guys?"

Mark said, "Yeah."

Joe asked, "Could I take the day off?"

Mark said, "Shut up, fool. Eat something. We have to open the office early today. Today will be another busy day from what I saw yesterday."

Jannet said, "Call us if you guys need help."

At 7:30 A.M sharp Mark and Joe walked out of the front door.

Shortly after they left for the office, the rest of the crew woke up. They sat around the pool and were having their breakfast.

Jannet said, "I hope you guys have a nice time at my parents's home last night."

Charles said, "Oh that was wonderful. I had a lot of fun."

Jannet asked, "How about you, Angie?"

Angie replied, "Oh I enjoyed myself. It was the first time I felt that way, I felt so good. It was fun."

Peter said, "And you've also said your piece."

Angie said, "Oh I feel so good I spit it out."

Rick said, "At first when you started, I had a bad feeling of what was to come."

Paul added, "Me too."

Angie asked, "And what was that feelings you guys had?"

Rick said, "That you had flirted with Prastan."

Angie asked, "In what way?"

Paul said, "Like paid him a visit in his room."

Charles said, "I had the same feelings too, Angie."

Prastan said, "You cannot blame the guys for thinking like that, Angie. The way you put yourself forward when you started."

Angie said, "Yeah right. Guys always think differently. Not every girl is wicked. You heard them, Jannet. If that would have happened, do you think I would have the courage to face you and to stay in your home? As I said, I did not know that Prastan was married. Any girl would have tried their luck. But he's a decent person. He rejected me from touching him.

Jannet said, "Okay guys. She said what she had in her heart. I agree with you, Angie. If I were in your shoes, I would have definitely tried to move that dark cloud that I have inside. You did the right thing, girl. Now let us all forget it and make some plan for today.

Prastan urged, "You guys get dressed. Today I'm going

to drive you guys around and show you what Allgreen looks like."

Rick said, "That's a good idea. We'll be proud to tell people that we have visited and toured the entire boundary of Allgreen."

Paul mentioned, "Hey, Prastan, you said that you will teach us some karate tricks so we can defend ourselves from the bad guys. Have you forgotten?"

Prastan said, "Of course not. We'll do that tomorrow."

Angie asked, "What dress should I wear, Jannet?"

Jannet responded, "Anything not too heavy. Today will be in the mid 80s."

They got themselves dressed and in a few minutes everyone gathered in the front yard once again, admiring the neighborhood. Jannet wore a simple dress. It was casual and not too flashy. Inasmuch Jannet had told Angie to wear something thin She still dressed in a red top and blue short pants.

Rick said, "You look good in that outfit, Angie," and then whispered softly in Jannet's ear "My God. She's a married woman."

Angie said, "This is my favorite outfit, Rick." This she said and hugged Charles and walked slowly towards the road.

Prastan asked, "Is everything okay, Jannet?"

Jannet said, "So far so good." She then turned and looked at her and whispered in Prastan's and Rick's ears, "She looked cute in that flashy outfit."

Rick said, "That outfit isn't appropriate." This he said while looking at her. He continued, "I had deeply considered that she's a young girl almost your age and that you're still young and have the flashy way of life. But damnit, she had just dug herself out from a messy situation. She should at least try to prove herself decent among everyone and be as simple as possible until she return home. Everyone here is a family friend. No one here will crush on her. Unless she still has him in her heart and is trying to catch his eyes in a particular way. She tried to convince everyone that she did not have any love relationship with him. No one knows what she has deep down her mind but herself. At a point I felt that it's all over and that you can now sleep easily, but it's quite unlike, you still have to sleep with your one eye open at her."

Paul and Peter came in and joined along, "Uh she looks hot."

Peter asked, "I wonder who eyes she's trying to catch."

Paul said, "You all knew."

Peter said, "But damnit she's a married woman. Charles fully recovered from his sickness. If he finds out that she still has her mind on Prastan, he will be heartbroken, knowing how nicely they're living."

Jannet smoothly polished the idea by saying "I'm wondering whether this is her style and way of life. Some people live like that. Maybe she's innocent and we all get it wrong. It would be unfair to criticize her because of her style. You know what? Let's forget that we ever thought of something like this." This she said and jumped in the SUV. She held the steering with both hands "Let's go, guys." Peter, Paul, and Rick sat in the rear seat. Prastan sat beside her. She drove up to the gate. Charles sat behind Prastan in the second row seat and Angie sat behind Jannet.

Jannet asked, "Where to, Prastan?"

Prastan said, "Let's show them Allgreen's Park where we had our first date."

Angie said, "Is that where you guys first caught each other's eye?"

Jannet said, "No. He came in the office looking for a job. When he returned his signed agreement to me our eyes lingered for a moment."

Charles added, "That was so sweet."

Angie asked, "And what happened next?"

Jannet said, "My pen slipped out of my hand, revealing my nervousness."

Peter said, "You bet. You must be really flattered."

Angie asked again, "And what happened next?"

Jannet said, "He told me he wished we could see each other again. Then he closed the door and headed towards the farm."

Angie asked, "Did you go crazy?"

Jannet replied, "Something I'll never forget, girl. I said to myself, poor thing, he so handsome and had to work in the field."

Rick said, "Interesting, keep going, let's hear some more."

Jannet continued, "When he said, he wished we couldn't see each other again I said to myself, *you bet.*"

Angie asked, "And after that?"

Jannet said, "We met one month later when he was called to the office for a promotion. I was packing stationery when I recognized the voice that I had treasured for a month, the voice that was disturbing my beautiful sleep. Mr. Martin had noticed my strange behavior and secretly investigated me. He fell in love with Prastan and thought that he was the perfect boy for me. I remembered when Prastan went at the door and signaled me to meet him. Mr. Martin noticed what was going on and wanted to see how clever I was and what excuse I would make to leave my desk. I went at the door and met Prastan—I mean my life." This she said with her right hand playing with Prastan left cheek.

Prastan said, "Stop it Jannet. You're driving." but inwardly he liked the idea.

Angie asked, "And what happened at the door?"

Jannet said, "He asked me to meet him at Allgreen's Park. That was our first date."

Prastan added, "You have forgotten to mention 10:00 A.M."

Everyone laughed almost on top of their voices.

Jannet said, "So, we are going there."

Rick from the rear seat, "This was the sweetest thing

I ever heard for a long time. We knew people love each other. But we never see people love each other like the two of you. People are right. God had created the two of you for each other. And that match was made in heaven. No one can separate the two of you from each other." This he said throwing the stone on Angie.

Paul said, "Only one person can do that." He hesitated for a few seconds to catch the attention of others and then continued, "Only God can do that."

Prastan and Jannet smiled inwardly. They knew that Peter, Paul, and Rick were throwing the stone on Angie. But at the same time unknowingly to them it was also referring to Charles.

They finally reached the park. They came out of the SUV and walked around stretching their arms and admiring the beautiful lake, trees, flowers, birds on the trees, birds flying overhead, and ducks swimming in the lake.

Jannet called the office to find out how everything is going, "Hello, Mark."

Mark answered, "Hi Jannet. Where you guys at?"

Jannet said, "We're at Allgreen's Park. How's everything shaping up?"

Mark said, "God blessed us. We're very busy. Business is blooming. But don't worry; we can handle it. Hey Jannet, Joe said not to show them the tree from which he fell down."

Jannet laughed loud, "Okay Mark. I heard you loud

and clear. By the way, we'll have lunch at the restaurant. You guys meet us there at 1:00 P.M."

Mark said, "Okay."

Prastan said, "Share the joke, Jannet."

Jannet tried to revive from her laughing. Everyone was curious and surrounded her to hear the joke and what was going on. She continued, "Mark said they're very busy but they can handle it, not to worry. He said Joe said not to show you guys the tree from which he fell down." Everyone laughed.

Charles said, "Joe and Mark are very funny. They make us laugh all the time."

Angie asked, "Hey, Charles, isn't Allgreen a beautiful place?"

Charles answered, "It is, I love this place it is so nice and clean."

Angie asked, "If you could find a good job here in Allgreen would you live here?"

Charles answered, "Of course." He wasn't serious.

Angie said, "Me, too." Hearing this, everyone glanced at each other.

Angie then continued, "Jannet, do you think Charles can find a job here?"

Jannet answered, "Yes, but it may take him a little while depending on what kind of job he's looking for."

Rick said, "Let assume that he finds a good job over here. What are you guys going to do with your house?" Saying this, he tried to discourage them.

Angie said, "We will rent it. And we can ask daddy to take care of it as a matter of fact. What do you think, Charles?"

Charles said, "Let me think about it, sweetheart."

Angie asked, "What do you have to think about?"

Peter said, "Charles is probably thinking about your dad. Remember he has no one else besides you guys. Isn't it right, Charles?" He tried to discourage them as well.

Charles said, "Yes, Peter, you're absolutely right. You never know when those bullies can attack the restaurant again. They may sometimes beat him or maybe kill him."

Paul said, "That's true, you never know. Those bullies are very dangerous and evil." He also tried to discourage them.

Angie said, "You guys don't have to be so pessimistic."

Charles said, "God forbid, you never know, Angie." And inwardly he questioned himself, *Why so suddenly she interesting in staying in Allgreen knowing that her father has no one else over there but us and knowing that those bullies are so dangerous. Damnit, I don't know what to say to myself. I don't think it's a wise idea to stay here.*
Jannet inwardly thought, *That's no problem if she wants to stay over here. They have to work, eat, and live just like everyone here in Allgreen. As a matter of fact life isn't easy anywhere.*

Angie asked, "What do you think, Jannet?"

Jannet said, "It's up to you, Angie, where you want to

live. Anywhere you go you have to work, eat, and live just like everyone." But inwardly she thought, *I don't think it's a good idea*"

Angie said, "That's true."

Prastan said, "Come on this way, let me show you guys the tree from which Joe fell down." He walked towards the tree, they followed behind, "This is the tree and he fell from that limb." This he said pointed his finger at the limb above.

Angie asked, "And where were you guys sitting?"

Jannet pointed, "Just here." She replied blushingly. She then looked at her watch "I have a few places more to show you guys, and then we're going to meet Mark and Joe at the restaurant."

They drove around Allgreen, and then they went to the downtown area where there are huge industrial buildings, office buildings, factories, government offices, and so on.

Charles observed, "Your downtown area is just like our downtown area."

Angie said, "Honestly speaking, yes. Except that over here is cleaner."

Peter said, "Well, on Monday we're going to start the fishing business again. You guys don't have to worry about buying fish again."

Jannet said, "Oh thank you, Peter. But how we are going to get the fish? As a matter of fact I can send Joe and

Mark at the beach for it but how we going to know when you guys are at the Allgreen's shore"

Paul said, "That's a good question."

Prastan said, "Jannet, let's go now; I'm feeling hungry."

Jannet looked at him and smiled, "Okay. I'm heading towards the restaurant. By the time we get there Mark and Joe should be there as well." This she said while glancing at her watch. She continued, "Let's get back to the point, Paul."

Rick added, "I have an idea. How about every Friday Mark and Joe reach us at Allgreen's shore, let say around 1:00 P.M.?"

Jannet said, "Every Friday. That will be too many fish. Besides, if we make an arrangement to meet on Friday, suppose you guys don't have a good catch?"

Charles said, "That's true. You've a point there, Jannet."

Prastan said, "I have a better idea."

Jannet looked at him again, "That's my husband." And after a few seconds asked, "What's your idea?"

Prastan said, "This idea that I have; I can't tell you."

Jannet asked, " Why not, Prastan?"

Prastan said, "This idea I have to show you. Look ahead to your right. Stop at that electronics and appliances store."

Jannet said, "No problem, my Lord." Everyone laughed.

Prastan said, "I'm not God, Jannet. I'm your husband."

Jannet said, "Well, for me you're both my husband and God."

Angie said, "Oh isn't that so sweet."

Charles asked, "Am I anyone God too."

Angie asked, "Is that a statement or a question?"

Prastan said, "Perhaps both." Jannet laughed.

Rick reminded, "We're waiting, Angie."

Jannet stopped the SUV in front of the store.

Peter urged, "Could we get an answer to that question before we get out of this SUV?"

Jannet said, "Angie, they're waiting."

Angie replied, "Let me see." This she said nodding her head "Okay, yes, providing you loved and treated me the same way Jannet is being treated.

Jannet said, "Oh Angie, come on. I'm positively sure Charles treated you like a queen."

Angie smiled and hugged Charles, "Okay lover boy, you're my God."

They laughed and eventually came out of the SUV and went in the store.

Jannet asked, "What are you looking for, Prastan?"

Prastan answered, "Prepaid cell phones for them."

Jannet said, "You're right. I should have thought of that?"

Angie asked, "Thought of what, Jannet?"

Jannet said, "Cell phones." This she said while she picked up two prepaid cell phones. They went to the cashier and purchased one thousand minutes for each phone.

Prastan said, "I'm done, let's go; I'm feeling hungry."

They went in the SUV and drove another fifteen minutes. When they reached the restaurant they parked the SUV in front as usual. After a few minutes idling outside, they went inside and sat at their favorite table at the far corner.

Prastan glanced at his watch, "They should be here by now."

A young waitress came to the table, "How may I help you guys today?"

Prastan said, "By telling us your name."

She replied, "Call me Sherry."

Prastan said, "Sherry is a beautiful name. Okay Sherry, bring me four cold beers, four shots of whisky, and two glasses."

Sherry said, "Absolutely, with pleasure, sir." This she said smiling at him.

Jannet asked, "You must be new here. I have never seen you here before. We came here often."

Sherry answered, "You're right. Today is my very first day here."

Jannet continued, "I guess they must be paying you good here."

Sherry replied, "Not really. But I have no choice." This she said and while walking away she whispered to herself, "My God she's so pretty and he's so handsome and cute." Everyone overheard it.

Angie looked at Jannet and smiled, "There comes your rival."

Jannet replied, "I got used to that. That isn't bothering me."

Charles looked through the window and said, "Here come Mark and Joe." They walked in and stood near the table.

Joe asked, "Have you ordered anything?"

Prastan mentioned, "Have a seat, I already did." Sherry had returned with a tray in her hand. She placed the beers, whisky, and glasses on the table one after another, "Anything else I may help you guys with at this moment?"

Jannet said, "Sure. Nine plates of chicken fried rice."

Sherry said, "Okay. That will take ten to fifteen minutes."

Jannet said, "That's no problem, Sherry." Joe and Mark looked at her. And in one voice said,, "Hi Sherry." She smiled at them, "Hi guys" and she walked slowly away.

Jannet added, "I like her." She overheard that and smiled in appreciation.

Mark looked at Joe and smiled.

"Joe said, "why are you smiling at me smile at her." This Joe said, and they had a seat. Sherry went and placed the order in the kitchen. The owner from inside waved his hand at Prastan and Jannet, "Hello Prastan, hi Jannet, hi Joe, hi Mark."

Sherry repeated after the owner "Her name is Jannet, oh she's so pretty. And who is that handsome guy?"

Owner said, "Who Prastan? Prastan married to Jannet. They are rich. They're the owner of Sunshine Farm."

Sherry said, "Wow! They are so young. And they're a perfect couple."

While drinking Jannet said, "I have to investigate that."

Prastan asked, "Investigate what?"

Joe added, "What, Jannet? Investigate what?"

Jannet said, "This is a girl thing."

Joe demanded, "Okay, let's hear."

Mark said, "Shut up,fool. Are you a girl?" Everyone laughed.

Sherry asked, "And those two guys that just came in?"

The owner replied, "Who—Mark and Joe? They are friends. They are Prastan and Jannet's best friends and they're working at the office with them."

Sherry asked, "And the rest of the guys?"

Owner said, "Oh, them. They are guests. They are living across the river."

Sherry said, "They are so friendly to me."

The owner said, "You bet they are."

Jannet said, "I bet she's asking the owner about us. They're talking about us."

Angie asked, "How did you know, Jannet?"

Jannet replied, "I can read their lips. But as I said, I like her. And I have to investigate why she said she has no choice but to work here. She's too young to work in a place like this restaurant."

Prastan added, "I agree with you, Jannet."

Sherry returned with the food and as she placed the plate one at a time on the table she asked, "You guys need anything to drink?"

Prastan said, "Bring us another round of drinks."

Sherry replied, "Sure, Prastan." This she said smiling and she returned to the bar.

Peter said, "You're right, Jannet. She was asking the owner about us. How did she know Prastan's name. No one has mentioned Prastan name to her."

Jannet said, "She likes us. And she knew all about us already."

Joe asked, "How are you so sure, Jannet?"

Angie sipped her drink, "That's what you called the girl thing."

Joe nodding his head, he asked, "What's girl thing?"

Mark said, "You fool, you don't know what a girl thing is." This he said sipping his beer.

Joe said, "Girl thing. No, I don't know." At least he was being honest to himself.

Mark whispered himself, "Neither do I."

He turned at Peter, Paul, Charles, and Rick, "What is a girl thing, guys?"

All of them replied in one voice, "We have no damn clue."

Mark tried to defend himself from Joe. "A girl thing is a girl thing; only a girl can know a girl thing."

Joe said, "That's poppycock. You don't know yourself." Everyone once again laughed.

Sherry returned with the drinks smiling innocently, she placed the drinks one at a time on the table.

Jannet really wanted to know why she said she had no other choice but to work here. She thought probably they are very poor or it has to do with some sorts of situation.

Jannet asked, "How old are you, Sherry?"

Sherry replied, "I'm twenty-two."

Angie said, "I'm twenty-two as well. How old are you, Jannet?"

Jannet said, "I'm twenty-one, girl. We're getting old."

A woman was passing by at the same time and overheard Jannet, "Then what must I say, little angel. I'm sixty-five years old and I'm not giving up. I still got it."

Joe said, "You heard that, Jannet." Everyone laughed.

Sherry looked at Joe and smiled. She then walked slowly away.

Joe said, "Wow, first time a girl ever smiled at me."

Sherry heard him and continued smiling. Jannet

looked at everyone and smiled. She called, "Sherry, one moment please. Are you working tomorrow?"

Sherry answered, "I don't know. The boss said he's giving me a tryout today. If he thinks that I can do the job, then he will hire me. If not—"

Prastan asked, "If not, what?"

Sherry said, "Then today is my first and last day. He told me everything about you guys, I mean good things and it seems like you guys knew each other very well. Will you guys say a word for me before leaving. I really need this job." She bent her head.

Prastan looked at everyone. Jannet, Joe and Mark knew that Prastan didn't like to hear words like that. They knew that he must remember where he came from and where he started from.

Jannet said, "Tell me the truth, Sherry. Do you really like this job?"

Sherry replied, "No. But I can't help it. I have looked everywhere and this is the only job I found."

Jannet mentioned, "You have emphasized that you really need this job. Why?"

Sherry replied, "My dad had a slight stroke due to his high blood pressure, and my mom cannot work because she is sickly. I had drop out of school because of poverty. So I really need this job to take care of my parents. I have no brother no sister to help me."

Prastan said, "Sherry, please don't lie to me that you don't have a brother."

Sherry said, "I'm not lying, Prastan." She pulled out a few bucks from her pocket. This is all the money I have. I have to buy high blood pressure tablets for my dad tonight on my way home." This she said while drying her tears with the back of her right hand.

Prastan said, "Excuse me guys, I'm going to the restroom. Don't go until I return from the restroom, Sherry." Prastan went to the restroom. On his way he asked the owner, "Are you going to hire her?"

Owner nodding his head and said, "I wish I could, Prastan but right now I really don't need anyone. I am only giving her a day work to help her out because I felt sorry for her. Poor thing had to quit school to work just to take care of her parents."

Prastan said, "Okay, I'll take care of her from this moment. She will work for my company as of today. So she's is no longer working with you anymore. She's my employee now. Is that okay with you?"

The owner said, "Not only okay. I am happy as well. You're a good person, Prastan. God will always bless you."

Jannet looked at Sherry and smiled, saying, "Congratulations, Sherry."

Everyone in one voice asked, "For what?"

Prastan returned to his table, "Okay, I feel much better now. Yes, Sherry." This he said and he pulled over a chair next to Jannet, "Sit here, Sherry."

Sherry said, "I love you guys but I'm on duty. If he sees me he'll fire me."

Prastan said, "Sit for one minute. He cannot fire you. You call this customer appreciation."

Sherry said, "Okay."

Prastan asked, "Now tell me. Where did you get this few bucks from? Wait,wait, don't tell me. Let me see if I get it right. You have sold your chain. You have sold your chain to buy tablets for your father. Am I correct?"

Sherry looked into the eyes of Prastan and wept bitterly. "You are a godsend person on this earth. How did you know that I sold my chain?"

Everyone looked at Prastan to hear what he has to say.

Prastan said, "You're a young girl. And for the first time working in a place like this, if you had a chain you'd definitely wear it."

Sherry asked, "How do you know that I had a chain?"

Prastan said, "Simple, there is a chain mark on your neck and there is no chain."

Sherry said, "I need the money. I cannot steal and I am too young to beg. Put yourself in my shoes, Prastan. What would you do?"

Prastan bent his head down. And when he raised his head he looked into her eyes and said, "I would have done the same."

Sherry said, "I must go now before I lose my job." This she said while attempting to leave.

Prastan said, "You already did."

Sherry said, "What? He told you that." She wept and then continued, "Oh my God. Why did he do that?"

Prastan said, "Because I asked him to."

Sherry asked, "Why, Prastan?"

Jannet added, "Because from this moment you're our employee. Today is your first day working with us And you'll be working in the office with Joe and Mark. Congratulation, aren't you guys going to congratulation Sherry on her new appointment?"

Everyone clapping hands, "Welcome, Sherry, to Sunshine Farm."

Joe smiled, not realizing that everyone eyes were at him. When he did, he said, "What? What?"

Prastan asked, "Have you anything to say, Sherry?"

Sherry said, "I'm so happy. God has sent his angels to help me and my parents."

This time Prastan went at the bar. He bought a cold beer and a plate of fried rice for Sherry.

Everyone mentioned in one voice, "Jannet, now we understood why you said, 'congratulations.'"

Sherry asked, "But, how did you knew Prastan was going to hire her?"

Jannet smiled and said, "We have each other's heart. The two of us are one, let me put it that way. As everyone said, we belong to each other."

Prastan said, "Let me continue from where I left off earlier. You said that you don't have a brother. I didn't doubt you. What I really meant was, we all here are your brothers and sisters, Okay."

Sherry said, "Yes, sir."

Everyone laughed.

Jannet said, "He dislikes it when people, 'sir' him. Just call him, Prastan. Now come on, everything will be okay, eat and drink this beer."

Sherry asked, "May I say something?"

Prastan said, "Let me say it for you. Permission granted."

Sherry said, "Yes, permission granted."

Prastan said, "You want to say how you will get to work and you don't know this, you don't know that. Am I right?"

Sherry smiled, "Absolutely right. As I said you're like a godsend person."

Mark said, "Let's double up, Joe. We have to go back to the office."

Joe replied, "You're right."

Jannet said, "Mark and Joe, you guys take Sherry to the office and start training her on the job. After work you guys take her home and—" This she said while she glanced at her.

Joe said, "I know, I know. Every morning we have to pick her up and every night we have to drop her off."

Jannet said, "Perfect. Oh yes, on your way taking her home tonight I want you guys to stop at the drug store and make sure she get that prescription for her father.

Mark, let that bill charge on our account. And also keep
an eye on her."

Joe asked, "On, keep an eye on what?"

Mark said, "Okay, Jannet. I know."

Joe asked, "Know what, know what, Mark? Am I
missing something here?"

Mark said, "Shut up fool. Let's go. Come on, Sherry,
let's go." Sherry glanced at Joe and smiled. Mark and Joe
walked out the door. Sherry hugged Jannet and gave her a
kiss. Jannet asked, "What is this for?"

Sherry said, "I just don't know. All I know that I am
happy and I love you guys. I feel as if I knew you guys
from a young age," she said and gave Prastan a kiss on his
cheek.

Jannet said, "Before you go, Sherry. Mark and Joe are
very good boys. They are Prastan's best friends, and they
are my adopted brothers and my best friends too. Have
you heard what Mark have just said? 'Shut up, fool. Let's
go.' That's the way they behave all the time. But they don't
mean it. I'm having a lot of fun with them and sometimes
they drove me nuts."

Prastan said, "They can't live without each other.
When they argue just pretended that you're not there."

Sherry said, "Okay." This she said and she hugged
everyone, "I may not see you guys again. You guys take
good care."

Prastan said, "Sherry."

Sherry answered, "Yes, Prastan."

Prastan said, "Saturday morning."

Jannet objected, "Stop that, Prastan. I wanted to say that."

Prastan said, "Okay, no problem. I'll reserve my energy." Everyone laughed.

Jannet said, "Saturday morning everyone hear besides Prastan and I will be leaving. Tomorrow night we will give them a farewell party."

Joe and Mark asked themselves outside, "What took her so long?" They returned inside.

Joe urged, "Sherry"

Jannet said, "Sorry about that, guys. I was just telling Sherry that Saturday morning our brothers and sister will be leaving, and tomorrow night we will be throwing a farewell party for them."

Mark added, "I knew you guys would do that."

Prastan said, "You guys must place a sign on the window. Close Friday at noon."

Joe asked, "So we are closing early tomorrow?"

Prastan said, "That's right."

Jannet said, "And—"

Joe said, "Don't tell me; I know."

Jannet asked, "Know what?"

Joe said, "I must drop her off and then pick her up for the party."

Angie and Charles in one voice, "Correct."

Joe said, "Okay, no problem." This he said while

glancing at Sherry with a blushing smile. Sherry also smiled at him blushingly.

Mark said, "Okay guys let's go; we're running late."

When they walked out the door, Angie said, "May I say something if you guys permit me."

Everyone in one voice answered, "Go ahead feel free."

Angie said, "I think that Joe and Sherry …."

Jannet said, "Me too. I have noticed."

Prastan said, "So what? We guys have noticed too. Guys, come on, we all are young people."

All the guys in one voice, "Of course, we have noticed them blushing and smiling at each other."

Angie said, "That was fast, at first sight."

Jannet said, "He always said that no girl will love him. And I always told him that she is out there somewhere."

Angie said, "We have heard that."

Jannet said, "I remembered my first glanced at him too. Oh, Prastan, you have forgotton something."

Prastan asked, "Forgot what, Jannet? Oh, yes." He took out the cell phone from the bag. "Charles, this prepaid cell phone is for you and Angie. It has one thousand minutes. You guys must call us now and again."

He then turned and looked at Peter and continued, "Peter, this is for you guys; it has one thousand minutes also."

Rick said, "Perfect, when we make a good catch we will call you guys."

Prastan said, "That's right. And I will send Mark and Joe for it. And anytime you guys want to come again and visit, just call."

Jannet added, "And we'll be there."

Prastan stretched out his arms, "So what's next?"

Charles said, "I feel tired. I think we should go home now and relax a little. Is that okay with you, guys?"

Peter said, "Fine with me."

Paul mentioned, "I feel tired myself."

Prastan asked, "How about you, Rick?"

Rick said, "We need some rest. Remember tomorrow morning is our karate training."

Prastan said, "That's true."

Jannet said, "Angie, when they are going to practice kicking I will make a sketch of you."

Angie said, "Really, you know drawing?"

Jannet said, "I'm not that good, but I know a little."

Prastan said, "I didn't know that you're an artist."

Jannet mentioned, "Likewise you, I never knew that you knew karate. Until you kick those bullies' ass. And I never knew that you could sing so well."

Rick said, "Since you have mentioned it Jannet, could he sing a song for us tomorrow night?"

Prastan said, "Okay, tomorrow night I will sing a song of friendship for you guys."

Everyone gave a slight clapping of hands. They finally went home and threw themselves on the sofa relaxing.

At the office Mark, Joe and Sherry were busy. Sherry

felt very comfortable among them. They showed her what to do and how to do it. She became a great help to them. Once in a while Joe and Sherry glanced at each other and blushed. Mark had noticed and pretended not to. He wanted to see Joe's reaction.

Jannet called the office to find out what's going on, "Mark. How is everything going over there?"

Mark said, "Good, we have everything under control."

Jannet said, "Glad to hear By the way. How is Sherry doing?"

Mark replied, "Very good. She is helping out a lot."

Jannet reminded, "Keep an eye on, Joe."

Mark said, "You bet. He's very glandsive. If you know what I mean."

Jannet said, "I read you crystal clear. I am happy for him anyway. Okay carry on. By the way, let me speak with, Sherry."

Mark said, "Okay." He gave Sherry the phone, "Jannet's on the line."

Sherry said, "Hi Jannet. How are you?" Jannet said, "I'm fine. How about yourself? Do you like the job?"

Sherry said, "Yes, thank you guys for helping me out. I'll never forget this kindness. I will always honor you guys and work honest and faithful for you. I'm speaking this from my heart."

Jannet said, "By the way, Sherry, I want you to bring

your mom and dad tomorrow night at the party. I want to see them."

Sherry said, "Okay, Jannet. I will. And once again thank you much and God bless you both." This she said and hanged up the phone.

Jannet said, "She's a nice girl."

Angie added, "I can see she's a nice person. And it looks like her family financial background is poor."

Mark said, "Joe, since we have everything under control why don't you take Sherry and show her the farm and introduce her to the manager, supervisor, and the employees."

Joe smiled at Mark and said, "Not a bad idea. Sherry, get a bottle of water; it will be hot out there. We should be back in two hours' time, Mark."

Mark laughed, "Take your time, I can handle it here."

They went in the car. Sherry sat in the front besides, Joe.

Sherry said, "It's a nice car. Is this yours?"

Joe answered, "Actually, this car belongs to Mark and me."

Sherry asked, "How much did you guys paid for it?"

Joe answered, "Actually, Prastan had bought this car for us. And they also gave us their house."

Sherry said, "Wow! I can see it in them; they are kindhearted."

Joe smiled, "You bet."

Sherry asked, "Tell me something, if they gave you guys their house, where are they living?"

Joe smiled, "Tomorrow you'll see. They bought a mansion. As a matter of fact Mark and I knew everything about them and they loved us and trusted us. We are good friends."

Sherry asked, "How did you guy became such good friends?"

Joe said, "Well, it's a long story."

Sherry pleaded, "Tell me, oh please, Joe, please." This she said smiling while she placed her left hand on Joe's right leg. Joe smiled at her, "You're the first girl who ever smiled at me, and you're the first girl had ever touched me. I always said to Jannet that if a girl loves me, it will be a miracle."

Sherry said, "Well, I suppose miracle do happen sometimes."

Joe said, "From what I'm getting, are you telling me that maybe you, you, you—"

Sherry said, "Yes Joe, for some reason I don't know but I feel like I fell in love with you. I don't know if you feel the same way about me. But if I offended you I'm very sorry."

Joe said, "I loved you too but I don't know how to say it to you. You see I'm not that educated like other people but I'm a good person."

Sherry mentioned, "I already knew about Mark and you."

Joe asked, "How come?"

Sherry smiled, "From your best friend's wife, from your boss, from your sister."

Joe asked, "Who, Jannet?"

Sherry said, "Who else would it be, Joe. Now back to my question."

Joe said, "I'm sorry, I really forget. What was the question again?"

Sherry asked again, "How did you guys became friends? I'm not inquisitive or, you may say, nosy. But I'm curious; you see, if we love each other, we must know about each other and when we know each other, we'll share our happiness and sorrows together."

Joe said, "You're right. That's the way Prastan and Jannet lives. They're madly in love with each other and only God can separate them."

Sherry said, "Well, since you guys are friends, why don't you guys follow their footsteps and live like them?"

Joe said, "You bet we will. Because if we don't we'll hurt their feelings, and we'd rather kill ourselves than to hurt their feelings. You see, Jannet came from a rich family." Only now he realized that he was getting to the point. He continued, "Prastan grew up as an orphan, very poor. One day Prastan went in the office for a job. The former owner Mr. Martin admired him, so he hired him. Jannet was the secretary. The very first time their eyes met, they fell in love and went crazy for each other."

Sherry said, "I can't blame them; he's so handsome and cute and she's so pretty and charming."

Joe said, "We're having problem with, Prastan."

Sherry asked, "What problem are you now talking about? He's a good person"

Joe laughed, "Anywhere we go girls are falling for him."

Sherry laughed, "You bet. And could you blame them?"

Joe said, "Of course, not. If I were a girl I'd fall in love with him too." They finally reached the farm. When the manager and supervisor saw the car they stopped what they were doing and walked towards the car. Joe and Sherry came out. Joe introduced them, "Sherry, this is Frankie, our manager, and this is George, our supervisor. Guys, Sherry is our new employee in the office"

Frankie and George shook her hand. "Nice meeting you, Sherry."

Sherry said, "Glad to know and see you guys."

Joe said, "Get in the car, guys." They drove around the farm and introduced Sherry to the employees, and after that Joe and Sherry headed back to the office.

Sherry said, "Okay Joe, you may continue."

Joe said, "Prastan, Mark, and I were working together so we became friends. Frankie was our supervisor and George was a regular employee."

Sherry said, "Okay now I understand how you guys became friends."

Joe said, "And you know what?"

Sherry asked, "What, Joe?"

Joe said, "I beat the hell out of Frankie one day."

Sherry said, "Oh no. Why?"

Joe said, "One day he went in the office and when he saw Jannet he fell in love with her. When he returned he overheard we were teasing Prastan about Jannet. Since that moment he started to pressure us. Prastan couldn't take it anymore and to save us from getting pressure, he told Frankie that he will forget Jannet."

Sherry said, "Oh no."

Joe said, "Prastan wrote a letter and sent it to Jannet. She fell sick and couldn't work.

Mr. Martin fired Prastan because he didn't expect that from him, though he loved him that much. Prastan fell sick also and couldn't work. So I beat the hell out of him. And as God smiled on Prastan and Jannet, they bought the company from the boss."

Sherry said, "They bought the company before or after marriage?"

Joe said, "They bought the company after they got married."

Sherry said, "God will always bless people like them. They are good people, Joe. Hey Joe, if Mr. Martin fired Prastan because of that letter, what did he do when you beat Frankie?"

Joe said, "He fired both Mark and me."

Sherry asked, "Why Mark? Mark didn't beat him."

Joe said, "No, but he said Mark should have stopped us from fighting and since he didn't, he assumed that Mark had encouraged me. So he fired both of us. But when the boss learned the truth of the story he hired us immediately and appointed Prastan manager for the company."

Sherry placed her hands on her chest, "Thank God. Have you seen what life is all about, today he owned the said company and he's such a good person; he made the man who almost destroy his life a manager."

Joe said, "And you know what?"

Sherry asked, "What, Joe?"

Joe said, "Prastan could sing very well and he's a good fighter. He knew karate."

Sherry said, "Wow! I would like to see him in action and to hear him sing as well."

They reached the office. Joe parked the car, and they sat in it for a little while. Mark noticed that Joe had pulled in and smiled.

Sherry said, "Joe, I want to thank you much."

Joe asked, "For what?"

Sherry said, "You have trusted me so much. Today is only my first day on the job and I know all about the company, its employees, Prastan and Jannet, and yourself. If you didn't love me you should have never told me this. Thank you, Joe, I love you too." This she said and she grabbed him around his neck and gave him a kiss."

Mark questioned himself. *What took them so long?* He

peeped through the window and saw them kissing. He smiled. "I'm happy for you, my dear friend." He picked up the phone and called, Jannet, "Hello, Jannet."

Jannet said, "Mark. Is everything okay?"

Mark said, "Yes, but you wouldn't believe this; I saw Sherry kissing Joe in the car."

Jannet said, "Really." Everyone overheard and came close to her, Prastan smiling. Jannet asked, "What are you smiling about? You don't know what he's talking about." The rest of the guys almost assumed the same as what Prastan was thinking and kept smiling too.

Angie asked, "What's the matter with you guys? Why are you guys smiling?"

Charles said, "Simple, guys see guys smiling and guys smiles too. You cannot understand. It's a guy thing"

Angie said, "Oh please. Don't give me that crap. Just because we said earlier that it's a girl thing, you're going to tell me now it's a guy thing."

This she said fanning her right hand and twisting her mouth, teasing him.

Mark said, "Jannet did you remember when you said to Joe that she's out there somewhere waiting for you, and Joe said if any girl loves him, it will be a miracle. There goes the miracle."

Jannet laughed, "What?"

Mark laughed too, "I'm happy for him. Oh boy, they're in the car kissing. Don't tell him I said anything."

Jannet laughed, "Oh my God, Oh my God. That's so sweet." This she said and hugged Prastan and gave him a kiss.

Prastan asked, "What's this for?"

Jannet said, "Joe and Sherry kissing in the car. That's so sweet, kissing on their first day. Oh boy, so sweet. What took us so long?" Everyone laughed and laughed.

Joe and Sherry went in the office.

Mark pretended innocence, "How is everything?"

Joe said, "So far, so good."

Mark said, "You bet. Sherry, now you know what the farm looks like."

Sherry said, "Yes, Mark."

Mark said, "Sherry, please write a sign and place it on the front door that the office will be closed at 12:30 P.M. on Friday."

Sherry said, "Okay, Mark."

At 5:00 P.M. they closed the office.

Mark said, "You drive, Joe." Sherry attempted to sit in the rear seat but Mark objected, "You sit at the front with Joe, Sherry. You have to direct him how to take you home." He considered his point as an excuse for Sherry to sit beside Joe.

Sherry said, "Oh thank you, Mark." She smiled at Mark. Mark smiled at her too.

Mark said, "Joe, don't forget to stop at the drug store."

Joe said, "Thank you for reminding me, Mark, I have almost forgotten."

After a few minutes Sherry pointed out a drug store to Joe. He stopped the car in front of the store.

Mark said, "You wait for us here. Let's go, Sherry."

Sherry smiled at Joe and said, "Joe don't leave the car; they write ticket like crazy here."

They went in the store. Mark charged the bill on the company account.

Sherry said, "Mark, you don't have to do that."

Mark replied, "If I don't, Jannet will kill me." They returned in the car.

Joe said, "That was fast. Is everything okay?"

Sherry answered, "Yes."

Joe said, "Okay Sherry, direct me how to get home from here." After a few minutes of driving Sherry said, "That's our house over there." Joe stopped the car in front of the house. Sherry's mom were in the front yard wondering about her. Being her first day at work and have never worked before she was quite worried. Sherry waved her right hand at Mark and Joe. They waved back at her and then drove away slowly.

Mom asked, "Dear, I noticed two boys in the car"

She then explained to her the entire events of the day.

Mom asked, "So you like him?"

Sherry said, "Yes, Mom, and he told me that he loved me too. And I'm working besides him. Isn't that so sweet?"

Mom said, "Yes, dear. But where is the prescription?"

Sherry said, "Oh my God, I forget it in the car."

Mark and Joe had noticed that Sherry had forgotten the prescription, and they turned around. Joe honked the horn in front of the house, and they came out of the car and stood beside it.

Sherry shouted, "Mom! They returned."

Mom said, "Why don't you ask them to come in; at least we'll get the opportunity to meet them and know them. What do you think, dear?"

Sherry said, "Not a bad idea for someone you really loved. I'll give it a try, Mom."

She ran out, "You guys want to come in for a few minutes? I want to introduce you to mom and dad."

Mark said, "We aren't in a rush. We could do that. What do you think, Joe?"

Joe said, "I see no harm in that. Let's go." They went inside. Sherry took the opportunity to introduce them, "Mom and dad, this is Mark, and this is Joe." This she said and held Joe in his right hand due to excitement, when she had realized it is the wrong place and at the wrong time she withdrew her hand quickly. Her mom and dad had noticed her but pretended not to.

Joe said, "We'll see you guys at the party tomorrow night. We must go now." This they said and they walked out of the door.

Mom asked, "What party, dear? What party are they talking about?"

Sherry said, "Prastan and Jannet invited us to the

party. They said they want to see and meet my parents. Mom and dad, you guys must go."

Scott said, "Who are those people, Sherry?" he asked her in a sweet and low voice.

Sherry said, "Dad, they are my boss. They are very good people, they are rich and they own the company. Joe had told me that Prastan grew up very poor as an orphan; maybe that's the reason he hired me."

Stella said, "God will always bless them, dear." This her mother said in a sweet and low voice.

Sherry said, "Could you believe that Prastan is one year older than me and Jannet is one year younger than me."

Scott said, "They must be godsend people dear. I mean so young."

Sherry said, "Joe had told me the same thing. He said everyone said the same thing about them that they are godsend, and their match was made in heaven. Besides, Prastan, he's so handsome and cute and Jannet, she's so pretty and charming. She's the prettiest girl I have ever seen in my life."

Stella said, "Okay dear, we will go at the party with you, though we don't have appropriate outfits for that kind of occasion. Maybe they will understand that." As she said this, she had noticed that her chain was missing from around her neck. She asked, "Where is your chain, dear? Don't tell me that you have dropped it?"

Sherry couldn't answer the question; she was most

astonished when her mom had asked her that question. She replied "I sold it, mom."

Scott said, "What ? Why have you sold your chain?"

Sherry said, "Yes dad, I couldn't raise the money to purchase the prescription. Prastan had noticed the chain mark around my neck and asked me the same question. And I gave him the same answer, dad. You know I can't lie. You guys always thought me to speak the truth no matter what it cost. They paid for the prescription, and I still have the money with me."

Scott disliked her idea and said, "You shouldn't have sold your chain, dear. I could have survived without the prescription. That was a beautiful chain."

Sherry said, "He's a street seller, dad. Probably he will sell it on the street for profit. Forget it dad; it was meant to happen like that. Probably God made it happen like that. I wouldn't say it's my bad luck. Maybe because of that Prastan and Jannet hired me. I have considered it my good luck. A job is the most important thing right now; one day I will buy a chain, dad."

Scott asked, "How will you go to work, dear? I mean to and from."

Sherry smiled at her dad, "They will pick me up and drop me off. They will also pick us up for the party and drop us home after the party, dad."

Stella added, "Aren't you seeing that God is answering our prayers, Scott. He's showing us his miracle in a mysterious way."

Scott said, "Maybe you're right."

Stella said, "The bank sent us a notice dear. You want to read it. We are behind three months of our mortgage payment."

Sherry said, "Mom and dad, now that I'm working everything will be okay. Put the letter in my bag, tomorrow I will call the bank and negotiate with them."

Joe and Mark on their way home were discussing their observations at Sherry's house.

Joe said, "It seemed like Sherry's parents are very poor. I felt sorry for them, espeically, her."

Mark added, "Me too. Sherry is a very nice girl."

Joe said, "I know. I want to tell you something, Mark."

Mark said, "Go ahead but don't tell me something that I have already knew. Tell me something that I don't know."

Joe asked, "What is it that you already knew?"

Mark said, "That you love her."

Joe smiled inwardly, "Are you kidding?"

Mark said, "Frankly speaking I'm not. Not Mark was kissing her in the car at the office parking lot. I am happy for you my friend. If you really love her, go for it."

Joe said, "So you saw me."

Mark said, "Yes, I saw you, you swine." And after a few seconds both of them laughed. They reached the mansion. Joe parked the car behind the SUV and they went in.

Jannet said, "Hello Mark. How is everything at

work?" This she asked smiling. She continued, "Hello, Joe, is everything okay?" This she asked and grabbed him and gave him a kiss on his cheek and ran away.

Joe asked, "What is this for?"

Everyone smiled at him.

Joe asked, "What is going on with you people?"

Everyone laughed. Joe looked at Mark, "Have you mentioned anything to them?"

Mark asked, "Why are you accusing me? I said nothing to them. Do you think I will lie to you? You're my friend; for you I will always speak the truth."

Joe asked, "What truth are you talking about?"

Mark said, "I wouldn't lie to you that you didn't kiss her." Mark knew Joe from the inside out. He knew that he was pretending that he disliked the idea but inwardly he was happy that everyone knew that he kissed, Sherry.

Jannet returned slowly and hugged, Joe "I'm happy for you, my dear loving brother. I hope everything works out good. She's a nice girl. Do you remember what I always said to you—that she's out there somewhere. Joe, Joe."

Joe said, "Yes Jannet, you've always mentioned that to me."

Jannet asked him, "And what you always said to me? That will be a miracle. Well, there comes the miracle." Everyone clapped hands and laughed; they felt happy for him. It was sunset. Everyone took a shower and then sat around the pool sipping a drink.

Jannet said, "Oh, before I forget." She called her mom, "Hi, mom."

Deecia answered, "Hello, dear. How are you? How is everyone?"

Jannet said, "Everyone is okay, mom. Hey mom, tomorrow night we'll be having a party for them. I will send either Joe or Mark to pick you guys up. I'm going to call Mr. Martin too."

Deecia said, "Mr. Martin went on vacation again, dear. He's out of the country right now."

Jannet said, "Vacation again, oh no. But at least I'm happy for him. He's enjoying his retirement. I can't wait to enjoy my retirement."

Her mom laughed, sharing that with her husband, James, "Your daughter is only twenty-one and she is worrying about retirement. Funny, my daughter is very funny."

Peter said, "Jannet, you're only twenty-one and you're worrying about retirement. What must I say, I'm thirty."

Rick said, "Say something, Joe. We are a little family here. How you feel about her?"

Joe said, "Okay, since you all know my story due to my friend, Mark." This he said and he looked at Mark.

Mark said, "But someone has to say something. Why are you looking at me?"

Joe said, "I really love her."

Everyone in one voice, "Yeah." they clapped their hands.

Joe said, "But."

Prastan said, "Don't give me that but, but what?"

Joe said, "It seems like Sherry's parents are very poor."

Mark supported, "Yes, it seems like they're really struggling."

Prastan said, "Probably that is the reason why she sold her chain." This he said and his face became sad. Everyone had noticed him. He walked away.

Jannet said, "He doesn't like to hear stories like that. I bet he's crying. You see, when his parents died he grew up struggling. He said sometimes neighbors gave him food. He's very emotional and soft-hearted. He can give away everything even his heart to people." She then turned at Mark and Joe, "You guys knew exactly what he's going to do, right?" Mark and Joe shook their head.

Charles and the rest of the guys in one voice, "He will take care of their problems."

Jannet said, "You bet. And for that God will always show him prosperity in life. This she said and she went and hugged him, "Your happiness, sorrow, and pain is my happiness, sorrow, and pain. So don't you ever forget thas. I have told you this the very first time we were together. I love you; you are my life. Come, let's go."

Mark said, "Guys, let's play some dominos." This he said while arranging tables and chairs.

Rick added, "Not a bad idea. Let me see what you Allgreen's guys have."

Joe said, "Oh yeah. My ten bucks against your one buck I beat you the first five games straight."

Rick said, "Deal. Come on Peter, you and I against Joe and Mark." They have a lot of fun and making some noise, but indeed Joe won the bet. The next teams were Charles and Paul against Joe and Mark. And as usual Joe had made the same bet his ten bucks against their one buck that he'd win the first five games straight.

Prastan, Jannet and Angie sat at a corner by a table not too far away from them. They were discussing Sherry.

Prastan said, "Jannet, tomorrow morning we'll go shopping. I want you and Angie to buy Sherry a beautiful dress and a nice chain. Tomorrow night before the party start giving it to her."

Jannet said, "That was my thought. I wanted to tell you the same thing."

Angie said, "You guys are alike, thinking the same way."

Jannet said, "I had told you the same thing earlier Angie, if you and Charles plan things together and make decision together you will see a change in life. Give it a try, trust me with this."

Joe wasn't concentrating on the game anymore. His thoughts were at Prastan's table and his ears were like antenna that picked up everything that was said. He knew they were talking about Sherry and he's so curious to know what they were talking about and he assumed that maybe they're probably talking about him also. Due to his inquisitiveness and not paying attention on the game, he lost the first game. Everyone knew that Joe's thoughts weren't on the game but across the other table. By now the foreigners knew him well and how nosy he was.

Mark reminded, "Joe, you have to concentrate on the game. Swing your antenna this direction on this table or else we will lose all the games."

Joe said, "I cannot concentrate."

Mark questioned, "Why?"

Joe said, "They're talking about Sherry and me over there."

Charles asked, "How are you so sure about that?"

Mark said, "Trust me with this, Charles, he knew. And once he knew that, he cannot concentrate anymore."

Charles said, "My God, Joe is something else." However, the game was over due to Joe's lack of concentration. Charles went over by Prastan's table.

Prastan asked, "You guys finish playing?" By then the rest of the guys joined them.

Charles said, "We have stopped playing the game because Joe cannot concentrate on the game. He has a feeling that you guys are talking about Sherry and him."

Angie said, "Yes, we're talking about, Sherry and him."

Jannet said, "You can't stop, Joe. He's like that, very

nosy but I like him, I like them, I like all you guys. Oh I am so happy."

This she said and kissed Angie on her cheek.. Prastan smiled at her happiness.

Prastan asked, "Mark, where is Joe?"

Mark said, "I believed he went to the rest room."

Prastan said, "Guys, if they love each other."

Jannet added, "Let me continue from there. Why don't we get them married?"

Angie mentioned again, "You guys always think alike. Charles from now on, you and I have to think like Prastan and Jannet."

Charles said, "No problem with me. When you want us to start?"

Prastan said, "At the party tomorrow night. I'll see what I can do for them."

They had a few drinks and later called it a night.

The next morning as usual Jannet and Prastan woke up very early preparing breakfast for everyone. They sat at the breakfast table having their coffee, eggs, and pancakes.

Jannet said, "I'm sorry that you guys leaving tomorrow. I knew that from Monday morning Peter, Paul, and Rick will start fishing. What you have in mind Charles? Have you thought of anything, business, or whatever? We'll miss you guys so much. However, any time you guys wanted to visit let us know."

Charles said, "We'll miss you guys too and back to

your question, Jannet. I'm thinking probably I open a small office selling property and auto insurance."

Paul encouraged him, " That's a good job for you, I suppose."

Rick and Peter, "That's true. You do have some kind of experience in that."

Angie added, "Yes, he did."

Mark said, "Okay you guys carry on with your breakfast and discussions. We have to go. Let's go, Joe, I have to pick up my sister-in-law."

Joe said, "Watch your mouth, watch your mouth. Don't start with me."

Everyone laughed and laughed. Before they drove off Jannet said, "Mark"

Mark waved his hand, "I know, I know." Pointing his finger at his eyes, meaning he'll keep an eye on Joe. After relaxing for a little while they went shopping. They went at the shopping mall. Jannet and Angie went in a store while the rest of the guys were outside leaning on the SUV. Jannet picked up a beautiful dress, a nice chain, and a watch for Sherry and also beautiful dresses for Angie and herself. She paid the cashier, and on their way out three men approached them selling a chain. Jannet glanced at Angie and whispered in her ear, "Wonder whether this is Sherry's chain." Angie whispered back at her "Maybe, you never know."

Jannet asked, "Let me have a look at the chain guys. Oh it's pretty. How much you want for it?"

The man replied, "Ten bucks."

Jannet said, "I just spent all my money. Let's go outside, I'll ask my husband to buy it for me."

The man in replied, "No problem." They went outside. Jannet showed Prastan the chain.

Prastan looked at the chain and glanced at the guys, giving them an eye contact message that probably its Sherry's chain.

Prastan said, "It's pretty. I could buy it for my wife, but I don't like to buy things on the street. Some people sold stolen articles. Please don't get me wrong I'm not saying that you have stolen it."

The man replied, "Sir, this is not a stolen goods. I bought this from a girl yesterday morning at the restaurant. She said she need money for prescription or something like that; I can't remember exactly what was it."

Prastan said, "Bingo, I'll take it."

At the office Sherry opened her bag and took out the letter that they received from the bank. She read the letter and her face became very pale. Joe and Mark were observing her, unknowingly to her. She called her bank and was negotiating a payment plan on the three months of mortgage payment due. But apparently the bank wasn't in her favor.

Joe asked, "Is everything okay, Sherry?"

Sherry replied, "Yeah."

Joe went near her, "What is bothering you, Sherry?

Ever since you read that letter your face became pale." She gave Joe the letter. Joe gave the letter to Mark.

Mark said, "Don't let this bother you, Sherry. There is always a way to solve a problem."

Joe asked, "What is it, Mark?"

Mark said, "She's behind three months in her mortgage payment." This he said while looking at Joe and then at her.

Sherry said, "May I ask you guys something?"

Joe asked, "What is it, Sherry?"

Sherry said, "I know it may sound very bad but not for my sake but for my parents sake. Can I borrow some money from the company to pay the mortgage and they can deduct in from my pay check every week?"

Mark called Jannet and explained to her. Jannet told Prastan.

Prastan said, "I can't let this happen."

Sherry said, "Oh, thank you, guys."

Prastan called the office, "Hello, Mark. How is everything?

Mark said, "As usual, so far so good."

Prastan said, "Is Sherry around?"

Mark said, "Yes, Prastan. Would you like to speak with her?"

Prastan said, "Yes, Mark, that is the reason I called."

Mark said, "Sherry, pick up line two. Prastan is on the phone."

Sherry said, "Hello, Prastan."

Everyone looked at Prastan wondering why he called the office.

Prastan said, "Sherry, I have to fill out some paper work regarding your employment. I need your house address." Everyone looked at Jannet and laughed.

Sherry said, "Okay, Prastan," and she gave him her house address.

Prastan said, "Thank you much. How is everything going?"

Sherry replied, "Everything is going good. And once again thank you for helping me. God will always bless Jannet and you."

Mark and Joe looked at each other and smiled.

Sherry asked, "Why are you guys smiling, did I said something wrong?"

Mark said, "No Sherry, we just admired the way you spoke on the phone, you spoke like you were on the job for years." They bluffed her.

Sherry said, "Oh thank you, guys." And she blushed.

Mark and Joe knew that Jannet normally handled all employment issues.

They knew that Prastan was up to something.

Prastan called the bank, "Hello. May I speak with Jim Curtis please?"

The secretary said, "Sure, why not."

Prastan said, "Thank you."

The secretary asked, "By the way, may I have the pleasure to know with whom I am speaking with"

Prastan replied, "Tell him, Prastan."

The secretary said, "Jim, someone by the name of, Prastan."

Jim said, "Give me the phone please. Hello, Prastan; how are you?"

Prastan said, "I can't hear from you, Jim. You are a busy man. By the way, I am having a party tonight. I want you and the family to come over."

Jim asked, "What time is the party?"

Prastan answered, "Start at six and prolong till midnight."

Jim said, "Sounds like a hell of a party. I'll be there."

Prastan said, "Hey Jim, can you do me a favor?"

Jim said, "For you, anytime. What is it?"

Prastan said, "I want you to check this property address and give me the history."

Jim said, "I'll do it for you. Okay, I'll call you back in an hour's time."

Prastan said, "Thank you Jim and see you tonight."

The secretary murmured inwardly, "Prastan, Prastan. He must be someone special."

Jannet said , " Okay guys let's go home; we have to make arrangements for tonight." In less than thirty minutes they reached home. Everyone threw themselves on the sofa. Jannet called the restaurant and ordered enough food for the party and asked for it to be delivered at 5:30 P.M.

Prastan called the office, "Hello Mark."

Mark said, "Yes, Prastan. Everything is going fine and we're about to close."

Prastan said, "I didn't call for that. When you guys drop off Sherry on your way back, drop in at the store and pick up enough liquor and beer for the party tonight."

Mark replied, "Okay, Prastan."

The phone rang. Jannet picked up, "Hello Jannet. This is Jim."

Jannet said, "Hi, Jim. Make sure I see you and the family at the party tonight."

Jim said, "You bet, I'll definitely be there or else Prastan will kill me. Let me speak to him please."

Jannet said, "Sure, Jim. Prastan, Jim is on the phone for you."

Prastan answered, "Hello, Jim. What you got for me?"

Jim said, "They're three months behind their mortgage payment and their current mortgage principal balance, let me see, yes, $4,100.00."

Jannet asked, "How much is the balance?"

Prastan said, "$4,100.00"

Jannet said, "Help them Prastan. Please don't let their house go. God will be happy with you."

Prastan said, "Hey Jim. Take the money from my checking account and pay off that mortgage and fax over all the papers over to me."

Jim replied, "No problem, Prastan, consider it done. But tell me something: are they related to you?"

Prastan said, "No, Jim. But I can't let their house go. I can't let them sleep on the street. We are all human, Jim. I can't let this happen. Pay off the mortgage for me, please. You know what, Jim? Bring the papers with you tonight; don't fax it over, and you give it to them. And let it be a surprise."

Jim said, "Okay, Prastan; you can count on that. You are a very good man. God will always shower blessings upon Jannet and you." This he said and hung up the phone.

Charles said, "Guys, where in this world will you find people like Prastan and Jannet."

Mark and Joe had dropped off Sherry at home.

Joe reminded her, "We'll pick you guys up at 5:30. Is that okay with you?"

Sherry said, "Yes, Joe." she blushed a little.

On their way home Mark, "I have a feeling Prastan called Jim to investigate Sherry's parents' house."

Joe asked, "What for?"

Mark said, "To find out about the three months mortgage payment and I have a good feeling that he will pay it for her."

Joe said, "I have the same feelings. Mark, we're very lucky to have a friend like Prastan. They loved us so dearly and they trusted us to the maximum extent. Don't you think that God has blessed us too?"

Mark replied, "You bet. You know what, Joe? We must always be honest and faithful to them. Look where we are today, working in the office besides them and we are above the manager. We must never let someone come between them and us, I want you to always remember this."

Joe said, "You bet." They soon reached the liquor store, and they bought their beer and liquor and went home.

All the guys were in the back yard practicing karate. Prastan demonstrated a few tricks and taught them how to defend themselves whenever the right times comes. He also explained to them to stay away from fight if possible.

Angie sat in a chair near the pool. Jannet had an artist brush in her right hand portraying her. After an hour of practicing, Prastan called the training session off. All the guys went in the pool and took a bath; then they went in the house and changed their clothes. After that they went and sat in chairs around the pool and were paying attention to the two girls. It seemed like Jannet having difficult time trying to make the color to finish off the topping on the cheeks. Prastan went near her "What happened, Jannet. Are you having a difficult time making the color?"

Jannet said, "Yeah, I can't believe it."

Prastan said, "Keep on trying; you will succeed."

Jannet said, "Hey Joe, you want to call mom and tell them that you're picking them up in thirty minutes time?"

Joe said, "Okay, no problem, Jannet."

Jannet said, "Oh yeah, on your way back, you can pick up Sherry and her parents also. What do you think?"

Joe said, "It makes sense."

The rest of the guys were sipping a drink.

Rick said, "You guys believe that the week finished so fast? Tomorrow we are going home."

Peter added, "When you're on vacation time always go fast."

Charles said, "At least we can say we have a wonderful time here in Allgreen."

Paul supported, "You can say that once more."

Jannet questioned herself inwardly, *Wonder what is going through Angie's mind right now. She's nice, I like her and want to be friends forever. I knew that she loved my husband before and she claimed that she never knew that he was married and she asked me to forgive her. I'm fine with that; if I were in her shoes I would have probably done the same. But, God knows her inside; I wonder whether she still loves him and pretended not, trying to give us an impression that it's over and trying to make us feel good.*

She then glanced at her watch and said, "Joe."

Joe said, "Yes, Jannet, I'm leaving right now." He then called on Mark, "Let's go, Mark."

Angie asking herself inwardly, *Oh Lord why I'm having difficult time in controlling my mind? I'm a married woman*

*and I am even older by one year than her. I had confessed
that I loved her husband at my first sight but I didn't know
that he was married. Oh Lord I've also confessed that that
love relationship that I had for him no longer existed; it's
all over. Lord, every time I looked at him my heart begins
beating faster, and I wanted to fall for him. How can I do
this to her and hurt her. They are very kind, they are so nice
to us. Look how much good they have done for us. Look
how nice we are living among them. I wanted to be her best
friend forever. They are a very happy married couple living
a respectable and decent life; they are progressing in life and
helping people. I can't let my mind overcome me and ruin
these godsend people's life. I can't destroy this angel life. Oh
Lord, please take away this evil away from my dirty mind
and fill it with love for her, with love for them. Jannet had
mentioned, dipped a glass of water from the right side of the
boat and dipped a glass of water from the left side of the boat
is the same water. Now I get the parable; the only difference
between him and my husband is that he's handsome, attractive, and decent; besides, man is man—they all have the same
thing. She's damn right. She's intelligent and smart, probably
she knew my mind and didn't want to tell me off but instead
she gave me the message in parable. And probably she likes me
and wanted to be friends and I'm neglected myself to see and
understand her. Why am I so stupid and dumb not to get it.
Living among them I've considered myself a flower floating in
a pool of milk. Why should I let this flower float in a septic?
Oh Lord if there is a wish in my agenda I wish to use it now.*

Oh Lord please erase all evil intention that I have in my wicked heart and mind, cleanse me, oh Lord, and show me the light of love, fill it with love especially for her."

Prastan asked, "Are you still having difficult time in making that color, Jannet?"

Jannet said, "It took the hell out of me but I finally get her face smiling."

Angie inwardly, *If she's talking about the color she may be right but if that's a parable referred to my heart she's absolutely right.*

Prastan said, "You see what I mean, Charles? I told you that you need a good vacation. You look good; you're back. How do you feel?"

Peter, Paul, and Rick in one voice said, "Yes, Charles, let us hear it from you. How do you feel?"

Charles said, "I'm back. Charles is back, I wouldn't lie to you guys; I'm feeling very good and healthy."

Jannet said, "I can see that, Charles; you look good." This she said and she placed both hands on her hip and admired the portrait, "You look pretty, you look gorgeous, you look …" She hesitated for a few seconds and then continued, "Wow!"

Angie stood up and admired the portrait, "Oh it's so pretty." She grabbed Jannet and kissed her, "Oh Jannet, I love you much; you've meant the world to me. Jannet my life belongs to you; you're my loving, sister."

Charles sipping his drink and inwardly, *God had sent*

me to Jannet. She's an angel sent from heaven to purify my dirty heart and my evil mind and to cleanse my soul and wash away all my sins. I have squandered all my money on luxury and comfort without even took a second thought whether it's the right thing I am doing or the wrong thing I am doing. I offered her that money in exchange for having pleasure with her. She's a girl chosen by God, a girl who elected to share pleasure with her own and not others. She kept that money and waited for my race to be over, a race that I can't win but I was always determined and involved in the race. I hurt so badly in that race, emotionally, mentally, physically and financially. Today I live to regret it; what I did was totally wrong. God has sent me to her with that money so she could cleanse me and save that money for me and to rescue me whenever the right time comes to restart me in a new life. He then looked at Jannet and Prastan and said, "From now on I'll try to follow their footstep and to live a life like them."

Joe and Mark reached at Mr. and Mrs. James. They were outside in the front yard waiting for them.

James said, "Hello guys, that was fast."

Mark replied, "Not exactly, we had a head start."

James said, "You guys are always busy. You guys need some vacation."

Joe said, "Working with Jannet and Prastan it's like having vacation every day."

James said, "You guys are driving the SUV now."

Joe said, "We have another stop to make."

Mrs. James asked, "What stop?" This she said and they went in the SUV.

Mark answered, "We have to pick up Sherry and her parents."

Mrs. James, "Sherry, do I know her?"

Mark said, "No. Jannet hired her to work in the office. Mrs. James they are very poor, I mean very poor. Her mom and dad are sickly; she sold her chain to buy tablet for her father."

James said, "Well, that is poor. And I'm very much sorry to hear that."

Mrs. James asked, "How did Jannet met with her?"

Joe said, "We were having lunch at a restaurant and she was working there."

Mrs. James asked, "How old is she?"

Joe said, "She's a year older than Jannet."

Mark exposed, "She likes Joe."

Mrs. James said, "That's the best thing I ever heard for the day. You see, Joe, Jannet always told you that she's out there. And you always said to her that that will be a miracle. And as I always said the Lord shows his miracles in mysterious ways. Isn't that so, James?" She had noticed that James wasn't paying attention.

In about fifteen minutes they reached Sherry's house. Joe honked the horn. Sherry and her parents came out. Mark moved himself over from the front passenger seat and sat beside Mr. and Mrs. James in the second-row seat.

Sherry sat beside Joe in the front and her parents sat in the third-row seat.

Joe said, "Sherry, Mr. and Mrs. Scott, this is Jannet's parents Mr. and Mrs. James."

They replied in one voice at the same time, "Nice meeting you Mr. and Mrs. James."

Mr. And Mrs. James said in one voice, "Nice knowing you all."

Mrs. James asked, "So how do you like your new job, Sherry?"

Sherry answered, "I like it. I must thank Prastan and Jannet for hiring me. They're so nice and kindhearted. God will always bless them and give them good health and strength. It's very rare to find people like them in this world."

Stella said, "I'm so sorry that my child had to drop out from school and work. She's the only one we have, she's the only hope we have got. We became old and sickly; who could have taken care of us? If she couldn't get this job, I don't know what would have happened to us. Everything is bills, bills, bills, and only bills."

Deecia said, "Everything will be okay now being that Sherry is now working. God will bless you Sherry. When you were a baby they took good care of you. And when we become old, we will be like babies once again in our lives. So the young babies have to take care of the old babies. When we're young and strong we have considered ourselves man, and when we got old, sickly, and helpless we became a child a second time. These are the three stages in life. One: When we were babies we slept most of our time. Two: When we were in our teen and full youth, we played a lot and not even remembered that there is a God; some of us got carried away in excitement and activities. And three: When we got older, weak and sickly we're asking God for help. God loves us all, he cares for us, and when we loved him and remember him, he will always be there for us. He will not come and help us but he will show his miracle in a mysterious ways. You see what I mean Sherry? He's helped your parents by sending you in this world to take care of them. Is in that something to think of."

They got to the mansion, and Joe pulled in the driveway.

Sherry said, "Wow! This house is a mansion."

They all went in. Everyone said, "Hi Sherry."

Sherry said, "Hi everyone." This she said and shook everyone hand. She went and kissed Jannet and gave Prastan a big hug. She said, "Mom and dad. This is Prastan and this is Jannet."

Mr and Mrs. Scott said, "Nice meeting you guys. Sherry had talked nonstop about the two of you. She praised you guys to the maximum extent." This they said and they shook everyone's hand.

Angie, Sherry, and Jannet moved to a corner; they filled their glasses with beer and sipped. Mr. and Mrs. James and Mr. and Mrs. Scott were at another corner.

Jannet, Angie, and Sherry went over next to them. Jannet poured a light drink of champagne in Mr. and Mrs. Scott glasses.

Angie asked, "What will you drink Mr. and Mrs. James?"

Mrs. James, "Tonight we will drink some hard stuff." Angie gave them both a drink of whisky.

Angie said, "Tonight we will have some fun, we are leaving tomorrow."

Jannet said, "Mr. and Mrs. Scott. I like Sherry and I will take good care of her. Don't worry everything will be okay from now on. These two girls here are my best friends, I loved them much." This she said and she smiled at Sherry and Angie.

Angie said, "I love you too Jannet. I owe you my life and you're everything to me. I'll worship you Jannet; you surely deserve to be."

Jannet said, "Oh come on Angie, don't say that. I am a human being; you can thank me if you feel like, but you only worship God"

Angie said, "Yes, I mean it." This she said and kissed her and then hugged her. Her tear drops flowed rapidly down her cheeks. The guys at the far corner in the house saw her crying.

Rubbing his eyes, Rick said, "Am I drunk?"

Peter said, "I didn't hear anyone say that. Who said you're drunk?"

Rick said, "No one said that but it seems like my eyes are deceiving me."

Charles asked, "What do you mean, your eyes are deceiving you?"

Rick said, "Look over there—Angie is crying." Everyone turned around. Charles went over near her, "Why are you crying, dear? What's the matter? Aren't you feeling well? Is something wrong?"

She grabbed Charles, "No, Charles, I am enduring friendship and love. I really, really love Jannet, and I'll miss her. They care for us; look what they have done for us. Our house was foreclosed. They bailed us out, gave us money and treated us with love and respect. Oh Charles, we owe them big, we cannot repay them but we can pray for them."

Charles said, "I knew, dear. Because of them my life has changed. We must try to follow their footstep and live like them. We should be proud to have friends like them. Everyone makes mistake in life. We made many mistake too but we just can't afford to repeat them. Let us change our way of life, Angie."

Angie agreed, "Yes, Charles. Let us promise ourselves that we will live a decent and respectable life from now on."

Charles said, "I promise."

Angie said, "Me too." By then all the guys walked up closer. Charles and Angie turned to Prastan and Jannet.

"We will love and respect you guys forever. We will be friends forever. Let us continue to live like this forever."

Paul clapped his hands, "Let this little speech of yours also be for all of us. We want to maintain this love, friendship, and respect forever." Everyone clapped hands "Yeah, yeah." The front door was unlocked. Jim and his wife came in when Angie, Charles, and Paul were saying their piece but didn't want to walk in and distract anyone's attention. They allowed them to complete what they had to say, then, they clapped their hands.

Jim said, "Wow! wonderful. That's the way people are supposed to live. I love that speech. Didn't you honey?" This he asked his wife.

Prastan and Jannet went up to them. Prastan and Jim shook hands.

Prastan said, "Thank you for coming guys; your presence is highly appreciated."

Jim said, "Jessica, This is Prastan and this is Jannet." Jessica shook Prastan's hand and gave Jannet a kiss on her cheek. And inwardly she said, "*She's so pretty and charming and oh boy, he's so handsome and cute.*"

Jannet held Jessica hand, "Follow me this way to the girls' section."

Jessica said, "This house is so huge, I can lost in this house."

Jannet took the opportunity and introduced Jessica

to everyone while Prastan took the same opportunity to introduce Jim to everyone.

Prastan said, "Attention please, attention. Before I say let's party, I would like to say something. Tomorrow morning you guys are leaving for home. On behalf of everyone from Allgreen, epically, Jannet and myself, I would like to say that we will miss you guys. I do hope that you guys enjoy your vacation here in Allgreen and any time you guys wanted to visit, consider yourselves welcome." Everyone clapped hands together.

Jannet said, "Sherry, would you please come forward please." Sherry smiled and blushing at the same time. Jannet looked at Joe, "Joe, why are you blushing?"

Joe smiled; Sherry looked at Joe and blushed.

Jannet said, "Angie, would you please bring it?"

Angie replied, "Sure Jannet." She went in Jannet's bed room and returned with a beautiful parcel wrapped with red gift paper and tied with a yellow ribbon. Jannet received the parcel from Angie and gave it to Sherry, "This is a gift for you, Sherry. It's a welcome gift for working for our company. Open it."

Sherry without knowing what was in the parcel said, smiling, "Thank you, Jannet." She slowly opened the parcel in front of everyone, "Oh my God. Oh my God, a dress. It's so beautiful. Oh my God and a chain, a watch. Oh my God, it's so pretty." She was so excited that she forgot herself and sprang on to Jannet like a wild cat and kissed her repeatedly. "Oh Jannet, I love you, it's so pretty.

I can't believe what I am seeing." She then called her mom and dad. She went and showed them the gift. Scott and Stella said, "We don't know what to say, dear. It's so pretty. You're right, dear, from what we heard from everyone here, Prastan and Jannet are indeed godsend."

Prastan said, "Sherry, come see what I have for you. You may like it." She walked up to him one step after another, "What is it, Prastan?"

Prastan said, "Close your eyes and open your hands." She immediately closed her eyes and opened her hands. Prastan put the chain in her hand, "Now, open your eyes."

Prastan asked, "Do you like it?"

Once again Sherry said, "Oh my God, oh my God. It's my chain. How did you get it?"

Prastan asked, "Are you happy now?"

She replied without hesitation, "Yes, yes." And she gave Prastan two kisses on his right cheek. She went and showed the chain to her mom and dad, "I don't know how he got it, but he got it." She was so excited it seemed like the night belonged to her and a bit carried away, she went and showed Joe. Everyone looked at them and smiled.

Joe asked, "What? What?"

Mark said, "Nothing, nothing. No one said a word."

Sherry's mom and dad smiled at the observation, looked at each other, and nodded their heads.

Prastan said, "Jim, it's your turn, it's all yours."

Jim said, "Okay." This he said and with his right hand signal the crowd to gather together. He then called Sherry and her parents, "Well, Sherry, I have here something very special for you and Mr. and Mrs. Scott. First let me take the opportunity to congratulate you Sherry on your employment with Sunshine Farm.

And I would also like to congratulate you for all the gifts that you've received. But I also have another gift a bigger gift for you and your parents. Do you ready to see that gift?"

Sherry said, "Yes, yes." This she said wondering what could it be.

Jim called on his wife, "Jessica, would you please."

Jessica said, "I would like to congratulate you all." This she said and she presented the envelope to Sherry, "Open it, Sherry."

She opened the envelope, "What's this? So many papers, it seems important."

Scott and Stella asked, "What is it, dear?"

Jessica said, "It's the deed for your house. Prastan and Jannet have paid off the bank for your house. Now the house is yours.."

Mr. and Mrs. Scott couldn't believe what they heard and saw. Sherry was astonished and remained speechless for a moment. She asked, "Is this a dream? Am I dreaming?"

Jannet said, "Absolutely not, Sherry. And I have good news for you guys. You guys don't have to repay this money to us. We're helping you guys. From now on you guys will live a decent and stress-free life. Aren't you guys happy?"

The three of them in one voice said, "Yes we are. And we will never forget this kindness as long as we live. We owe you guys big."

Prastan said, "Okay, let's party guys."

Rick said, "Not before you sing us a song as you promised."

Prastan said, "I have given my word; I won't take it back. My word is my honor. I am weak in making a promise but when I do I am strong to live up to it. But before I sing this song I want you guys to know that this song is based on our friendship. You don't go on the street and says hey you are my friend or you've met someone at the supermarket and called them friend. Friends are chosen with love, and it isn't easy to find; it's rare to find. And, my dear friends, whenever you find true friends treasure them in your heart, soul, and mind. When you have a friend it is a blessing from God. When you stand in front of the mirror you must actually see your friend in the mirror as yourself. You guys knew that Jannet had a very difficult time in making a color to paint Angie's portrait. Whenever you achieve that color, my friend, you must cherish it and don't let that portrait break. When friends are together they makes jokes, play games—they do many things together and have fun. If you're in a boat and your friend falls in the ocean, you must jump in the ocean to save him, don't let him drift away and drown.

Friends should be in your memory at all times, anyway you go or anyway you are. Friendship should always linger in your memories; that what you call a friend. When I first met you guys in the ocean we've considered each other friends. We felt that we're the best of friends and that we are above the rest of the guys. We felt that we can override anyone just like the ocean waves overflow the shore. And, my dear friends, we must admire this friendship; we must adore this friendship. And since we're faithful friends, we've felt that we're above, just like the clouds floating high above all. But, my friends, when this friendship is broken because of some reason or some dispute, believe me, it really hurts, it's really painful, and sometimes you cry bitterly. Friendship should be treated with love and dignity, and friendship should last forever until eternity. This is what you call friends."

Jim and Jessica clapped their hands very loud "Wonderful, wonderful, good speech, Prastan. You heard that guys; that is what friends are about. Love love."

Angie went and hugged Jannet, squeezed her and said, "You're my friend until my last day." Hearing this, everyone join with a loud clapping of hands.

Sherry went and hugged Jannet also and said, "You aren't just a friends and a boss, you're an angel descended from above. I'll worship you forever until my last day, my last minute."

again, clapping of hands. When the clapping stopped

Prastan with his sweet voice began to sing this beautiful song.

FRIENDSHIP

Friendship is a gift and a pride.
Throughout the world nation's wide.
It's like the season flowers that's rare to find.
And should be treasured in the heart soul and mind.

Friendship is loving and blessed of them all.
Should be in sight like mirror on the wall.
It's like a color that's difficult to make.
And should be cherished and should never break.

Friendship together makes a happy day.
With those things they'll do and say.
Its relationship meant a lot to me.
Even though it's beneath the deepest sea.

Friendship lingering in the memories now and again.
From the heart its flows and travels through the veins.
It's like the ocean's waves that over flows the shore.
And with a tender heart should always be adored.

Friendship floats on high over mountains and cloud.
When hurt its pain and cried that loud.
Its punctuated with love and dignity.

And should remain forever until eternity.

Friendship is a gift and a pride.
Throughout the world nation's wide.
It's like the season flowers that's rare to find.
And should be treasured in the heart soul and mind.

When the song finished, everyone once again clapped their hands. After that the party began. Jannet, Jessica, Angie, and Sherry stood by themselves being young girls.

Jannet said, "Sherry, I think that my brother Joe is deeply in love with you."

Sherry said, "He's a fine guy, I see no problem with him, besides, I love him too."

Angie urged, "So what are you waiting for?"

Sherry answered, "Inasmuch as I loved him, I really can't make a decision about getting married to him."

Angie questioned, "Why not?"

Jessica, who was the oldest among them asked, "Why not?"

Joe stood among the guys with a beer in his hand, but his thoughts, eyes, and ears were focusing on the girls. He knew that they were talking about him and since he could not hear what they were saying he was trying to read their lips.

Jannet said, "I knew what's your problem, Sherry. You're worrying about your parents. Am I right?"

Sherry said, "That's right. I mentioned that you're an

angel descended from above. You knew exactly what my problem is."

Jannet mentioned, "Sherry, we are young girls and let us face reality, young girls have to leave their parent's home one day. They cannot live with parents forever. They have to battle on their own someday. Use me as an example: my parents are rich, and I fell in love with a poor guy."

Angie added, "You mean, madly fell in love with a poor handsome, cute guy."

Sherry said, "Please, Angie."

Jannet said, "Girl, though we were married for a few years now I still can't take my eyes off him. He's so cute charming and sexy, uh."

Jessica said, "I know, I know, leave that 'uh' for later."

Jannet mentioned, "You're right though he's my husband I got carried away sometimes when I admired him secretly. Now let's pick up from where we've left off."

Angie said, "You don't have to worry about your parents, Sherry, as Jannet said, girls have to leave their parent's home one day. They don't have a mortgage to pay. We knew that they are sick. And I think that they will not tell you this but they would rather see you married before they die, I mean God forbid."

Jannet added, "That's right Angie, perfectly right. Sherry, you can support your parents; you're working now. If you don't want to leave your parents you can still marry and continue to stay with your parents."

Sherry asked, "Will he agree to that?"

Jannet said, "I'm his sister; leave that to me."

Sherry said, "Okay." She blushed.

Jannet, Jessica, and Angie hugged her, "Welcome to the new world."

Joe smiled blushingly. The rest of the guys glanced at Joe and laughed.

Prastan said, "Let's cheer, guys. This one is for Joe."

Joe asked, "What for?"

Mark said, " Don't pretend, fool, you read their lips."

Mr. and Mrs. Scott and Mr. and Mrs. James were at a corner. Deecia was telling Mrs. Scott that Mark had mentioned in the SUV that Sherry loved Joe.

Stella said, "He's a nice boy I think they will make a nice couple."

James said, "I'll ask Prastan to ask him. What do you think, Scott?"

Scott said, "Fine with us. We'll thank you for that. We'll be happy to see she got married before we die."

Deecia waved at the girls. They went over.

Jannet asked, "You guys having fun?"

"Yes dear." replied her mom. She looked at Joe and Sherry and continued, "Dear we were talking about Sherry and Joe."

Jannet said, "We were on the same topic, mom."

Deecia said, "Really."

Angie said, "Yes, and she agreed."

Deecia said, "Oh how sweet. Let us make use of this golden opportunity."

Jannet said, "Over here guys, come over here, please. Well, Joe, I have something to say, Sherry's parents are asking for you to get married to Sherry. What do you have to say? Sherry agreed, her parents agreed, everyone here agreed. what do you have to say?"

Joe blushed, "Okay."

Jannet asked, "Joe, when you guys get married could you stay at Sherry's home until her parents feel better if you don't mind."

Joe said, "I see no problem with that, Jannet."

Everyone in one voice said, "Yeah."

Prastan said, "We'll fix a date later. Let's celebrate this as well. Cheers, guys."

Joe said, "Before we toast to that, I've a special announcement to make and trust me this is very important to me in my life." Everyone looked at Joe anxiously waiting to hear what he had so special in his mind to say.

Joe said, "Ladies and gentlemen, what I'm saying here now I really mean it. Prastan, Jannet, and Mark are my friends. Prastan and Jannet are my bosses. We have loved each other and can't stay without each other. Prastan and Mark are like my brothers because I have considered them more than a friend. Jannet, I have considered my sister. Prastan and Jannet have made Mark and myself somebody in this world today. They have trusted us to the maximum extent with everything. We have considered their business our business, this house is just like ours. They gave us their car and house they made us work in their office besides them. Their happiness, sorrows, and pain are ours. Today, in front of everyone I would like to say this and this goes to the girl I love and to the girl I will be getting married to one day and that is no one else but Sherry." Hearing this everyone gave a loud clapping of hands although he still didn't get to the point as yet. He then continued, "Sherry, Mr. and Mrs. Scott, I want you all to hear what I have to say. After marriage at no time I will tolerate Sherry if she wants to separate me from my loving people. Am I making myself clear here, Sherry?"

Sherry laughed and went and hugged him, "Trust me, in the name of God,, that will never happen. Look what they have done for me. They gave me a very good job and I will be working besides you, they have bought me precious gifts, they have paid off our mortgage, and through them I've met you. Joe, I would like to reverse the same question to you. Should you at any time try to steer me away from them, personally, I would not tolerate your behavior. Am I making myself clear here in front of everyone?"

Joe said, "Absolutely. Thank God both of us are on the same page here or else."

Mark asked, "Or else what, fool?"

Everyone laughed except Sherry's parents.

Sherry's parents then looked at each other.

Jannet whispered at them, "Don't ever bother with them that's the way they behaved all day long; sometimes they drove me nuts, but no matter what I love them and will always keep them by my side." Joe and Sherry hugged each other. Sherry's mom had tears of happiness flowing down her cheeks. Everyone gave another loud clapping of hands.

Jim said, "Oh Prastan, before I forget, I want to tell you something."

Jessica said, "Jim, I thought I supposed to tell them. Have you forgotten?"

Jim said, "You're right dear I am sorry."

Jessica said, "Prastan, I think you should put a thought on this."

Jannet asked, "Thought on what, Jessica?"

Jessica said, "It's a car dealer business. The bank has seized the business due to default payment. The business has three locations, Jannet, three locations."

Jim said, "I think you should invest on this business, Prastan." Hearing this everyone was speechless and paid full attention on what Prastan had to say. Everyone's eyes were at Prastan.

Prastan asked, "Why was the owner default on his payment? Isn't the business making money?"

Jim said, "Of course, the business was making money, that's the reason why I am asking you to buy the business."

Prastan asked, "But if the business was making money, why did the bank seize the business ?"

Jim said, "The owner had told me that his employees weren't very honest with him; they've stolen from him. So he couldn't pay the mortgage."

Jannet said, "I'm very sorry to hear that."

Prastan asked, "How much the bank asking for the business?"

Jim said, "With all three locations included eighty cars. The cars are $225,000.00 and the three lots are $45,000.00 so we're talking a total of $270,000.00. Prastan if you buy that business you'll make money like crazy, believe me."

Prastan said, "That's a lot of money you're talking about $270,000.00. I don't have all that money. Will you qualify me for a loan that much?"

Jim laughed, "Have you forgotten I'm your friend too. Consider it done."

Prastan said, "I'm a businessman and would like to make an offer to the bank."

Jim said, "You have the right to make an offer. I see no harm in that."

Prastan asked, "If they accept my offer, can you arrange for the money. I'm offering $250,000.00 for that business."

Jim said, "I'll work on that offer for you my friend. And you know what I would like you to meet one of my doctor friend. I had mentioned to him about you and he's so anxious to meet you and be your friend."

Jannet added, "So we'll have a doctor friend also in this group. Perfect."

Prastan mentioned, "There's one little problem I'm seeing here."

Jannet, Mark and Joe in one voice asked, "What problem, Prastan?"

Prastan said, "Let assume we got the loan. Where will we find honest people?"

Jannet said, "We'll take care of that, honey; we'll work out something if everything goes well."

Jessica said, "Trust me, Jannet, everything will work out well."

Jim suggested, "Probably, Jessica could work for you guys if you don't mind hiring her. Not because I'm a bank manager means that I'm loaded."

Jannet said, "Really Jessica, would you like to work with us." This she said and grabbed her.

Jessica said, "Why not. I've joined your group, remember?"

Jannet released her, "So sweet." Due to this conversation the party was discontinued and everyone was now focusing on the new topic. Prastan and Jannet tried to work out a system to get the business running without dishonesty.

Prastan said, "Okay, let assume everything goes well."

Jim said, "Stop it just there, Prastan, everything will be okay, remember I am the bank manager, I am your friend and Jessica will be working for you guys. Doesn't that tell you something? Consider it done. Now, you may go ahead and plan yourselves."

Prastan said, "Okay, Joe, you will be the office manager for Sunshine Farm. You and Sherry will run the office. Can you handle that, Joe?"

Sherry said, "Yes, we can. I'll be on his back where our job is concerned."

Jannet said, "Oh thank you, Sherry."

Joe said, "Okay Prastan, I'll run the farm. But, what will Mark do?"

Mark said, "Shut up fool." Everyone laughed at their childishness. Jannet shook her head. "They'll never change."

Prastan said, "Mark, you will be the office manager for one location of the car business. Can you handle it?"

Mark said, "I'm your friend for a long time now and I'm learning the way how you tackle business. I'll exercise your tactics. Yes, I'll handle it."

Jannet mentioned, "Well, we have two businesses in good hands. Now, Jessica you will be the office manager for one location of the car business."

Jessica without any hesitation said, "Yes, I'll take it."

Jannet said, "Thank you, Jessica."

Prastan said, "Well now the problem begins. Where will we find an honest employee for the third location?"

Charles said, "Prastan, we love you guys much and we wish if we could be among each other. I am not certain whether business will work out good in my country. Look what you have done for us, you paid off our mortgage and you said not even bother to pay it back; you don't need the money. You gave us money and you and Jannet showed us so much love. If you want to hire me I promise I'll work for you very honest and faithful."

Jannet said, "Charles, you will be the office manager for the third location of the car business and Angie you will work beside, Charles. Will you guys accept the job?"

Charles and Angie in one voice said, "You bet."

Prastan "Guys, personally, I feel like we are exaggerating ourselves here and at the same time for you guys it may sound ridiculous. But, if we cannot find honest and reliable people to manage the business, I don't think that we should invest in the business. What happened with the previous owner, I don't want it to happen to me. In business you have to plan and make good decision. You can't plunge into business just like that without planning. Now the problem here is to find two honest employees one to be with Mark and one to be with Jessica."

Rick said, "I could work for you, Prastan, if you want to hire me."

Paul added, "Me too, Prastan, if you want to hire me I will work very faithful to you."

Peter mentioned, "Assuming Prastan hired you guys where will I find people to work with me? What will I do all by myself without you guys. Prastan needed only two persons; if he needed three I should work for him as well."

Jannet laughed, "Okay the three of you guys hired. Peter you will work with Jessica. Paul you and Rick will work with Mark."

Prastan said, "Everyone now has a job. Is everyone happy?"

Everyone in one voice said, "Yeah."

Jannet said, "I can't here you guys"

Everyone shouted, "Yeah."

Prastan said, "Well Jim, I have ruled out my business now everything is yours."

Jim said, "Prastan, I don't want to exaggerate but I'll have to make the decision and I have to underwrite the loan. My dear beloved friend you may consider your loan approved. Besides, I'm happy my wife is a manager for one of your branch."

Prastan said, "Guys, I know you all will be leaving in the morning but as soon as we get over this business I will not hesitate to inform you guys. Now, let the party continue." It was running close to midnight when Jim said, "I'll take a hike, Prastan. And remember to see me in my office Monday morning 8:00 A.M. sharp to start the paperwork. And by the way, when you sign the contract I'll take the opportunity to introduce you to Dr. Nick."

Prastan said, "No problem, Jim"

Jim said, "And by the way guys, have a safe journey home."

All in one voice, "Thank you Jim, thank you, Jessica."

Jessica said, "See you guys soon."

Jim and Jessica walked out the front door. After that they ended the party and went to bed.

Early on Saturday morning as usual Prastan and Jannet woke up took a shower and went in the kitchen. Her mom and dad were already in the kitchen preparing breakfast.

Jannet said, "Morning mom, dad. You guys are early."

Mom and dad said, "Good morning dear, morning Prastan. You guys are late."

Prastan said, "According to Jim last night we will definitely get the money to do the business. But—"

James said, "No 'but' son." He hesitated, " but what?" You're doing the right thing, son. You guys are young, do it now before you get old. And believe me, I don't know about your mother but I am very much proud of you guys."

Deecia said, "What are you saying? I am proud of them, I mean, very proud."

Prastan said, "I am worrying about accommodations for Charles, Angie, Rick, Peter and Paul.

Definitely, they will have to get a place to stay if they decided to work with us permanently here in Allgreen. And since they have their own boat they can go and come.

I have an idea but I really don't know how you guys will take it."

Jannet said, " May I assume what your idea is?"

Prastan said, "My pleasure, feel free."

Jannet said, "Since we have this huge mansion and the two of us alone. You are suggesting that mom and dad should stay with us and rent their house to Rick, Peter, and Paul. Am I correct?"

Prastan replied, "Absolutely, how come the two of us always think alike?"

Deecia said, "Because you guys are made for each other"

James added, "You've got that right."

Deecia said, "I see no problem with that, after all we're living for our children. And—"

Jannet asked, "And what?"

James added, "And our grands."

Jannet said blushingly, "Dad."

Deecia added, "What dad? One day you guys will have to get your own little family and we'll play our own little grands."

James said, "Well, personally, I see no problem with your idea. At least your mom and I can do something in the house while you guys are at work. I can take care of the yard and pool and your mom can cook and clean inside the house."

By this time everyone woke up and while some were busy packing some were busy brushing. At the breakfast table, Jannet said, "Well, good morning everyone. We do hope you guys had an enjoyable vacation here with us in Allgreen. And at the same time we are glad that you guys have decided to work with us here in, Allgreen.

At this point" This she said while sipped her coffee. She continued, "We are trying to make accommodation where you guys will stay if you guys have decided to work with us here in Allgreen permanently."

Everyone in one voice, "Definitely, we will work permanently."

Prastan mentioned to them, "Mom and dad will move over with us and Rick, Peter, and Paul will pay a small rent to them for their house. At least they have to pay property taxes and insurance."

Jannet added, "Mom and dad's house will be very convenient for you guys because it has three bed rooms. And Mark and Joe you guys can move in with us and rent your house to Charles and Angie. Hey, what do you think?"

Rick, Peter, and Paul said, "It's a brilliant idea; we accept the deal."

Joe and Mark said, "We'll always respect your decision."

Charles and Angie said, "That's a brilliant idea and we also accept the deal."

Mark asked, "What will happen when Joe gets married?"

Sherry said, "He'll move in with us."

Mr and Mrs. Scott said, "Look at that, There is nothing to worry about now, Prastan."

After breakfast they have decided to hit the road. Joe, Mark, Sherry, and her mom and dad went in the car.

Stella said, "Dear, you guys can please drop us at home first."

Sherry said, "No problem mom." This she spoke with some sort of privilege while she smiled at Joe. Joe smiled at her and said, "No problem."

He then turned at Prastan, "Hey Prastan, We're leaving now, I'll give Mr. and Mrs. Scott a ride home. I'll see you guys at the beach at the dock."

Prastan said, "See you at the dock."

Rick, Peter, and Paul went in the SUV and sat in the third row seat. Charles and Angie sat in the second row. Prastan was at the wheel and Jannet besides him. Mr. and Mrs. James stayed back at home doing some cleaning up.

The morning was very pleasant: clear blue sky with a calm wind , birds flying here and there.

Angie said, "Allgreen is a really beautiful place. If things work out well, we can sell our house and live here permanently. What do you think, Charles?"

Charles said, "I'll live anywhere you want to live, dear, once you are happy, I'm happy. I had promised everyone that I'll be a changed man, and I want to live a simple and decent life. I want to keep my promise."

Jannet said, "I'm so proud of you, Charles. And I'm also happy that you feel better. I think Allgreen is for you guys. What do you think, Rick?"

Rick said, "Perfect, and I will marry and settle down here." Hearing this everyone laughed.

Prastan questioned, "So what will happen with your dad, Angie?"

Angie said, "That restaurant business is too dangerous for him to run all by himself. May be sooner or later, I'll ask him to move over with us. The house is a two-bedroom house."

Prastan said, "Not a bad idea. What will Mike do by himself?

Jannet asked, "What will happen with the restaurant?"

Angie replied, "He can rent it out."

Prastan said, "That will be the biggest headache for him; might as well sell it."

Angie said, "That's true. He will listen to me; I'm the only one he's got."

They reached the beach. They parked the SUV and went to the dock.

Tony said, "Hey, Prastan, good morning, I was just thinking of you." He waived his hand and said, "Good morning, everyone."

Everyone in one voice replied, "Good morning, Tony."

Joe had arrived. He parked the car behind the SUV. They all embraced each other.

Charles said, "Thank you very much for everything, Prastan and Jannet. And we will be waiting to hear from you as soon as possible."

Rick, Peter, and Paul said, "Thank you Prastan and

Jannet for everything. And we do hope the business come true."

Prastan said, "You guys will hear from me Monday night."

All in one voice said, "Thank you much once again for everything." This they said and then went in the boat.

Mark and Joe said, "See you guys soon."

Rick turned the boat around and moved slowly into the deep.

Prastan said, "Thank you so much, Tony." This he said and he gave Tony a hundred buck for his kindness.

Tony said, "Thank you, Prastan, and see you later."

They walked out to the shore. Mark and Joe stood near each other.

Sherry stood almost fifteen meters away from them all by herself. Jannet and Prastan stood almost fifteen meters away from them also. They were all looking at the boat and waving as it drifted slowly into the deep.

Sherry waved slowly at them. Inwardly, she asked and questioned herself, *If Charles and Prastan aren't relatives and they weren't friends before likewise Angie. Why did Prastan pay off that huge amount of mortgage for them? I wondered whether it has anything to do with Angie or whether she had flirted with him secretly. I doubt it because he's a very respectable young man and beside, neither Angie nor myself can't compare ourselves with Jannet, she's far prettier than us. I don't think that Prastan will fall for us when he's married* to the prettiest girl I have ever seen on earth. At the same time I can't blame any young girl if they flirted with him or got carried away by him. He's so handsome, cute, charming, and sexy. He paid off my mortgage too. Is it because he is very kindhearted and a good man and felt very sorry for poor people like us since he grew up very poor? Or is it he did this favor for me because he's expecting something from me in return. Oh boy, he doesn't need to do favors for girls. I'm sure girls are dying for him. My God, what am I thinking? I'll soon get married to one of his best friends, Joe, and besides we'll be working for his company. I wonder whether Angie had slept with him before. They're so kindhearted and loving. Do I have the ability to hurt Jannet? Do I have the heart to hurt this beautiful loving angel? At this point Sherry is uncertain of herself whether she can solve the problem by answering her own question, "Oh boy"

Angie waved back to them at the shore. Inwardly she questioned herself, why did Prastan pay off Sherry's mortgage? Why did he hire her the first day he met her at the restaurant? I knew that he's a good guy and he's handsome, cute, charming, sexy, and attractive young man. Why did he pay off our mortgage? He and my husband aren't relative nor they knew each other nor they were friends before. I'm wondering whether he loves me. May be he did. Suppose he really did; what am I supposed to do? I did inform everyone at one point that I loved him before and then made an oath that that will be discontinued. They're so innocent and kindhearted. Do I

*have the ability to hurt Jannet by cheating with her man? Do
I have the heart to hurt this beautiful loving angel? I wonder
whether Sherry will try to return his kindness forcefully on
him whether he like it or not by throwing herself on him?
Inasmuch as I promised to discontinue the love that I had for
him, I wonder whether I should return his kindness forcefully
whether he likes it or not by throwing myself on him?* At this
point Angie is uncertain of herself whether she could solve
the problem by answering her own question, "Oh boy."

As the boat drifted slowly into the deep leaving
Allgreen shore behind Peter, Paul, and Rick kept admiring
beautiful Allgreen.

Peter said, "I only hope things work out well. If we get
that job, we will be better off in life and we don't have to
call ourselves fishermen anymore. Besides, I like Allgreen;
it's a beautiful place."

Rick said, "Everything will work out good; I have a
good feeling about it."

Paul added, "I have the same feeling as well."

Charles kept admiring Allgreen while all of his
thoughts were on his past way of life as he remembered
and recalled all the things that he had done that destroyed
his life. And at the same time he focused his thoughts
on Allgreen and dream of living a new and decent life in
the future. He recalled at one point when he had lusted
for Jannet and so desired to have pleasure with her when

she had denied him and eventually she had changed his life into a decent person. He also recalled when he fell sick and lost everything he had, that the same money he had offered Jannet to have some pleasure, that the same money and some from them, they dug him out from the sinking financial hole, just the way she dug him out from the world of a rotten life that he was sunk in. He then thought inwardly, *I thank them a lot for dugging me. This will be a hidden secret between the three of us until our last day but I wonder how Angie felt about the bail out and what she must be thinking about the bail out. Oh boy.*

Joe and Mark walked up to Sherry.

Joe asked, "Are you okay, Sherry? You seemed lost in wonderland." Hearing this she tried to revive from her lost and to break the peculiar of her awakened sleep that was filled with weird thoughts and imaginings.

She then responded, "Oh yes, I'm fine. I'm just wondering."

Joe asked, "Wondering about what?"

Sherry said, "Wondering that God has sent us in this beautiful world. And our duration on this earth is a destination. We have a journey to travel through happiness and sorrows and we have so many things to do and say, so many decision to make whether it's good or bad; only God knows what is written in our destination and whether any decision we made is appropriate or not."

Mark added, "I agree with you, Sherry." This he said and the three of them walking towards Prastan and Jannet.

When the boat reached the deep, it took off with speed heading towards the opposite shore. Jannet looked at the boat until it disappeared in the river as if it was swallowed by the water. Tears dripped down her cheeks while she dried it with the back of her right hand.

Prastan asked, "Are you okay, Jannet?"

Jannet replied, "Yeah, it's the tears of happiness. It's a girl thing. Girls are very tender and emotional. They can be easily got carried away. But as you said a hundred times that we came in this world for a short period of time. And the good and evil that men do lived after them. Prastan, I will continue to do good until my last day no matter what it takes." Prastan is a very smart young man and a quick thinker. He had realized that Jannet is foreseeing her faith and has decided to comfort her and to guarantee her that her dreams will always come true.

He threw his right hand around her shoulder and they walked slowly one step after another towards the SUV.

Prastan asked, "Do you remember when we were dating before we got married?"

Jannet said, "Yeah, how could I ever forget that?"

Prastan continued, "Do you remember I said, 'Jannet I love you, Jannet I cannot live without you, Jannet you are my life'?"

Jannet with tears slightly running down her cheeks said, "Yes, Prastan, I have treasured those words for the rest of my life. I can never forget those words." This she said while she grabbed him around his waist.

Prastan said, "Me too. And no human on the face of this planet earth can take those words away from me. No human can come between us to split us. I will always love you until my *last* day. God made us for each other and only he has the right.

ONLY GOD CAN SEPARATE US "

They stopped and faced each other followed by a sweet kiss and a tight hug while standing on the wet sandy shore.

After that they took a deep breath and repated the word, "Only God can separate us."

CHAPTER THREE

JANNET said, "Let's go home, guys. I really need to have some rest; I'm so tired."

The sun seemed to be climbing faster and faster, leaving the earth beneath. A few clouds floats overhead traveling southwest.

Jannet complained, "My God, it's very sticky" This she said as she went in the SUV and turned the AC on, a few minutes later she whispered, "I feel much better now."

In less than thirty minutes they reached home. Deecia said, "You looked very tired, dear, sit down and have some rest for God's sake." It's a mother's feeling.

Jannet said, "You bet, I'm tired. Vacation is very good and enjoyable but it seems like I have worked as twice as hard, than on my job."

James added, "That's the reason why I don't like to take vacations. But sometime you really need a vacation too, to just get out of the job into a new atmosphere and relax the brain."

Deecia asked, "Where are Mark and Joe?"

Prastan said, "They gave Sherry a ride home. They should be here in a few minutes; I guess they must be tired too."

Shortly after Mark and Joe pulled in the driveway. They came out of the car.

Deecia said, "Well, we have clean up all the messes in the house, and I have prepared lunch for you guys."

Joe asked, "I heard you said lunch, Mrs. James?"

Deecia said, "That's right. You've heard me right."

Joe said, "I'm hungry, I'm starving, I'm dying."

Mark said, "Anytime you hear 'food,' you're hungry, you're starving, you're dying."

Deecia added, "When he got married there will be no such words again from him."

Mark said, "Yeah right. Who, Joe?" Everyone laughed.

When the boat reach the other side of the shore Mike was already there waiting for their arrival. Rick docked the boat. They went out. Angie kissed and hugged her dad. Mike then welcome them home. They shook hands and then went in the bus.

Mike asked, "So, how was the vacation?"

Angie said, "Oh dad it was fun, shared fun, and nothing but fun all the time."

Mike said, "That's good. That's the way vacation should be. So you guys walked a lot? How does Allgreen look?"

Charles said, "Oh, it's beautiful, really beautiful."

Rick added, "Prastan is a very popular guy in Allgreen. Anywhere you go, anywhere you turn, people knew him."

Peter added, "He's rich. He owns Sunshine Farm and he's got twenty-five employees."

Mike asked, "So how are the boys Mark and Joe?"

Angie said, "They're fun. They're working in Sunshine Farm's office."

Mike said, "Peter, I'm sorry I wasn't paying attention. I was fully engrossed in excitement. What were you saying? Say it again if you don't mind, please."

Peter said, "I said that Prastan is rich; he owns Sunshine Farm and has twenty-five employees."

Mike said, "Wow! And he's so innocent and simple."

Angie said, "A few days ago Prastan hired a young girl about my age to work in the office."

Mike said, "That's so nice and kindhearted of him. At least she will be able to help herself and maybe her family too."

Angie said, "And guess what, dad.,that new girl I'm talking about, she loved Joe and she's going to get married to him soon, oh boy." This she said and clapped her hands. She then continued "Dad, dad, they got a mansion."

Paul added, "That is a huge house, seven bedrooms, four baths and three-car garage."

Mike said, "Wow! And they are like ordinary people; you just can't believe that they're rich."

Angie said, "Hey Paul, you didn't mention the pool."

Paul said, "Oh yes. That's a real beautiful pool."

Angie said, "I have learned to swim in the pool, dad."

Mike said, "I can really imagine all the fun you guys have in Allgreen."

Angie said, "Dad, I'm your only daughter, I'm the

only one you have in this wide world. What will make you happy about me, dad?"

Mike said, "Your question sounds very difficult but it's very easy to answer. For me, once you're happy and living happily that all that matters to me. Did I answer your question?"

Angie said, "Yes, dad. You really did."

Mike said, "Well, now is your turn to answer my question." This he said with both hands on the wheel and concentrating on his driving.

Angie asked, "What question, dad?"

Mike said, "Well, you have never in your life asked me a question like this. What's up your sleeve?" Hearing this everyone laughed. Angie looked at Charles. She didn't know how to begin telling her dad about their new job and what they had decided.

Charles said, "Dad, Prastan and Jannet are very good people. Look what they have done for us. They have paid off our mortgage. They have bought a boat for Rick, Peter, and Paul. They have paid off Sherry's mortgage."

Mike asked, " Sherry?"

Angie said, "Sherry is the girl Joe is going to get married to."

Mike said, "Oh I see. Now you guys get to the point. Don't beat around the bush."

Rick asked, "How's business Mike?"

Mike said, "Don't remind me about business. Business is very slow, very, very slow. If it continues like this I may have to close it down and look for a job somewhere. Now, get back to the point, Charles. You're about to tell me something."

Everyone looked at Charles. They wanted to know how he was going to reveal the news to him.

Charles said, "Dad, Angie wanted to tell you something but she don't know how to begin."

Mike said, "I can't understand. But, why, is she's scared?"

Charles said, "She feels that she may hurt your feelings and maybe sometimes break your heart."

Mike said, "Wait, wait a minute. My daughter killed someone?"

Charles replied, "No dad. It's good for us but we don't know how you will take it."

Mike said, "Have you mentioned good for us? What do you mean by saying good for us?"

Charles said, "Dad, Prastan have decided to buy a car dealership. It has three locations. If he gets the deal, he said he'll make me the manager for one location and Angie will be my assistant."

Mike said, "Wow! That is good news. That's very good. Consider yourselves lucky. This place here is getting worse and worse every day. If you guys can do better in Allgreen, probably I'll sell this damn restaurant and move also."

Angie placed her hands on her chest and said, "Thank

God." She then continued "Dad, Prastan appointed the bank manager's wife Jessica as manager for one location."

Peter added, "And I will be working besides her."

Mike said, "Really."

Charles said, "And he made Joe the manager for Sunshine Farm office and Sherry will be working with him."

Mike said, "Wow!"

Angie added, "And he made Mark the manager for another location."

Paul added, "And Rick and I will be working with him."

Mike said," Are you guys serious or are you guys making fun of me?"

Angie said, "We're dead serious, dad; this is no joke."

Mike said, "But you guys have just said that Prastan has decided to buy a car dealership which means that he didn't buy it yet. Am I right?"

Angie said, "You're absolutely right dad. But the manager and Prastan are very good friends. He's in charge of the approval of the loan and he guaranteed Prastan that he's going to definitely get the loan. Besides, dad, his wife will be working for Prastan as a manager."

Mike said, "Well, now that makes sense to me. So when is he going to get the loan?"

Charles said, "He is going to the bank Monday morning."

Mike asked," How you know for sure?"

Charles said, "Because he had an appointment with Jim."

Mike question, "Who's, Jim?"

Angie said, "Jim is the bank manager."

Mike asked, "Is that the same bank manager's wife you guys are talking about?'

Angie said, "Yes dad."

Mike said, "Well, definitely he is getting the loan."

Charles mentioned, "Prastan said he's going to call us Monday night to let us know whether everything is okay or not."

Mike said, "Everything will be okay. He's a very smart guy. That guy will become a millionaire one day."

Peter added, "We are happy for him. He grew up in poverty. His parents drowned in Allgreen's river when he was twelve years old. And from what we heard he struggled in life a lot. I really love that guy"

Angie inwardly said, "Me too. But I don't know, I asked God if I ever had a wish, I would wish that the love that I have for Prastan must be discontinued and I've promised myself not to break Jannet's heart. But if that bitch Sherry will try to flirt with him secretly, I would not tolerate that. If I can't get him, no one else can'., Besides, Jannet."

Not everyone is strong enough to live up to their promise, not everyone is capable enough to live up to their promise. Written words are subjected to corrections, whereas, spoken words are wind. Inasmuch you may sincerely desire and so wanted to keep to your promise, but if you are emotionally fragile, you can be easily broken and got carried away by temptations.

Paul added as well, "That is the reason why he's helping people."

Rick said, "He's not only a handsome guy, he's also kindhearted. Likewise, Jannet, she's not only a pretty girl but she's also kindhearted as well." Finally they reached home.

On the following Monday morning Mark and Joe went at Sherry to pick her up for work. When they reached there Mark moved himself over from the front passenger seat to the rear seat giving Sherry the opportunity to sit beside, Joe.

Sherry said, "Hi, Joe, good morning."

Joe replied, "Good morning, Sherry. How are you this morning?"

Sherry answered, "I'm fine Joe." She then turned at Mark, "Hi, Mark, good morning."

Mark replied, "Morning Sherry. It's Monday. You guys know that Prastan and Jannet will run late today."

Joe had forgotten all about it. He asked, "Why?"

Mark said "Have you forgotten they're going this morning at the bank to meet Jim concerning that loan they were discussing Saturday's night?"

Joe said, "Oh yeah, yeah."

Sherry said, "I'm not curious but, you guys really think that Prastan will get the loan?"

Mark said, "He's rich and popular, besides, he's a good customer at the bank and well known too. I see no good reason why they would turn him down."

Joe said, "What made you asked that question, Sherry? Do you have any doubt in mind whether he will get the loan or not?"

Sherry said, "I have no doubt but he's so young, just twenty-three years old."

Mark said, "I get your point. I knew it's a huge amount of money and, he's so young but, that has nothing to do with it. Prastan's credit is good; besides, Jim is the main man in the bank and, he and Jim are very good friends, so I see no problem."

Joe said, "The richer Prastan becomes is better for us. Check this out, who will make us managers for their company if we do not have good qualifications or some sort of degree or whatever."

Mark said, "Let me use you as an example, Sherry. If not for Prastan where would you be right now? Now, let me answer that question for you. You would have either been laid off or still working in that stupid restaurant. If the deal comes out successful, tomorrow Joe will be confirmed as manager, and you will be confirmed as assistant manager. Isn't that a blessing from God?"

Joe said, "Check this out, Sherry. Besides hiring you,

look what he has done for you. Look what Jannet has done for you. Through them we have met each other and we will get married sometime anytime or anytime sometime, whatever."

Mark said, "Don't give me that bull, sometime anytime or anytime sometime. Your statement is no good; according to your statement it could be tomorrow or it could be ten years from now. Isn't it right, Sherry?" She didn't answer the question but instead she blushed smilingly.

Sherry said, "That's true, they have done a lot for me. I will never forget it." And inwardly, *I understood obviously that he hired me but why he paid off my mortgage? Suppose he really wants something from me in return as a favor. What am I supposed to do if he asked me? Girls are falling and dying for him. I have my financé sitting beside me and we will get married sometime, anytime, or anytime sometime as he said, my God. Prastan is so cute sexy and irresistible, I'll be glad to hold him. I wouldn't be the first to cheat; many cheaters are out there. For him., Oh boy. But place myself in Jannet shoes. She's so sweet, innocent and so kind to me. Oh boy, this is a corrupted decision. Though I'm poor I still have my dignity and pride. I'm not going to stretch out my hand for him though I'm passionate. But what if he does stretch out his hands to me? Lord, what decision should I make?*

Sherry still couldn't solve this imaginary problem that she had created for herself. Prastan will not cheat on Jannet for any reason. He loves her too much. They both love each other to the maximum extent and only God can separate them. Prastan grew up very poor and now that he became rich, he intended to help people and no question about it. Jannet knew this and is supporting him as well.

When they reached the office customers were in line in front of the office door. They said, ", *hello* and *morning* to everyone." While Mark and Joe were taking care of the customers Sherry went and brewed a pot of coffee. The morning started out very busy. One customer asked, "Will Prastan and Jannet be in today?"

Mark said, "Sure, but they will run late sir, is there something I can help you with?"

The customer said, "I want to talk with Prastan, but thank you anyway."

Mark said, "No problem, sir. If it's important you could come back any time after noon; he'll be here by then."

Prastan and Jannet went in the bank and slowly walked up to the receptionist's desk.

Prastan said, "Good morning sweetie." The young female, who seemed in her mid-twenties smiled at him, "Good morning handsome. How may I help you?"

Prastan said, "We're here to see, Jim."
She asked, "Do you know where his office is?"
Prastan said, "Of course, I do."
She replied "Good luck, handsome."

As they walked towards Jim's office the receptionist whispered, "My God, she's so pretty; they were made for each other."

Jannet overheard her and smiled inwardly, " *You can say that again*".

Jim said, "Good morning Prastan, morning Jannet. Have a seat please. You guys are behind fifteen minutes." This he said glancing at his watch. He then continued, "That doesn't matter. I have used those fifteen minutes and prepared all the paperwork. Now, do you walk with your documents?"

Jannet said, "We have the deed for our business."

Prastan added, "We have also walked with the deed for the house."

Jim asked, "Do you have any mortgages or lien on the business or house? I know that you don't have but I have to ask this question, company policy you know."

Prastan replied, "No mortgages, no lien."

Jim asked, "I need a favor from both of you and I will be highly appreciate if you guys could help me out."

Jannet asked, "What favor you need Jim? We are friends and if there is anything we can do to help you and make you happy, we will not hesitate. Besides, helping people is our desire.," she hesitate for a few seconds while she caught her husband's eyes and she smiled; she then continued, "It's my husband goal and we feel happy when we help people."

Jim said, "You see, one of the car location is very close

to my house. I will be glad if you guys could let Jessica work there." Prastan and Jannet laughed.

Prastan said, "We'll be glad to, Jim, but right now we cannot make that decision. We do not have the loan."

Jim said, "Don't you guys mess with me. Here's your loan, approved, approved." This he said and stamped all the documents. Prastan and Jannet were smiling and laughing.

Jannet said, "Jim, would you please close your eyes?"

Jim said, "Even if my eyes are open I wouldn't see anything but what the heck if you ask me to I will." He closed his eyes.

Jannet was so happy that she gave Prastan a sound kiss.

Jim asked, "Can I open my eyes now, Jannet?"

Jannet said, "Yes, Jim."

Jim said, "I knew, you have kissed him."

Jannet said, "I'm sorry Jim, I can't help it."

Jim said, "That okay. He deserves it."

Prastan asked, "So what's next, Jim?"

Jim said, "You're asking me? You tell me. When you want to close the deal?"

Jannet and Prastan looked at each other.

Prastan asked, "Could we close the deal on Friday?"

Jim said, "That's fine with me."

Jannet said, "Jim, now we can answer your question. Jessica has been confirmed as Manager for the location of your desire."

Jim said, "Oh thank you guys very much. As I said before, not because I have this position means that I'm rich. Now that you guys made Jessica a manager we can afford to live a better life."

The phone rang. Jim picked it up.

The receptionist said, "Jim, Dr. Nick is here to see you."

Jim said, "Send him in." This he said and put down the phone. He then continued, "I'm glad that he came."

Dr. Nick said, "Hello Jim, good morning. And who's this handsome young man and this beautiful angel?" This he asked while admiring the young couple.

Jim requested, "Have a seat, Nick."

Nick said, I hope that I'm not in the middle of inter-rupting what's going on here."

Jim said, "Of course not, but you'll be glad to be here at this moment."

Nick said, "Sound interesting to me."

Jim said, "Nick, do you recall I had mentioned to you of one of my friends."

Nick said, "The rich guy, Prastan and his wife Jannet."

Jim said, "Yes."

Nick asked, "So when you will arrange for us to meet? You've been talking so many good things about them. I want to be their friends too just like you. We all will make good friends."

Jim said, "And good friends help each other."

Nick said, "That's right."

Jim said, "Well, these are the good friends that I'm talking about."

Nick asked, "Who, Prastan and Jannet?"

Jim said, "Yes, they have just helped me out. They have hired Jessica as manager for one of their car dealer locations."

Nick said, "Wow!. They are really good people indeed. Wait a minute. Have you said one of their car dealer location?"

Prastan and Jannet looked at each other smiling.

Jim said, "That right. They have bought the three car dealer locations on the east coast."

Nick asked, "How much did they pay for it?"

Jim said, "Quarter of a million."

Nick said, "God really blessed those couple. I'm a doctor and I don't even have a proper car."

Jim said, "I'm definitely sure they will help you. As I said they are good people."

Nick asked, "Then when the hell you will arrange for us to meet?"

Jim laughed smiling, "I already did."

Nick said, "Really, my car is falling apart, maybe they will sell me a car very reasonably. So when we're going to meet?"

Jim said, "Right now."

Nick asked, "What do you mean, right now?"

Jim introduced them, "Here's the couple you have been so anxious to meet. This is Prastan and this is Jannet."

Prastan said, "Hello Dr. Nick, nice meeting you, I'm Prastan."

They shook hands. He then continued "And this is my beautiful wife, Jannet."

Jannet shook his hands as well. "Nice meeting you Dr. Nick."

Dr. Nick was astonished for a moment when he knew that those young couple were the persons he was so anxious to meet and couldn't believe that this beautiful young couple is so rich.

Nick asked, "So you guys owned Sunshine Farm too?"

Jim said, "That's right."

Prastan said, "Okay Jim, we must go now."

Dr. Nick said, "From now on we are friends so you guys call me Nick."

Prastan said, "Nick, We will take over the company this Friday. Monday morning see Mrs. Jim. I mean our manager Jessica and see what kind of car you need. And I would like to invite you guys Saturday night; we will celebrate this beautiful occasion. See you guys later."

Prastan and Jannet slowly walked out of the door.

Nick said, "They are so young, wonderful and kind-hearted. May God bless them both."

Jim said, "You see what I mean. Today my wife became a manager for their company. That's what friends are for."

Prastan and Jannet overheard them and smiled. It was approximately 10:00 A.M. when they reached the office.

The first question Prastan asked, "How is everything going, guys?"

Joe answered, "Very busy, Prastan."

Sherry said, "Hello Jannet, hello Prastan. Would you guys like a cup of coffee?"

Jannet said, "Oh yes, Sherry, that will be nice. Milk and light sugar for Prastan."

Sherry asked, "And you?"

Jannet said, "Milk and two spoon of sugar." Mark said, "Oh yes, before I forget, Prastan one customer said he would like to see you. I think he want to discuss some kind of business with you. I asked him to come back any time after noon."

Prastan said, "No problem." While they were sipping the coffee Mark, Joe and Sherry were looking at them wondering to know whether they succeeded with their business. Prastan and Jannet knew that they were curious about the loan. Jannet looked at Prastan. And as usual they always understood each other. Even if they looked at each other one knew what the other wanted to say. Prastan shook his head granted her permission.

Jannet said, "Well Joe, congratulation you are confirmed Manager for this office and Sherry you will be his assistant. From Monday Joe you will be sitting in Prastan's chair and Sherry you'll be sitting in Jannet's chair." Mark, Joe and Sherry clapped their hands.

Joe said, "This clapping of hands is not for our

promotions but for your success. Congratulations to both of you."

Prastan said, "We will close the deal on Friday. Saturday night we will have a celebration for this. Sherry, you must bring your parents at the celebration."

Sherry said, "Thank you, Prastan."

Jannet said, "Oh, I have to call mom and dad and share the good news with them. And Prastan, don't forget to call Rick and the boys."

She called her mom, "Hi mom, good morning."

Mom answered, It better be." And after a moment of hesitation, she asked, "Where are you at right now?"

Jannet said, "I'm at work. I'm at the office right now."

Mom asked, "Aren't you guys supposed to meet Jim at his office this morning regarding that loan?"

Jannet said, "Yes, mom, we did."

Mom questioned, "You did? And what happened, dear? What is the outcome of it?"

Jannet said, "We have got the loan, mom, and we're going to close the deal on Friday. You and dad have to make arrangement to move over with us latest by Friday."

Mom asked, "So what are we going to do with our stuff, dear?"

Jannet said, "Just forget it and leave it behind. They are older than me anyway. Just pack your clothes only. Peter, Paul, and Rick will move in Sunday."

Mom asked, "When they're coming dear?"

Jannet said, "Prastan what them to come over here Saturday so that they can start work on Monday."

Mom said, "Sweetheart, you have got yourself a real businessman."

Jannet said, "And what about me, mom? I'm a businesswoman too."

Her mom laughed, "Yes, dear, you are and, stop flattering me businesswoman. Now let me share this good news with your grumpy father."

Jannet objected, "No, mom, he's not grumpy. He's pushy."

Mom said, "You are right, dear. I can see where you have got it from; I'll talk with you later." This she said and put the phone down.

Jannet then turned at Mark and Joe. She placed both hands on her waist and smiled at them.

Joe said, "Oh no."

Jannet laughed, "Oh yes, brothers."

Joe said, "Oh no, I'll miss my room." Everyone laughed at him.

Mark asked, "So when we have to move over, sister?"

Jannet shook her head "Any time but before Saturday, brother." They were teasing each other at the same time. Sherry was excited to see how they are getting along so nice like real brothers and sisters and so desired to share that kind of love with them, but her imaginary thoughts and day dreaming of Prastan is still corrupted her. Although she was laughing and smiling with them and sharing her happy facial expression, inwardly her conscience was eating her as she repeatedly asked herself the same question over and over all the time: *Why did Prastan pay off my mortgage? Did he look forward for a favor from me in return? How can I do this to Jannet? How can I do this to Joe? What if they happen to find out? What if Prastan stretches out his hands to me; should I reject him? Suppose I rejected him; will I hurt his feelings? If I flirt with him secretly will this be fair to Jannet and Joe? I'm confused, I'm confused.* Sherry's confused herself over a situation that would never occur, a situation that was just a weird thought and merely day dreaming that she had imposed upon herself.

Peter, Paul, and Rick were in the river fishing. The cell phone that Prastan bought them rang.

Peter said, "That must be Prastan. He said he's going to call us Monday night." He glanced at his watch, "But it's too early. Wonder if the bank denied him?"

Paul and Rick said, "Hope not."

Peter said, "Hello, Prastan."

Prastan said, "Hello, Peter. What's going on? How is everything?"

Peter said, "We're in the river fishing."

Prastan said, "Well, stop fishing. You guys go home and rest. You guys will have to start work on Monday. I need you guys over here Saturday at least by noon. I will send Mark and Joe to pick you guys up around noon. See you guys soon."

Peter said, "Yes, yes." The three of them were over joyed. They turned around the boat and head back home.

Jannet called Angie. "Hi Angie, how are you?"

Angie said, "Hi Jannet, I'm fine. We are at the restaurant helping out dad. How is everything going?"

Jannet said, "I have good news for you, girl. We have got the loan. We will buy the business Friday morning."

Angie said, "Yes, yes. Oh girl I am so happy."

Jannet said, "Prastan has just spoken with Peter. He wants you guys to come over Saturday morning. I think he wants you guys to start work on Monday."

Angie said, "Girl, you got yourself a real businessman. He doesn't waste time. When he said business, he meant business."

Jannet said, "Well, I will see you on Saturday."

Angie said, "You bet." This she said and slowly put the phone down. She ran and hugged Charles, "We have got the job, we have got the job."

Mike asked, "Really, I told you guys he will get the loan. So what are you guys going to do now?"

Charles said, "We will rent the house."

Mike said, "I knew someone looking for a place to rent. He's a very nice person."

Angie asked, "How many of them, dad?"

Mike said, " His wife and him and they have two children who may be eight and ten years old."

Charles said, "No problem, dad; contact them. We want you to handle everything."

Mike said, "That's no problem. So when will you guys decide to go?"

Angie said, "He wants us to start work from Monday. Jannet said to go over Saturday morning."

Mike said, "Good luck. They're very nice people, if they find you guys very honest they will like you guys very much, and they will treat you guys well."

Charles agreed, "That's true, dad."

The phone rang. Charles picked up "Hello. Hi Peter."

Peter said, "Did Prastan or Jannet called you guys?"

Charles said, "Yes, Jannet did."

Peter asked, "You guys start to make arrangements. We have to be there Saturday by noon."

Charles said, "We started making arrangement. Dad has someone to rent our house."

Peter said, "That's good. We were fishing when Prastan called us so we are heading home to start make necessary arrangements to leave on Saturday. See you later."

Mike mentioned, "If things work out good in Allgreen, I could probably rent out this business and join you guys over there."

Friday morning quite as usual Jannet and Prastan woke up early to make a head start of the day's event. She made breakfast while Prastan was taking a shower. After Prastan showered she immediately went and took a shower. When she came out from the shower Prastan laughed.

She glanced at him, "What? "

Prastan smiling, he said "Nothing, nothing."

Jannet asked, "If it's nothing, then why are you smiling?"

Prastan said, "That was the quickest shower you ever took."

She laughed, "Important matters are ahead, boy." She smiled. When they finished their breakfast they went to the office. Mark, Joe, and Sherry were already in the office.

Jannet and Prastan in one voice said, "Good morning, guys."

"Good morning." they replied

Prastan said, "You guys are early this morning, I mean very early," he glanced at his watch.

Joe said, "Important matters are ahead." Everyone laughed.

Jannet said, "Guys, we are going at the bank to close the deal." While walking out she turned back, "And don't." Before she could complete what she had to say Joe said "I know, I know. We have to move over today."

Jannet said, "You read my mind, brother."

They reached the bank.

Jannet said, "Hi Jessica, what brought you here so early?"

Jessica said, "Jim asked me to come along in case they ask you guys for a witness."

Jannet said, "Oh that's so wonderful. You guys are very thoughtful."

Jim said, "Good morning, Prastan, morning, Jannet. Please come right in. I have got all the papers on my table just awaiting signatures. Have a seat, guys."

Prastan said, "Where is everyone else?"

Jim asked, "What are you talking about, Prastan?"

Prastan said, I mean who is representing the sellers?"

Jim laughed. "You mean, who is representing the bank."

Prastan said, "That's right"

Jim said, "I am, my dear friend." This he said and pushed the papers onto him and Jannet, "Both of you guys sign at all the yellow arrows." When they finished signing all the papers Jim asked Jessica to sign at the bottom as a witness, "Well, Prastan and Jannet, congratulations, you are now the new owner of the business." They shook hands.

Jim asked, "So what next?"

Prastan said, "Let's go and check out the business. Jessica, congratulation, you're now a confirmed manager."

Jannet said, "Congratulation, Jessica. Start working on Monday."

Jessica said, "Oh thank you guys so much."

Prastan asked, " Aren't you going with us, Jim."

Jim said, "No problem. I can't refuse my wife's employer." They all laughed together.

They went and visited the three locations. The first location was very close to Jessica's home.

Jannet said, "Jessica, since you're residing not too far

away from here, I think this location will be very convenient for you."

Jessica and Jim in one voice, "Oh thank you guys very much."

Jim said, "If business isn't working well at the bank, probably, you can hire me as well."

Prastan said, "I'll make you general manager when it comes to that situation."

Jim said, "I heard a lot of stories about angels, but now, I am seeing them in front of me." Of course he was referring to Prastan and Jannet.

Friday seemed like a very short day as the day went by very fast. Jannet and Prastan, after visiting all three locations, went back to the office. Jim went back to the bank. Jessica went home happily and started to prepare herself in advance for Monday morning. She whispered herself, "*I'm a manager, I'm a manager. Oh thank you Jannet, oh thank you Prastan. May God always bless you all.*"

Prastan and Jannet walked in the office smiling.

Joe said, "Well."

Jannet said, "Well, we are in business. Joe, starting Monday you fully in charged of this office, and Sherry, make sure you keep an eye on him."

Sherry said, "You count on that Jannet. I promise. You heard that, Joe?"

Joe asked, "Heard what?"

Sherry said, "When I gazed you down don't say what. That will be part of my job." Everyone laughed.

Jannet said, "Mark, I know that you have no knowledge of the car business, none of us here do, but we will surely learn and one day we will definitely be perfect."

Prastan said, "Guys, let take for example, when we first started this farm business. We had no knowledge about it, but look at us today. Today we are masters of it. Joe, you have knowledge of this business so you will be doing just fine. Mark, as Jannet just said, we will surely learn one day. Now, tomorrow which is of course Saturday, Mark, you and Joe will go and pick up our crew at Allgreen's beach and make sure you guys ask Tony to dock the boat on a long-term basis."

Jannet said, "Sherry, make sure you don't forget to bring your mom and dad to the party tomorrow night."

Sherry said, "Okay Jannet, and if you need me to help you tomorrow morning. it will be my pleasure to come and assist you. I know you will have many things to do."

Jannet said, "Of course, I will need help."

Joe said, "So when we are going to move over?"

Jannet reminded, "Tonight, my loving brother." This she said smiling and nodding her head at him.

Joe said, "Okay my loving, sister." He teased back at her.

They closed the office at 5:00 P.M. and went home.

Mark asked, "So what we should bring over, Jannet?"

Jannet said, "I don't know. But that's a good question. What do you guys have?"

Joe said, "Let me think."

Mark laughed.

Joe asked, "What? Why are you laughing?"

Mark said, "Because you never think."

Sherry covered her mouth with both hands, laughing.

Prastan said, "We will find out. Let's go with the SUV and the car."

Mark rode with Jannet and Prastan in the SUV. And Sherry rode with Joe in the car. When they reached the home, Jannet recalled her old memories. She started to point out to Sherry, "I used to have my flower plants here, I used to have my shoes etc. etc."

Prastan said, "Okay guys, leave everything for Charles and Angie. Just pick up what is really necessary for you guys. Tomorrow when you guys pick them up, bring them home. Sunday morning you guys can take them to their new homes."

Jannet called her mom, "Hi mom."

Deecia responded, "Hi dear. Is everything okay? I didn't hear from you since this morning. Did you guys close that deal?"

Jannet said, "Yes mom, and we were so busy that why I didn't call you earlier."

Deecia said, "That no problem dear. So when do you want us to move over, tonight or Saturday morning?"

Jannet glanced at Prastan.

"Tonight will be better," Prastan whispered to Jannet.

Jannet said, "Tonight, mom. As we said leave

everything behind just walk out with what is really necessary. Leave everything for Rick,Peter, and Paul. They are
so nice, mom."

Deecia said, "Don't reminded me, dear, I know."

Jannet said, "We are at our old mansion, mom. It
brought back some of my old memories. When Prastan
and I first met I told him that his little hut would be my
mansion."

Deecia said, "But you had never told me that, dear. So
you were very sneaky to me."

Jannet said, "Some of the things I have kept to myself
secretly, mom, secretly."

Deecia said, "I'm your mother. And I want to update
you with something that you didn't know. I was watching
all your moves with the far corner of my eyes. And believed
me dear you cannot teach old dogs new tricks. Besides,
dear, I used to lie as well."

Jannet laughed, "Okay, mom, you won. Now, since
we are close by we can come pick you guys up now.
Tomorrow night we will have a party; at least you and
dad will help out a little. I have invited Dr. Nick, Jim and
Jessica, Henry the realtor, and Sherry's parents over and of
course our new employees from overseas Charles, Angie,
Rick, Peter, and Paul."

Deecia said, "Okay, dear, by the time you guys get
here we should be ready."

They went and picked them up and on their way
home they dropped off Sherry. Sherry had invited them

to go inside her house as a matter of appreciation, but it was running late, and they have decided not to."

Joe asked, "What time do you want me to pick you up in the morning?"

Sherry asked, "What time you need me, Jannet?"

Jannet said, "Whenever it is convenient for you."

Sherry said, "Pick me up at 9:00 A.M., Joe."

Jannet said, "See you tomorrow, Sherry."

Sherry said, "Bye everyone, see you guys tomorrow."

When they reached home, Jannet had pointed out room to everyone.

Jannet said, "Okay, mom and dad, this bedroom is yours. Mark, this bedroom is yours, and Joe, this bedroom is yours."

Saturday morning Prastan and Jannet woke up early as usual. They went in the bathroom to shower and then went in the kitchen. Once again they were surprised to see that James and Deecia were already preparing breakfast for everyone. Jannet and Prastan in one voice said, "Good morning, mom and dad."

Mom and dad, "Good morning; you guys should have slept a little more; remember tonight is the party, and you guys have a long night ahead."

Jannet said, "Don't worry, mom; we can handle it."

Mom said, "That's what I thought also."

James said, "Well, what are you guys waiting for?

Grab yourselves something to eat. By the way, what time these guys coming?"

Prastan asked, "Whom are you talking about, dad?"

James said, "Charles and his crew."

Prastan said, "Oh them. They should reach Allgreen's shore around noon. Mark and Joe will leave here around maybe 11:00 "This he said looking at his watch.

Joe woke up. He knocked at Mark's door.

Mark said, "What?"

Joe said, "Get up lazybones."

Mark said, "Watch your mouth. I'm not a lazybones. You woke up because you smell food. Isn't that so?"

Joe said, "What food are you talking about, lazybones? I smell nothing."

Jannet looked at her mom and dad. She said, "There goes again. But you know what, it doesn't bother me I have got accustomed to it; that is routine for them."

Joe slowly inched into the kitchen, "Good morning. You guys are early this morning."

Everyone in one voice said, "Good morning, Joe."

Jannet asked, "Have you slept well, Joe?"

Joe said, "What can prevent me?"

Prastan said, "I guess, Sherry."

Joe said, "Stop it, Prastan. Stop it."

Mark shouted from the inside of his room, "Well, what goes around comes around. Have you forgotten you used to tease him about, Jannet. Now it's your turn, brother."

Jannet laughed placing her right hand on her mouth.
Joe whispered, "I smell food."

Mark said, "I heard that. I knew that you smelled food."

Joe said, "Damn, you have ears like a cat." Everyone once again laughed.

Jannet said, "You see what I mean, mom and dad. My day goes by very fast with them around."

Deecia said, "I wonder if Sherry got accustomed to this by now."

Jannet said, "By now, of course she is."

Deecia added, "I believed you because when Mark told him he never thinks, she covered her mouth with both hands and laughed."

After breakfast they sat on the sofas around the pool relaxing.

Prastan said, "Well, guys, I have a change of plan." This he said while glancing at his watch. He then looked at Joe, "Don't forget you have to pick up, Sherry at 9:00?"

Joe said, "I know, I know. But what is the change of plans?"

Prastan said, "You and dad will go and pick up the guys."

Joe said, "No problem." He then looked at, Mark, "And what will Mark do?"

Mark said, "Watch your mouth, Sherry." Everyone laughed again.

Prastan said, "Mark will go with me to pick up liquor and beer for tonight. We will have lots of running to do here and there."

James said, "That's true. Anytime there is a special occasion time goes by very fast."

Joe glanced at his watch, "Let me go and pick her up."

"Do you need company?" Mark asked, teasing him with a smile. "I guess not."

"Oh Mark. Let him go all by himself he need some privacy, at least," she said nodding her head at Joe and teasing him as well.

Joe said, "I don't know what you're talking about. What privacy are you talking about?"

Prastan said, "Would you guys give him a break." This he said laughing and smiling. Joe got up jumped in the car and left.

Prastan said, "Well, I only hope that everything goes as well as has been planned."

Jannet turned at him, "What do you mean, Prastan?"

Prastan said, "I mean this quarter of a million dollars business that we have invested in."

James said, "Oh come on, you're a smart guy. You can handle it. That will be a piece of cake when you settle down."

Jannet said, "Trust me, Prastan, everything will be just fine."

Deecia added, "Think positive, son. You are very

smart. You guys will make it, just like your dad has just said."

Prastan said, "I have an idea."

James said, "Look at that. That's what I mean. I knew you have ideas and besides, you have a smart wife to back you up."

Jannet asked, "What idea do you came up with, Prastan?"

Prastan said, "Joe will need this car to run the farm. He will have to pick up Sherry and drop her off every day to and from work."

Mark questioned, "And—"

Prastan said, "And we will have to give you a ride to work. As soon as business picks up I have to get you your own car."

Jannet asked, "What about those guys?"

Prastan asked, "You mean Charles and his crew?"

Jannet said, "Yes."

Mark asked, "What about Rick?"

Prastan asked, "What about?"

Mark said, "How will he survive without a car?"

Prastan said,"Simple. Everyone will need a car to go to work to and from. And remember we own three car lots. Does that answer your question?"

Mark said, "Crystal clear."

Prastan said, "We have promised Dr. Nick to sell him a car at a very reasonable price but I had given that deal to Jessica since Jim had introduced us to Dr. Nick. Besides,

Jessica was there when the topic came up. However, Rick can sell himself a car." This he emphasized while he tapped him with his right hand on his left shoulder.

Jannet said, "So you're saying that two cars will be sold on Monday."

Prastan replied, "Sorry, dear, you are wrong."

Jannet was a bit confused for a moment and asked, " What do you mean, 'I'm wrong,' Prastan?" Mark, Mr. and Mrs. James leaned back looking at Prastan waiting for an answer to Jannet's question.

Prastan said, "Since Mark, Rick and Paul will be working together Paul can sell himself a car as well."

James said, "Look at that."

Jannet asked, "And what about the rest?"

Prastan mentioned, "Well, since Jessica and Peter will be working together, Peter can do the same—sell himself a car."

Jannet mentioned, "I think that Jessica will need a car too."

Mark added, "Well, she can do the same and sell herself a car."

James said, "That's right."

Jannet asked, "What about Charles and Angie?"

Deecia added, "Well, definitely they have to get a car as well."

James said, "And since they will be working together as you guys said, they can do the same—sell themselves a car."

Prastan said, "Tonight at the party I will explain this to them. And I will also ask Dr. Nick to have a look at Sherry's dad."

Jannet said, "I have another idea."

Prastan asked, "What idea?"

Jannet mentioned, "Why don't you invite the farm manager and supervisor to the party tonight?"

Prastan asked, "You mean Frankie and George?"

Jannet said, "Yes."

Prastan said, "Believe me I was thinking about that. And they need car as well."

Jannet punched him on his left arm, "That was my idea." Then she said, "Ouch. Its hurts" Rubbing her fingers.

Prastan said, "Okay, go ahead and invite them for the party."

Jannet did a little quick math and then the said, "So we are talking here that eight cars may be sold on Monday."

Prastan replied, "That's right."

Jannet said, "Wow! Eight cars will be sold on the very first business day. Wow!"

James turned and looked at his wife Deecia, "Am I hearing correctly, eight cars may be sold on the first business day."

"That's right, dad. You heard that correctly," she said and hugged her dad.

James said, "You see that, Deecia. God has blessed

them and sent them in this world. Can I get a job too?"
This he said smiling.

Jannet said, "Sure, why not, dad."

James asked, "What is it? What is it?"

Jannet smiled and said, "Your job is to pray for us."

James said, "Oh, I've been doing that before you were born."

Mark said, "That's a good answer; I wasn't expected an answered like that, Mr. James. You heard that, Jannet. And I hope you do the same whenever the time comes." Everyone laughed at Mark's statement.

In less than an hour Joe and Sherry had returned. Everyone in one voice said, "Good morning, Sherry."

Sherry said, "Good morning everyone, hi Jannet, hi Prastan, hi Mr. and Mrs. James, hi Mark." This she said and went and hugged everyone.

Deecia said to James, "She's so nice."

James glanced at his watch, "Let's go Joe, they should have arrived by the time we reach there."

Jannet added, "That's true." Joe and James took the SUV and drove away.

When they reached Allgreen's shore, they drove on the beach slowly. They had noticed *Prasjan* approximately a mile away in the river speeding towards shore.

Angie said, "I can see something moving on the beach. Maybe that's them"

A minute later as *Prasjan* got closer to the shore she said, "That's them. I recognized the SUV."

Rick headed towards the dock along with Joe. They reached the dock almost the same time.

Tony said, "Hey, hey, hey. Good morning guys."

Everyone in one voice said, "Good morning, Tony."

Tony said, "Nice seeing you guys again. What brought you guys back so soon?"

Peter said, "Prastan had bought three car dealership and we will be working for him."

Tony said, "That's very good news. I'm very proud of him. He's a smart guy."

Paul added, "So does his wife, Jannet."

Tony said, "Hey Joe, ask Prastan for me if he can help me out, you see my car is very shaky and since he owns three car dealership he can help me get a good car."

Joe called, Prastan, "Hello Prastan."

Prastan said, "Hello Joe."

Joe said, "They have just arrived. And Prastan, Tony asked if you can help him out. He said that his car is very shaky. Here, speak with him." He gave the phone to Tony.

Tony said, "Hello Prastan, congratulations my friend."

Prastan said, Oh thank you so much, Tony. How may I help you, my friend?"

Tony said, "I really need a car; my car is very shaky."

Prastan began to speak louder so that his voice could be heard by the crew. Jannet looked at him wondering why he was speaking almost at the top of his voice. Prastan looked at Jannet and placed his left index finger on his lips. She shook her head smiling. They understood him, so did, Joe.

Prastan continued, "Okay Tony, I want you to come to our party tonight. I will ask one of my, manager, to take care of you. Monday you can have your new car and you can work and pay. Feel better now."

Tony said, "Oh thank you so much, Prastan. I'll see you at the party tonight. Tell Jannet hello for me."

Prastan turned off the phone and smiled at everyone and said, "I gave the crew a message."

Jannet said, "So now we are talking nine cars will be sold on Monday."

Deecia said, "As we said, God blessed you all. That does not mean that we will stop pray for you all. We will continue to pray for you all, as my daughter said our job is to pray and nothing else."

Mark smiled and said, "You're a genius, Prastan"

Jannet said, "That's my man." After realizing that her mom was there, she said, "Oops."

Prastan said, "Mark, let's go to the store to pick up liquor and beer."

Jannet said, "Okay, Sherry. Let us see what we can do in the meantime. Where should we begin, mom?"

Mom said, "Don't worry, dear. If you're going to order all foods then we just have nothing to do."

Joe gave Tony two hundred bucks.

Tony asked, "What's this for?"

Joe said, "For a long term docking."

Tony said, "Don't worry with that, I can't charge my friend. Hey Rick dock the boat at the far end away from others."

Charles and Angie went in the SUV and sat in the second row seat while Paul, Peter and Rick made themselves comfortable in the third row seat. As Joe drove off slowly, he honked his horn and waved at Tony, saying, "See you tonight."

Angie said, "When we start working I suppose all of us will have to get our own car. We can ask Prastan to sell us and we can work and pay as well."

James smiled inwardly, "I'm positively sure he will if you guys just open your mouth and ask him. From what I know he loves you guys very much as well as my daughter." Joe smiled inwardly and whispered himself, *Business, business, business.*

James glanced at Joe and smiled.

Charles asked, "So we're having a party tonight?"

James said, "Well. I think we all deserve a party. Look at it both sides, guys."

Rick said, "You are perfectly right, Mr. James. They helped us a lot and we will always pray for them. God blessed them."

Peter said, "Today we will be working for him. He

made me assistant to the manager and one day he will make me manager."

James said, "That's right. Once you guys work honest and faithful everyone will benefit."

Joe said, "Check this out, guys. I barely know to read and write. Who the hell will hire me as a manager without a degree but my friend did. He loves me and Mark very much. They trusted us with their business, money etc. And, besides, they trusted the love that we have for them."

Angie asked, "So, how is Sherry doing, Joe?"

Joe said, "She's doing just fine. As Prastan said she will be working with me at the office."

Angie said, "That's so nice." This she said while painting her lips with red lipstick and powdering her cheeks.

Charles said, "I see only one little problem here."

James asked, "What little problem are you talking about, Charles?"

Joe asked, "What problem, Charles?"

Charles said, "We will have to rent a house. It is not like we are guess anymore; we will be working for Prastan and Jannet's company. Though we will be working and living like family, we still have to get our own place."

Peter supported, Charles and said, "Likewise us. The three of us have to find a place also and as soon as possible."

James said, "That's true guys and I don't want to

give my mouth liberty inasmuch as I could but I had a feeling that Prastan and Jannet had foreseen that situation and had already made some sorts of arrangement for you guys."

Joe said, "They are business people and they always plan ahead."

Rick said, "I'm so proud of them, they are so clever and smart."

Paul added, "And kindhearted too."

Peter said, "Damn, this Allgreen is a really beautiful place."

Joe said, "Well, you'll be working here now. This will be your home if you really want to consider it that way. This is home for all of you guys. You guys have good jobs; besides, you guys have us. Remember, at some point in time you guys will get married and raise your own little family. This is the perfect place to raise children: quiet, safe, and peaceful."

A few minutes later they reached home. Joe pulled in the driveway.

Rick said, "Back to the mansion."

They came out of the SUV. Jannet, her mom and Sherry went outside to welcome them home. They kissed and hugged each other in front of the house and then went inside. Then they eventually ended up relaxing by the pool.

Jannet called Prastan, asking "Where are you guys?"

Prastan said, "We are on our way home."

Jannet said, "They have just arrived. See you soon." She turned off the phone and then continued, "I suggest that you guys should take showers and freshen yourselves up before they reach home."

Angie asked, "Is there anything I could help you with, Jannet?"

Jannet said, "Sherry came over this morning. We actually got everything under control. Thank you so much, Angie."

Everyone went and took a shower and fresh up themselves. Prastan and Mark had arrived.

Mark asked, " Could we get some help here, Joe." This he said placing his hands on his waist.

Joe said, "I'm coming, lazybones, I'm coming."

Mark said, "I'm not a lazybones. Sherry, talk with your man before I break his bone."

Sherry laughed and said, "Sherry isn't going between the two of you. I don't want to get involved. I know you guys very well. I advise no one to get between the two of you."

This she said while she grabbed Jannet around her waist laughing.

Prastan said, "Welcome home everybody." This he said and hugged everyone. "Since we have everything under control let us all cool off ourselves with an ice-cold beer." This he said and he gave everyone a beer in their hand. "Let us all be proud of ourselves to have a good relationship like this. Let us all continue to live this wonderful life that we are all living. And let us all thank God for everything."

This he said while he threw his right arm around Jannet right shoulder and he raised his left hand up to the Lord above.

Joe said, "Sherry, I think I should drop you home."

Jannet said, "You guys, don't be late. And Sherry, make sure you bring your mom and dad."

Sherry replied, "Okay, Jannet."

The phone rang. Jannet picked it up. "Hello."

" Hello, Jannet. This is Dr. Nick."

Jannet said, "Oh hello Dr. Nick. Nice hearing from you. I only hope you're not changing your mind. We want to see you at the party tonight."

Dr. Nick said, "Definitely, you'll see me tonight. Hey Jannet, I am wondering whether I could bring along a friend if you and Prastan don't mind. He is the inspector of police."

Jannet answered, "We'll be delighted to welcome him. As a matter of fact any of your friends, that's no problem."

Dr. Nick said, "Thank you so much, Jannet. We'll see you guys tonight, by the way. What time is the party again?"

Jannet said, "6:00 P.M."

Dr. Nick confidently mentioned, "See you then."

At 5:00 P.M. the farm manager Frankie and supervisor

George came in. A few minutes later Jim and Jessica came in. After that Dr. Nick and the police inspector came in.

Jannet asked, "Prastan did you inform Henry?"

Prastan said, "Damn, I forgot. Call him and ask him to come over."

Jannet said, "Okay."

At 6:00 P.M. Joe came in with Sherry and her parents, followed by Henry.

Prastan looked around and said, "Well, I think only Mr. and Mrs. Martin are missing here."

James reminded, "They must be enjoying their vacation in Paris right now."

Jannet added, "I think they deserve it."

Another car drove in and it sounds like it had a transmission problem.

Joe said, "That must be, Tony."

Everyone went at the pool side. Some of them sat in chairs whereas some with drinks in their hands walked around the pool and were admiring the beautiful mansion.

Prastan and Jannet stood beside each other.

Prastan announced, "May I have your attention please." Everyone stop doing what they were doing and looked at him. He looked at everyone and then continued, "My loved ones, this party that we are having here tonight is not for Jannet nor I. This party is for all of us. And you know why, because all of us here are happy. And if you're not happy, I'll make you happy tonight. Everyone clapped their hands.

He then pointed his right hand at Charles, Angie, Peter, Rick, and Paul and said, "Guys, I would like you all to meet some of my good friends from over here in Allgreen. Please meet Dr. Nick."

Dr. Nick then introduced the police inspector to Jannet and Prastan "This is Inspector Roberts."

Prastan continued, "And this is one of my friend Roberts, he's a police inspector; this is Henry Earl, he's a realtor; this is Jim, he is a bank manager; and this is his wife Jessica."

You guys have met them before. You guys have met our farm manager and supervisor before, Frankie and George. He then placed his right hand on Tony's shoulder, "and this is Tony, custom officer and dock captain." He then bent his head down for a minute.

Jannet asked, "Prastan, Prastan are you okay?" This she said and she placed her left hand on his right shoulder. Prastan had recalled his past life how he grew up and how he had struggled in life. Though he became rich, he didn't want to forget where he came from. Everyone eyes were on him. They knew that he probably got carried away by some sort of emotions. He tried to regain control over his thoughts and emotions and to revive from his sad way of feeling. Jannet knew Prastan inside out and can foretell his situation. She cheered him up with a hug and said, "Forget it, I knew that you had recalled your past. Remember we always said it over and over that everything that happened in a man's life is meant to happen. God knew what is best, he knew what is best for everyone." This she said as she pointed her right hand at everyone.

The crowd murmured, "That's true. You're perfectly right, Jannet." This they said almost in one voice. Prastan then hugged her, "How do you always know what is in my mind? How did you know how I was feeling?"

Mrs. James said, "Because the two of you were made for each other. She is only our daughter but she was born for you. God made the two of you for each other."

Mark and Joe in one voice said, "And only he can separate you all " Hearing those words Prastan fully revived from his emotions. And with his face upright he smiled at everyone. He then received a sound kiss from, Jannet. A kiss of happiness and joy, she said, "The Lord wanted me to kiss you." And once again everyone clapped their hands.

Prastan said, "Okay, if you guys would permit me to say my piece, I will hesitate no further. My dear In- Laws, my beloved wife, my dear friends, Mr. and Mrs. Scott, Frankie and George, not forgetting Sherry and my two loving brothers Mark and Joe. I never forget where I came from and how I grew up in my life. I want to thank Mr. Martin. He always been like a father to me ever since I met him, he always stood up for me. When Jannet and I first met he was there and he's always there for us. I'm so sorry that he isn't here today. However, without his love for Jannet and me, we would not have been here today. For some reason he loved Jannet and me so much; only God knows why. And we loved him too. He's like my father. I remembered one day I hurt Jannet's feeling. He called me into his office, and he lectured me. I could see my father's image in front of me, and I looked at him without saying a word; inside, I was grieving, but he was carried away by his own emotion and didn't notice me. I wanted to say sorry and repent, but I was stunted emotionally by just admiring him. I loved him so dearly and I wish he could be here tonight to stand by us."

Jannet had known about the incident but she didn't know this part of it. Prastan and Jannet had tear drops slightly flowing down their cheeks, and while attempting to dry them off, they heard the voice of Mr. Martin, "Wait." Mr. and Mrs. Martin walked up to them, "We have heard it all." and they dried the tears off Prastan's and Jannet's cheeks. Everyone was emotionally caught in the middle of it and they were drying their tears as well.

Martin said, "We came in last night and wanted to see you guys, so we came here; now you may explain."

Prastan and Jannet then explained to him about the deal that Jim had offered them and the whole story of it. They then took the opportunity and introduced them to everyone.

Martin said, "Very good I am always proud of the two of you. Okay, now you may continue from where you have left off."

Prastan said, "Jannet and I only own this company. Basically, you guys own this company.Eemployees are the foundations of this company. You guys can build this company if you guys work as a team and keep your job as long as you wanted to or you guys can destroy this company by not working hard and honest and walk on the street after that. It all depends on you what you wanted." He turned at Jannet and said, "Say something to them, Jannet."

Jannet said, "Prastan is absolutely right. Everything is in your hands. Either we strive towards production and live happily or we strive towards failure and live in poverty. So you guys tell us. What you guys want to strive toward, production or poverty?" Everyone in a loud voice shouted, "Production."

Prastan and Jannet in one loud voice said, "Yeah, let the party begins."

Everyone enjoyed themselves eating and drinking and having fun. Prastan then introduced Dr. Nick to Mr. and Mrs. Scott. He had explained their situation to him for a word of advice.

Dr. Nick said, "Jannet, I would like to examine Mr. Scott. Is there a room we can go to?"

Jannet said, "Sure, Nick, over there." She pointed at the room. After the examination Dr. Nick prescribed medication for him. He said, "This will make him feel better."

Jannet took the prescription and gave it to Sherry, she

said. "Buy this first thing Monday morning before going to work."

Sherry said, "Thank you, Jannet."

Prastan announced, "Attention please, attention everyone." Everyone held their glasses in their hand and was looking at him. He then continued. "Well, to all employees. Monday morning is a working day for everyone. I know for the fact and you guys know for the fact as well that all of you guys will need a car to go to work. Since we have our own car dealership, I will let you guys buy car at a real good price and you guys can work and pay. What do you guys think?"

Everyone almost in one voice said, "That's wonderful."

Charles was the first one to say, "We need a car, Prastan."

Everyone was enjoying themselves, eating, drinking, and having fun as the party went well past midnight.

During the party Jannet had noticed Angie stood at a far corner admiring Prastan secretly. She whispered to herself, *My God, I knew she had a crush on him before and she had promised to forget it but it seems like she is still falling for my man. Please God give me some faith with these girls.* She knew from the bottom of her heart that her husband loved her dearly and desired no other girl but her. On one occasion on the dance floor she had noticed that Sherry when dancing with, Prastan, she had squeezed him inappropriately and in a passionate way. She only hoped that she isn't going to fall for him also. *Joe, Charles and*

my husband are all men together, the only thing about my
husband is that he's cute and attractive; let me hope that in
the long run these two girls wouldn't give me a headache.

When the party was over everyone went home. Joe
and Mark gave Sherry and her parents a ride home.

Mark said, "Sherry, you're a good dancer. Where did
you learn to dance like that?"

Sherry smiled and said, "Watching TV"

Mark had noticed Sherry when she squeezed Prastan
and decided to pay more attention at her. And inwardly,
he said, *"My friend Joe is just good for her. She is not going*
to mess with my sister's life." When they returned home
everyone went to sleep.

Joe said, "Let's get some rest, Mark."

Mark replied, "That's true. We have lots of work to
do in the morning."

Joe asked, "What are you talking about?"

Mark said, "We have to move everyone over to their
respective home."

Joe said, "Oh yeah, yeah."

Prastan and Jannet were in their room and they over
heard all their conversation.

Jannet called on Prastan, "Prastan."

Prastan asked, "What, Jannet? Try and get some rest;
you are very tired. You really need to have some sleep."

Jannet said, "I know but—"

Prastan asked, "But what?"

Jannet said, "As soon as we settle down in this business, we must try to get Joe and Sherry married."

Prastan said, "That's true."

Jannet added, "And when they get married Sherry is going to stay with us." This she said trying to feel Prastan's opinion.

Prastan said, "Hell no. The only women will be staying in this house is your mother and you." She laughed.

Prastan asked, "Why are you laughing? I'm dead serious."

Jannet reminded him, "I saw Sherry when she squeezed your butt with her both hands. I only hope she wouldn't turn out to be like, Angie."

Prastan said, "Jannet, you're my girl, you're the first girl I ever loved, and you will be the only girl for me, no one else."

Jannet said, "I trust you so much Prastan, and I knew that you wouldn't cheat on me but I don't trust those girls."

Prastan said, "You don't have to trust them. You have to trust me and have confidence in me."

Jannet added, "That's true."

Early on Sunday morning Prastan and Jannet woke up from bed, they brushed their teeth and then they went in the shower at the same time.

Prastan said, "Would you like to scrub my back, Jannet?"

Jannet smiled and said, "Sure Prastan. Let me do it

before someone else may want to do it." She smiled again blushingly and when she finished she said, "It's your turn now."

Prastan smiled.

Jannet asked, "Why are you smiling? better not misbehaved in here."

Prastan said, "I won't."

Jannet asked, "Then why are you smiling?"

Prastan said, "I think it should be like this from now on."

Jannet laughed and said, "Hell no." She blushed for a while, then, she said, "Maybe." After the bath they went in the kitchen and as usual Mr. and Mrs. James were already in the kitchen making breakfast for everyone.

Jannet and Prastan in one voice said, "Good morning, mom, good morning, dad."

Mr. and Mrs. James replied, "Good morning" as they dragged their voice along.

Deecia said, "You see what a good night's rest can do. You guys look so fresh compared to the past few days."

Jannet said, "Very observant, mom, very observant."

James said, "Since you guys are up, you guys can take my place in the kitchen. I have to water those beautiful flowers at the front yard."

A few minutes later everyone came crawling out after they had a healthy breakfast and after a few minutes of relaxation. Jannet said, "Well guys, it's time for your new homes. But first we will move Peter, Paul, and Rick and then Charles and Angie." It was a moment of astonishment for them.

Joe said, "Okay guys." This he said clapping his hands like an instructor. He continued, "Put all your belongings in the SUV."

Peter, Paul, and Rick threw their bag on their shoulder and went in the SUV along with Prastan, Jannet and Mark. Charles and Angie took their bags and went in the car with Joe and Sherry. Jannet drove the SUV out of the driveway, and Joe followed behind. In less than half an hour Jannet pulled in her parent's driveway, "Well, Peter, Paul, and Rick you guys will stay in this house. This is my parent's house. It has three bedrooms and two baths."

Peter asked, "And where will your mom and dad be staying."

Prastan said, "They will stay with us. Besides, we really need them since we are going to be extremely busy now."

Jannet give them three keys, "Go ahead, guys. It's your home."

Peter, Paul, and Rick looked at each other. Paul went and unlocked the front door, and they all went in.

Angie said, "Oh, it's so beautiful."

Prastan said, "Show them you room, Jannet." He teased at her.

Jannet said, "Oh please, Prastan, give me a break." This she said punching him on his right arm as usual and blushing at the same time. Peter, Paul, and Rick had chosen their room. And after a few minutes of rest and relaxation, Joe said, "Let go, Charles, let's go, Angie." He then turned at Peter, Paul, and Rick. "Let's go, guys, at least you will see Charles and Angie's new home as well."

Jannet drove out the driveway, and Joe followed behind. In less than half an hour Jannet turned in the street. Charles had recalled the street and was almost sure where they are heading but kept quiet. Jannet parked the SUV in front of the house and Joe pulled in behind her. They came out of the car and SUV and looked at the house from the street. Jannet gave Angie the key for the house. Angie, Sherry, Joe, and Mark went in the front yard. Peter, Paul, and Rick followed behind. Angie went and unlocked the front door and they all went in.

Angie said, "This house is good enough for us. I like it."

Joe added, "It's a two bedrooms and one bath."

Sherry asked, "You came here before?"

Joe replied, "Yes. And as a matter of fact Mark and I used to live here."

Mark added, "This was Prastan's house. This is the house they gave us."

Angie asked, "And they took it back?"

Joe said, " No. We will be staying with them in the mansion and you guys will stay here in this house."

Angie went in the bedroom unknowing Sherry was

behind of her. She whispered to herself quietly, "At least he gave me his house. I hope he give me his heart someday."

Sherry overheard her and pretended not to. When Angie turned around and noticed that Sherry was behind of her she almost dropped dead. Sherry tried to convince her that she didn't heard what she had said by asking, "I'm sorry Angie, have you said something?"

Angie whispered to herself, *maybe, she didn't heard what I have said. Oh thank God.* She placed the bag on the bed She became less scared of her bad feeling that probably Sherry must have over heard her. "Oh, I was saying I like this room."

Sherry said, "Oh I see. It's a nice room, I like it myself." And inwardly she said, "*You bitch, you still get him in your mind and you still loved him. If the opportunity knocks you'll cheat on Charles without even looking back.*"

Charles's tears dripped down his cheeks. Jannet and Prastan glanced at him.

Jannet asked, "Charles. Are you crying?"

Prastan asked, "What's the matter, Charles. Are you okay? Is something wrong?"

Charles replied, "I am okay, Prastan."

Jannet asked, "Then why are you crying?"

Charles said, "A few years ago I came to this house and I had a crush on you. Today, I will be living in this same very house. I'm so ashamed of myself."

Prastan said, "Charles, I agreed with you of your shame about your past life. But now you should be proud of yourself that you are now a respectable man and desire to live a decent life. Only the three of us knew about this. As Jannet said, God has sent you to her so that she can change your life. And that is very true. That money you left on the table and told Jannet to have that this money is from your brother. We never touched that money. That is the same money your sister Jannet and I took and we put some from our side and paid off your mortgage."

Jannet said, "Charles, forget your past life. You're not the first or the only one who has made a mistake like that in life. No man is perfect. Everything was meant to happen the way it did. So let bygone be bygone. Turn over the page and start a bright future. You have considered me your sister and now I want you to act like my brother. You will have to convince others that I am your adopted sister. And for those who do not know, let them believe that I am your real sister."

Charles looked upward and took a deep breath. He then looked at both of them and said, "You guys have given me a new life and I would never let you guys down. I will live a decent life, a good life, a respectable life. I want to live a life like my sister Jannet and my brother-in-law, Prastan. You guys did so many good for me and put me back on my feet. I would be lying if I said I will repay you guys but I will repay you guys with my love, honesty, and kindness." This he said and he hugged Prastan and Jannet. He then continued, "It's my new country, it's my new home, and I'll start with my new life. Let's go inside."

They went in the house.

Jannet called, "Angie, Sherry."

Prastan smiled.

Jannet looked at him, "Stop it, Prastan, stop it."

Prastan asked, "Stop what, Jannet?"

Jannet said, "You know." Prastan covered his mouth with his hands and went straight in the kitchen.

Jannet said, "Girls, this was my room" then she pointed at the ceiling and said "When I got married and came to this house, one night the rain fell heavily and the ceiling leaked so we had to move the bed over to this wall."

Sherry and Angie laughed. She then continued, "No wind, no rain, no lightning storm can separate me from Prastan. I loved him at first sight, and I'll love him until my dying day." This she said having a feeling that someday Angie and Sherry will put a crush on her man. So she threw that parable on them but apparently they aren't smart enough to understand.

Sherry said, "That's so sweet."

Mark said, "Well, Charles this is your new home."

Charles and Angie in one voice, "Oh thank you guys for your kindness and everything."

Angie kissed Jannet and then hugged her, "Oh thank you, Jannet."

Sherry said inwardly, *Yes bitch, you're the most dangerous snake I ever saw; you could bite her at any time.*

Prastan said, "Okay guys, it's time to go. By the way,

Mark will pick up you guys in the morning since you guys are living in the same area. And Joe will pick up Sherry since she is living in the opposite area. Mark when you pick them up bring them to your office. And Joe you give us a ride before you go to your office. Any question?" Everyone in one voice said, "No question, Prastan."

Joe said, "Let's go, Sherry, I'll drop you home. I really need some rest."

Sherry said, "I'll see you guys tomorrow. See you in the morning, Jannet."

Jannet said, "You take good care. And don't forget, when Joe pick you in the morning make sure you buy that prescription for your dad."

Sherry said, "I will Jannet. Thanks for reminding me."

Jannet then gave Peter, Paul, and Rick a ride home. When they reached in front of the house Prastan, Jannet, and Mark in one voice said, "Good luck guys. See you in the morning."

On their way home, Prastan said, "It seems like they are happy. What do you think, Jannet? What do you think, Mark?"

Jannet replied, "It seemed like all the guys are happy but I can see it in Angie."

Mark said, "Well, she has to get accustomed to it. She can't expect to live in our house."

Jannet said, "Hell no." She knew that Sherry and Angie are in her age group and that they are older than her by just a year. She also knew that they loved them for who they are and for all the kindness that they have done for them, but she was certain that they were been carried away by Prastan's charming looks.

Though she trusted her man to the highest extent, she would keep an eye on those girls. She placed herself in their shoes and thought she probably would have had the same feelings like them. She murmured, "I have to secure my property, guys."

Prastan asked, "What property are you talking about?"

Mark laughed and laughed.

Prastan asked, "And why are you laughing like that?"

Mark said, "Wait a minute. I never knew laughing is a crime. If a girl squeezed my butt it would be fun. But if a girl squeezed your butt that's a crime because you're a married man."

Jannet laughed and laughed. "Have you seen that too, Mark? I thought I alone saw that."

Mark asked, "Wait a minute, you saw that too?"

Jannet said, "Of course I did, I have to keep an eye on my property."

Prastan said, "You guys think I am going to fall for those girls. No way. I'm bound to my sweet wife until my dying day." This he said and he threw his left arm around Jannet's shoulder while she was driving.

Mark said, "Angie is totally a stranger; if she had a crush on Prastan, we could understand that. But Sherry,

Sherry will soon get married to our brother; she cannot do a thing like that. If she does, she will kill two birds with one stone. She will kill my sister and she will kill our brother. And if she does and Prastan tolerated it, then Prastan will kill three birds with one stone: he will kill his beautiful wife and his two faithful friends. I will definitely keep an eagle eye on her. I wouldn't hesitate to slap her if she ever had this intention. No one will come in our lives and try to separate us. If Joe knew this, he's a mad man, he'll kick her ass, trust me. Besides, if I notice she continues with this attitude I will put a stop to her. We all trusted you Prastan and we know that you wouldn't tolerate a thing like that; you wouldn't cheat on Jannet— we all knew that. But at the same time we must educate them and put a stop to nonsense." They finally reached home.

CHAPTER FOUR

WHEN Mr. and Mrs. James finished preparing lunch, they went and sat in separate chairs beside each other relaxing at the pool side.

James said, "Well, Deecia, tomorrow will be a challenging day for our children." He then turned to her expecting to get a response from her, but instead he got nothing. After a moment of silence, he called her attention. "Deecia, have you heard what I have just said?"

She replied, "Of course, James. I think that they are smart, especially, Prastan, and I feel that they will do just fine."

James said, "I think so myself."

Jannet, Prastan, and Mark walked in through the front door. Jannet said, "Mom, dad."

Deecia asked, "Jannet, is that you?"

Jannet said, "Who else would it be, mom."

James said, "You guys are early; I had been expecting you guys much later."

Prastan said, "I think that everyone needs a good rest. Remember tomorrow will be the first day of our new business."

Deecia said, "You guys must be very sweaty. I will arrange lunch while you guys can take a shower. By the way, where is, Joe?"

Prastan said, "He took Sherry home. He should be here shortly." Immediately after, Joe drove in the driveway.

James said, "Here he comes"

Joe walked in through the front door.

Mark asked, "What took you so long, Sherry?"

Joe said, "Stop it Mark stop it. Don't make fun of me, okay?"

Prastan and Jannet laughed. Joe looked at them. "And what's the matter with the two of you. I was jammed in traffic."

Jannet said,"Yeah right."

Joe said, "Stop it Jannet stop it."

Prastan said, "Well boy, it's your turn now. Remember how you used to tease me every day at work? Well, tables turned around now."

Mark asked, "Did you go inside?"

Joe said, "Watch your mouth, Mark."

Jannet were about to enter into the shower. She shouted, "Did you say hello to Mr. and Mrs. Scot or weren't they at home?"

Joe said, "Stop it Jannet,stop it. Go take a shower."

Prastan teased, "Yeah, were they at home?"

Mark teased, "Probably they went shopping." This he said smiling while he glanced at him.

Joe said, "I'm warning you guys, stop it."

Mr. and Mrs. James looked at each other smiling, "These kids are something else."

This they said in one voice and shook their heads from side to side.

Although they were teasing Joe, it really doesn't matter to him. He heard it through one ear and passed it through the other.

Joe said, "I smell food, I'm hungry."

Mark said, "Bet you are."

Deecia said, "Why don't you guys go and take a shower, in the meantime I'll put your lunch on the table."

After everyone took a shower, they all sat around the table and had a hot, delicious lunch. After that they threw themselves on the sofa relaxing

Prastan said, "Well, starting tomorrow, Joe, you will use the car."

Jannet added, "And you have to pick up Sherry in the morning and drop her off after work." She then tapped Prastan on his left lap with her right hand and asked, "And what about, Mark?"

Prastan said, "Well, we will have to give Mark his own car tomorrow and that will be on the house."

Joe suggested, "Mark could take my car."

Mark said, "Hell no. I need a clean car."

Joe asked, "And what do you mean by clean car; it is a clean car."

Jannet said, "What Mark means is, he wants a car that nobody kissed inside."

Joe had no choice and said, "Whatever. It's a damn

good car and it will be better than the one that you will have."

Peter, Paul, and Rick were relaxing on the sofa at their home.

Peter said, "How can we repay Prastan and Jannet?"

Paul answered, "There is no way we can ever repay them."

Rick said, "Of course, we can repay them, and we can start repay them starting right now."

Peter said, "Sorry to say this but your statement makes no sense at all. In what way we can repay them, Rick?"

Rick smiled and answered, "With our love, our respect, our honesty, our dedication, and our prayers."

Paul said, "That's true, and if they find that we are honest and faithful to them they may help us get up in life. Remember, we are single now and one day the three of us will get married and settle down by ourselves."

Peter added, "Very true and probably he can buy houses for us and we can work and pay him as well. By the way, guys, we have to cook food for lunch and dinner as well." They went in the kitchen. Rick is a master of cooking, and within an hour the three of them cooked food for lunch and dinner.

Charles and Angie were relaxing on the sofa at their house.

Charles said, "Prastan and Jannet are very kindhearted

people, they are so simple, noble, peaceful, smart, and they always plan things together, make decisions together. I have considered Jannet my sister and Prastan my brother."

Angie supported his statement, "Very true. Do you think we could ever repay them?" But inwardly, she thought, *I can repay Prastan if he wants me to.*

Charles said, "Yes, we can repay them."

Angie asked, "In what way, Charles?"

Charles said, "With our love, our respect, our honesty, our dedication, and our prayers."

Angie replied, "Maybe."

Charles asked, "What do you mean 'maybe'?"

Angie said, "I mean maybe you are right."

Charles said, "Let's go in the kitchen and see if we can cook something for lunch and dinner as well." Charles made his way in the kitchen and Angie followed behind. The pantry was filled with groceries. They looked at each other.

Charles said, "These people are godsend."

Angie asked, "Are you saying that we should worship them?"

Charles said, "I never said that. But we should respect these people, especially Prastan and Jannet."

Angie said, "Maybe you're right." *He deserved to be loved and respected.*

Charles said, "I found some yellow rice here; I think we should cook yellow rice and beans."

Angie said, "Sound good to me." And after a moment
of silence, she said, "I'll prepare some sandwiches for
tomorrow's breakfast." Within an hour they finished
cooking for lunch and dinner. Charles went in the shower.
Angie started to redecorate the bedroom and living room.
When Charles came out of the shower Angie went and
took a shower. Charles sat in a chair at the table waiting
for her so that they could have lunch together. He remembered the incident with Jannet and him. He remembered
when he unlocked the briefcase and made the crush on
her, and for a moment he imagined everything that had
occurred that day, and his tear drops slightly dripped
down his cheeks. As he dried them with his right hand, he
whispered to himself, *Forgive me my sister. But as you have
said that God had put it that way so that you can changed my
life, and it was meant to happen that way. After one time is
another. God please forgive me and let me be a good person, I
want to be a good person, oh God.*

Angie came out. "I'm hungry."

Charles added, "Me too. Come on let's eat." While
eating Angie said, "I never took it that seriously, but they
really are nice people."

Charles asked, "What are you talking about?"

Angie said, "I mean Prastan and Jannet. *"And inwardly,
I'm not really intended to break Jannet's heart neither to cheat
on you. But if Prastan should ever stretch out his hand to me I
will take it, and as I said many times, I wouldn't be the first,
nor the last.* Angie had no knowledge that she was being

deceived by her imaginary dreams and hence got carried away by her emotions.

Charles said, "Oh yeah, they are really nice people."

Angie started to laugh.

Charles asked, "What's the matter with you?"

Angie said, "You already started to talk like them." This she said and she continued to laugh.

Charles asked, "And so what?"

Monday morning everyone woke up early and start preparing themselves for the first day of their new business. After breakfast Joe was about to walk out of the door to go and pick up Sherry when Jannet reminded him of the prescription for Sherry's father.

Joe said, "I had almost forgotten, Jannet. Thanks for reminding me."

Mark asked, "How come you have forgotton about the prescription and not to pick up Sherry?" This he said teasing him.

Joe said, "Stop it, Mark, stop it." And he walked out of the door. Everyone laughed.

Jannet said, "Don't press him too much, Mark. He's in a different world right now." When she had realized that her mom and dad were around she said, "Oops" and covered her mouth with her hands. Prastan laughed and her parents smiled at her.

Joe picked up Sherry and went straight to his office at the farm. Mark went with the SUV to pick up Peter, Paul,

Rick, Charles, and Angie. He then brought them home. Mr. and Mrs. James had prepared breakfast for everyone. Mrs. James had laid the table and asked everyone to have their breakfast.

Angie said, "Oh thank you so much, Mrs. James. But we have already had breakfast at home."

Jannet said, "Eat something at least to make her happy." This she whispered in her ears.

Angie said, "Okay, Mrs. James, we'll eat something."

After a healthy breakfast they went out the front door. Prastan held the SUV steering wheel, and Jannet sat beside him. Charles and Angie sat in the second row seat while the remaining four guys sat in the third row seat. Prastan drove to Mark's office. When he reached there he parked the SUV in front of the office. He grabbed his cell phone and immediately called Roberts, the police inspector and Tony, the dock captain. They desperately need a good car. A few minutes later Manager Jessica and her husband Jim came in. Jannet took the cell phone from Prastan and called Joe at his office, "Hi Joe."

Joe said, "Hi, Jannet. How is everything going?"

Jannet said, "Too early to say, Joe, I want you to go at the farm and bring Frankie and George at Mark's office. And ask Sherry to run the office until you return."

Joe asked, "As has been planned."

Jannet said, "Yeah brother, business is business." They both laughed. As soon as Jannet end the conversation the phone rang. "Hello."

Her mom said, "Jannet."

Jannet said, "Hi mom."

Mom said, "Your dad and I want to come over. Would you please send Mark for us."

Jannet said, "Okay mom. He's on his way." This she said and end the conversation. She turned at Mark, "Please, go and pick up Mom and dad; they are restless."

In less than an hour everyone had arrived. Mr. James placed a sign by the road side saying, "Grand opening. New ownership, check it out."

Prastan asked, "Dad, how do you come up with this idea?"

Mr. James answered, "Ever since my children bought over the business."

Jannet hugged her dad and gave him a kiss and said, "Oh thank you, dad."

Dad said, "Don't mention it. You don't have to thank me sweetheart. I want to be a manager too."

Prastan laughed and said, "You are above the managers, dad. You're our legal adviser." They all laughed together.

Moments later a few drive- by auto shoppers saw the sign and decided to check it out. One of them loudly said, "I have passed two dealers not too far away from here but they hadn't open yet."

James said to them, "It's the same company, sir. Today is the opening, after here we'll go over there."

Auto shopper said, "Who bought the company?"

James replied, "My children, Prastan and Jannet."

The auto shopper asked, "Is that the same Prastan and Jannet who own Sunshine Farm."

Joe said, "That's right. And from now on I'm the new manager at the office."

The auto shopper said, "Everyone's talking good about them. May I see them?"

Joe pointed at them "Look over there."

The auto shopper said, "My God they are so young and cute." This he said and went up to them, "Are you the same Prastan and Jannet I heard all over Allgreen people talking about?"

Prastan and Jannet looked at each other with a smile.

The auto shopper continued, "I desperately need a car. I got a very good job and I need a car to go to work. No dealers want to sell me a car because I have no credit. Anywhere you go they ask for credit. That's the only word they knew, credit, credit.."

Prastan said, "No one is born with credit. Everyone has to start from somewhere. Go find your car." Prastan turned around, the crowd started to increase. He raised both hands in the air and clapping, "Everyone, I mean everyone who wants a car or really needs a car for work or for the family, go find your car." Inspector Roberts had chosen a nice car, as had Jim, the bank manager and Tony, the immigration dock captain.

Prastan said, "Haven't you guys made up your mind as yet?"

Roberts said, "This one is nice but this may cost a fortune."

Prastan said, "Mark, Joe, Jessica, Charles, and Angie show these customers around and try not to lose a deal. And at the same time look for your car as well. Frankie and George, I knew you guys desperately need a car, so go find your dream car." He hesitated for a few seconds and then continued, "Okay, Jim, Roberts, and Tony let's go in the office." Prastan grabbed hold of the inventory list and scanned through the cost of the cars. "Guys, these are very good cars, I can make at least three thousand profit on each one of these car but since we are very good friends you guys pay for all the paper work, the cost for the car and give me one thousand on top of it for the business. And work and pay every month. And I need no down payment from you guys."

The three of them in one voice said, "Wow!"

Prastan said, "Jannet, start the paper work."

Mr. James said, "That's a good deal. Well the three of you guys are very good friends. And a friend's duty is to help each other."

Roberts said, "Okay, I'll pick up my car tomorrow. And if you need my help to get anyone a driver's license don't hesitate to send them to me. I must go now. "

Tony said, "I'll pick up my car tomorrow as well.

Thank you so much Prastan and Jannet." At the same moment Jessica walked in with a customer. She said, "Prastan, I have a client who wanted to buy a car."

Jim said, "Jessica, I'll drive the new car to work; you can take the old one."

Jessica said, "But I'm supposed to have the new one."

Roberts said, "Remember I am a police inspector; if you guys have a dispute, I can solve the problem right now." Everyone laughed and then he walked out of the door. Jessica sold a car the very first day to a customer. Mark sold a car to another customer. Joe also sold a car to a customer, and Charles sold a car to a customer and also bought one. Jannet sold Frankie and George their car. At this point ten cars were sold on the very first day. Everyone thanked Prastan and Jannet. Prastan gave Mark a car from the house. Mark took over his office, Joe had returned to his farm office, and Frankie and George had returned to the field

Jannet said, "Rick, I suppose you will need your own ride."

Rick asked, "Can I buy a car and work and pay as well?"

Jannet said, "Why not, see what car you like. In this way you, Paul, and Peter will be independent and free."

When Joe reached the office he called Jannet, "Hi Jannet, it seems the car business is doing well."

Jannet replied, "Yes brother, Now Rick, Peter, and Paul have their own cars."

Joe said, "Wow! Sister that will make thirteen cars sold for today."

Prastan said, "Okay guys." Glancing at his watch, he said, "Let's go to the other locations. Peter bought his car and followed the SUV along with as Jessica and Charles. The second location was Jessica and Peter's office. Prastan and Jannet had explained a few things to them and wished them good luck in the business. They then drove to the third location, followed by Charles and Angie. He also showed and explained a few things to them and wished them good luck as well.

Prastan, Jannet, Mr. and Mrs. James went in the SUV and drove home. When they reached home they threw themselves in the sofa relaxing.

Jannet said, "Wow! The very first day and we have sold thirteen cars."

James added, "And it's only noon."

Prastan picked up the phone and called Inspector Roberts.

Roberts asked, "What's up, Prastan? Did everything go well after I left?"

Prastan said, "Oh yes, It's only noon and we sold thirteen cars."

Roberts replied, "Your business will do just fine. I will also send customers to you."

Prastan said, "Thank you Roberts. I need a favor. I need five driver's licenses for my managers."

Roberts said, "Give me their names and addresses and ask Joe to pick them up, let's say, by 2:00 P.M."

Prastan said, "That's fine and thank you." He then gave him the names and addresses.

Roberts said, "That what friends are for."

Prastan called Joe at his office "Joe."

Joe said, "Hi Prastan."

Prastan said, "I want you to go at Inspector Roberts office at 2:00 P.M. and pick up those licenses and then go and hand them out."

Joe said, "Consider it done." He then hung up the phone. "That was fast, faster than I ever thought."

Sherry asked, "What is it, Joe?"

Joe said, "They all got their driver's licenses already."

Sherry said, "That guy is good. He knows people."

Joe said, "Oh, he's very popular."

Sherry said, "He really loves you guys."

Joe said, "We loved them too. Mark and I cannot live without them, and they cannot live without us, either. It's like we were born and grew up in the same home."

Sherry added, "I can see that." And after a moment of silent playing with her pen in her right fingers, she said, "They did a lot for me as well, and I don't think I can repay them." Sherry knew for the fact that Prastan and Jannet are very nice people, people to admire, people to talk about but for some crazy and imaginary ideas of hers got her mind corrupted and untrusting of herself. She always had a positive feeling that someday Prastan may stretch out his hands to her. And considering all that he had done for her, not to mention how cute and attractive he was, she would definitely accept his hand and welcome him considering it a genuine payback rather than to say thank you.

At 1:45 P.M. Joe said, "Sherry you handle everything until I return. I'm going to inspector Roberts's office to pick up those licenses." He made his first step towards the door.

Sherry said, "Joe." He turned around slowly and looked at her. She gave him the prescription paper, "We have forgotten? Please, pick up the prescription for dad."

Joe said, "Damn, you're right. I have forgotten completely though Jannet had reminded me this morning." Joe went and got the licenses and delivered them to everyone, he went and bought the prescription. He finally returned to the office almost 4:00 P.M. He said to Sherry, "Good news Sherry. Mark and Paul sold another car also Jessica and Peter. And I am not sure but I believe, I believed that Charles and Angie sold two cars as well."

Sherry happily said, "Yes, yes. That's very good. We all depended on his business to survive. The bigger his business grows the stronger we are. What do you think, Joe?"

Joe said, "You're right. We all depend on them. Without them I don't know where Iwould be right now."

And after a moment of hesitation, he saked, "Were you busy?"

She smiled and replied, "All the time. Business is good. Thanks to, Prastan and Jannet. We are somebody respectable now. People can look at us as respectable persons now."

Joe said, "I'm glad you see it that way, Sherry. Look at Mark and me. Who the hell would have hired us and made us managers? People have degrees out there and still can't find good jobs. By the way, here's the prescription, Sherry. And make sure that you don't forget it in the car tonight."

Sherry smiled and after nodding her head she asked, "I want a driver's license too. One day I will buy my own car. How long you will pick me up and drop me off?"

Joe said, "You're right, besides, pick up and drop off. This is Allgreen, people depend on transportation. I'll talk with my sister tonight. By the way it's time to close."

The first day the car business did very well. Charles and Angie went home with their new car. Charles said, "We'll do just fine Angie. When we finish paying off this car, we will concentrate on buying a small house. How long you think we can stay in this house? This is Mark and Joe's house. Inasmuch as they are staying with Prastan and Jannet they don't need the house. This house belong to them not us."

Angie said, "You're right. The business is making good money, seventeen cars sold in the very first day. Besides, Sunshine Farm is bringing in money also. You think they will buy a house for us and let us work and pay?"

Charles said, "I believe so but it's too early to make that move. If he's so kind to pay off our mortgage, he'll definitely do that for us.

Angie and Sherry inwardly and secretly have their own crazy ideas that since Prastan had done so much for them, he probably did it for a reason. And considering the fact that they are within the same age group that he probably will stretch out his hands to them some day in return for his favors. And considering how cute and charming he is, they will not let him down.

Jannet, on the other hand, had a bad feeling about Sherry and Angie—that if they had the opportunity, they could fall for her man. However, she trusted Prastan and knew than he will never fall for those girls. Jannet is the prettiest girl in Allgreen and she loved Prastan very much. She's a simple girl, quiet, smiling, and an easygoing young girl.

At 6:00 P.M. Mark, and Joe arrived sharing their good news. They all gathered around the pool corner relaxing, recapping the day's activities and sharing joy and happiness. Prastan sat in a chair gazing into nothingness. Jannet went behind him and grabbed him around his neck and asked, "What's the matter, Prastan? We have done very well for the first day. Haven't we?" This she said rubbing her left cheek against his right cheek.

James asked, "What's the matter, son? Don't worry about anything; you guys will do just fine."

Joe added, "Stop that, Prastan. We don't want to see you like that. When you're sad we are sad, and when you are happy we are happy. Mark and I are not managers for your company. We are Prastan and Jannet. You guys are inside of us. Look, I am not educated to put forward myself in the right way, but what I mean is that you guys have meant everything to us, so to speak. Mark and I cannot live without you guys." As he said this his eyes filled with tears so did Mark's. Prastan couldn't take those words so he stood up. Jannet hugged him. He then stretched out his hands open and allowed Mark and Joe to fit themselves in as well."

Mr. and Mrs. James looked at each other.

Mrs. James said, "We have four loving children."

James said, "What must I say. We should have considered ourselves lucky. Let us thank God for everything."

Prastan released them and with his right hand tapping on Joe's left cheek and his left hand tapping on Mark's right cheek, "Nothing is bothering me. I have my loving wife and she will be the only girl in my life until my dying day. I have my loving in-laws and my two loving friends. You guys are my family. I have nobody in this world but the five of you." Hearing those words Jannet cried and hugged him tighter and tighter around his waist. After a moment he asked everyone to pay him some attention. With Jannet by his side he calculated, "Guys, we have four businesses, the farm which I am not worrying about, Joe is there. I am not worrying about Mark's location. The other two car locations although we trusted them, we have to keep an eye on them just to guide them along."

Jannet added, "That's true."

Prastan continued, "As far as I calculate if all four businesses—after deducting all business expenses—if each business can bring in $1,000.00 profit per week that will be $4,000.00 profit per week; hence we can pay off the loan together with the interest in less than eighteen months.

James emphasized, "Eighteen months." He stood up waving his hands, "You guys can do it, you guys can do it." This he said and he walked a few steps here and there.

Rick, Paul, and Peter went home happily thinking alike that they will work very faithfully and honestly with Prastan and Jannet and that someday they will also ask Prastan to buy them a house and they will work and pay him as well.

Jessica went home discussing with Jim about the business showing excellent progress.

Jim said, "I'm happy for them, Jessica. If the bank business goes bananas I can work for him as well. So I am asking you to work honestly and faithfully with them, you never know."

Jessica added, "That's true. I will never show them an ugly face. They are so young, simple and kindhearted."

So it was said and so it was done. With everyone's co-operation, epically Joe and Mark and with the encouragement of Jannet's parents, they accomplished their dreams before the eighteen months were up. They had paid off the loan and were free from all debt.

Charles and Angie doubled their car payment every month and had paid off for their car in less than eighteen months.

One Sunday morning, Prastan, Jannet, Mark, and Joe sat by the pool corner enjoying the morning breeze. As the sun rose slowly leaving the earth beneath, its reddish reflection in the pool made the blue water sparkling and glazed. Jannet couldn't take her eyes off of it, and her thoughts were in some kind of wonderland. She remained speechless for a little while. Prastan, Joe, and Mark had noticed that Jannet had been carried away by some unseen force and had decided to pay more attention to her.

As they looked at each other, they gave signals that something must be bothering her as they glanced at her. Prastan was about to call her attention when she awakened. She immediately turned at Joe and said, "Joe, I think it's time now for Sherry and you to get married."

Mark supported, "I second that."

"Why don't you get married?" Joe murmured.

Mark said, "I will, as soon as I find a girl."

Joe said, "Well, try and find one and you get married. Leave me out of this. Besides, this Mr. Joe is not going to live with no in-laws." This he said and tapped his chest with his right hand. James walked in, "Who's bothering you, Joe? You guys leave him alone."

Joe said, "Nothing is bothering me Mister James. It's a beautiful morning and they have nothing good to say. Now, they spoiled my good mood."

Mrs. James walked in with a tray, "Come on guys, you guys stop bother, Joe. Here is breakfast, come on, eat." She placed the tray on a table and looked at the sun, "It's a beautiful day."

Jannet said, "It is, it's a real beautiful day and beautiful day calls for happy moments."

Prastan smiled, "Joe, your sister is right. I think that you should get married now."

Mrs. James said, "By the way, I had forgotten to mention. Mrs. Scott and I had spoken a few days ago and she had mentioned about Sherry and Joe. She said anytime we are ready she is ready. She also mentioned that Scott is waiting for that day to see his daughter got married."

James said, "I am a father too. Father and mother have a different kind of feelings. I agree with everyone, you should get married now, Joe." Joe sat in his chair, Jannet went behind of him and hugged him. "You're not going to let your sister down and break her heart."

Joe said, " Okay, okay. But I am not going to stay with in-laws."

Prastan glanced at Jannet.

Jannet said, "We will buy you a beautiful wedding gift."

Joe asked, "What gift?"

Jannet replied, "We will buy you a beautiful house."

Joe said, "It's a nice and simple way to get rid of me, right?"

Prastan said, "Wrong. You will always be in our lives and in our heart forever no matter where you are. You could stay with us forever. This house will still be like yours because you will still have the key to this house."

Mark said, "Yeah, young people also need privacy."

Joe said, "Is that true, Jannet?" This he asked smiling.

Jannet blushed and then everyone laughed, considering that Joe had agreed.

Charles and Angie drove in. They went through the side gate. And as they were heading towards the back yard at the pool, Angie asked, "Where is everyone? I can smell food." By then they met face to face. Charles said, "Looks like we came at the right time. Wow! That smells good. What you guys having for breakfast?"

Mrs. James said, "Come on, you guys have something to eat as well. I have prepared everyone's favorite—mash potatoes, eggs, and pancakes, and I brewed coffee."

Charles asked, "Mmm, you guys have extra?"

Mrs. James replied, "Of course, I wouldn't have offered you guys if I don't have extra. And if I didn't have extra, definitely, I should have prepared something for you guys to eat."

Angie mentioned, "Oh that so nice of you, Mrs. James."

Jannet asked, "So how is it, girl?"

Angie replied, "We cannot complain. By the way guys, I had spoken with my dad."

Prastan said, "Tell me he's doing well."

Charles replied, "Not really."

Jannet asked, "Is there a problem, Angie?"

Angie said, "Well, regarding his health and strength he's doing well. But—"

Jannet asked, "But what?"

Angie replied, "The restaurant and bar business slowed down."

Prastan said, "Sorry to hear that. Why don't you guys ask him to come and live in Allgreen?"

Angie said, "We did."

Jannet asked, "And?"

Angie said, "He has decided to sell and come stay with us in Allgreen but since the economy fell he will lose almost forty percent on everything he owned."

James said, "Sorry to hear that."

Angie said, "Prastan and Jannet I want to ask you guys for a favor."

Jannet asked, "What is it, Angie?"

Angie looked at Charles.

Charles said, "Since dad has decided to come and stay with us, we will need a three-bed room house."

Angie said, "We saw a house for $5,000.00. If you guys can buy it for us we can work and pay you guys just like we did with the car."

Charles said, "Dad said that my house value dropped dramatically as well that I may get five thousands for it if I'm lucky. So when we get that money we will definitely give you some of it to boost our payment."

Jannet and Prastan looked at each other.

Prastan said, "Okay. And when do you guys want to buy the house?"

Angie and Charles, "Oh thank you guys so much. Any time it is possible for you guys."

Prastan said, "We'll give you the money." He then turned at Jannet "Make it six thousands, they will have to pay closing costs as well."

Jannet went in the house and brought $6,000.00 and

gave it to them. She said, "Congratulation on your new house."

Mark looked at Joe and laughed. Everyone looked at Mark and knew that he had something to say to Joe, and they braced back to hear what was coming next.

Joe asked Mark, "Why are you looking at me, laughing and smiling. Haven't you seen me before?"

Jannet looked at everyone and laughed, "There he goes again."

Prastan and Jannet knew exactly what Mark was coming out with.

Mark nodded his head. "So?"

Joe asked, "So what? I'm not leaving here. You go and stay in the house. Prastan gave you the house."

Mark said, "Oh no. No, no. They gave both of us the house."

Joe said, "Well, you go and stay in the house."

Everyone laughed.

Mark said, "I'm not the one getting married. Besides, you will need privacy, privacy boy, privacy."

Angie clapped her hands, "Joe's getting married "

Mark teased, "Congratulations, Joe."

Joe said, "Congratulations my foot. I'm not leaving here."

Jannet went behind him as usual and rubbed him on his head, "One day you will have your own little family, brother."

Mark added, "Yes, your own little family. And they will call me—"

Prastan butted in, "And they will call you, Uncle Mark."

Mark said, "Uncle Mark. Wait a minute, Uncle Mark sounds like I'm very old. I have never thought of that. You know what? I will teach them to call me Mark and if they call me Uncle Mark. I'll spank them."

Joe said, "You're supposed to love them not spank them." This he said not realizing that he had committed himself, and when he finally realized it, he said, "Oops."

Everyone laughed.

On the following Saturday Charles and Angie bought their dream home. And with the help of Mark, Joe, Jannet, and Prastan they moved over on Sunday. Mark and Joe had now regained their house. In the evening Jannet called Sherry, "Hi Sherry."

Sherry answered, "Hi Jannet nice hearing from you again."

Jannet asked, "What are you doing right now, girl?"

Sherry said, "Nothing of importance, just bored and killing precious time."

Jannet asked, "Are your mom and dad home?"

Sherry said, "Yes, Jannet."

Jannet asked, "Let me speak with your mom, please."

Sherry said, "Sure Jannet, sure. Is something wrong, Jannet?"

Jannet said, "Nothing to worry about, girl."

Sherry called, "Mom, Oh mom, Jannet is on the phone. She would like to speak with you."

Stella said, "I'm coming, I'm coming. Is something wrong, Sherry? Have you got any problem at work?"

Sherry held the phone, "No mom." Jannet overheard the conversation and smiled.

Stella grabbed the phone from her, "Hello, Jannet."

Jannet said, "Hello Mrs. Scott. How are you?"

Stella replied, "I'm fine, Jannet."

Jannet said, "Nothing to worry about Mrs. Scott. I have good news. I'm sending over Joe for you guys right now. We want to get these young people married."

Stella said, "Oh thank you so much, Jannet. Scott will be so happy. He knew ever since from the day she was born that this day would one day come. He's been waiting for this day. Oh, he'll be so happy."

Jannet said, "Okay, I'll see you in a little while. Let me speak to Sherry, please."

Stella gave Sherry the phone and went and shared the good news with her husband, "Get dressed. Joe will be here soon." They were so happy and excited.

Sherry also overheard the conversation and smiled, "Hi Jannet."

Jannet said, "Joe will soon be on his way. It's your turn, girl. See you soon."

Sherry said, "Okay, Jannet."

Mrs. James said, "Go Joe. Go bring your family."

Mark added, "Yes Joe, go bring your family. Meanwhile, I'll try to figure out some names."

Joe asked, "Figure out what names?" Everyone laughed.

Joe said, "I know all of you want to get rid of me. There is no love for Joe anymore." This he said, but jokingly and not serious. Hearing those words from Joe Jannet walked away slowly. Joe walked out the front door. Prastan and Mark looked at Jannet. They knew that she was hurt by those words and rushed out behind Joe. As Joe attempted to open the door Mark grabbed him on his shoulder. He turned around and looking at Prastan's and Mark's faces, he knew that something was wrong, "What? What?"

Mark said, " You have broken our sister's heart by saying those words."

Prastan said, "I guess she must be crying bitterly. You knew what kind of heart she has, Joe."

Joe said, "Oh no." This he said and ran inside the house. He grabbed and hugged Jannet. "I didn't mean to hurt your feelings, sister. I was only exaggerating about myself. Any decision you make for us is good for us, everything you have done for us is good for us. Stop crying; don't break my heart. You know me better." This he said while drying her tears with his hands. At the same time she dried his. Jannet then hugged him again, "Go bring my sister-in-law and parents. It is my desired to see both of you get married, like us. Go Vick." She smiled and teasing him with his nick name.

Joe smiled as well. "Okay, Chuck" They remembered the old days when they were looking for Prastan and they had to changed their names to Vick and Chuck. Everyone smiled and laughed. Prastan looked at everyone and shook his head, "We all came in this world for a short time. Let us continue to love each other the same way until we are separated."

James said, "You can say that again, son. As we have said many times, we are one little family."

Joe said, "I'll be back in a little while." This he said and walked out the door.

In less than thirty minutes Joe had reached Sherry's house. He honked the horn, parked the car, and then walked slowly towards the front door. Sherry peeped through the window. "He's here, mom."

Mom said, "Who's here?"

Sherry said, "Joe."

Mom said, "Okay dear."

Scott asked, "Did you expect someone else, Stella?"

Stella said, "Give me a break."

Sherry smiled and said, "Old age." She unlocked the door and let Joe in. She gave him a hug and a fast kiss. She said, "So."

Joe said, "So what?"

Sherry said, "I wasn't expected this so soon."

Joe said, "I know but my sister insisted. She wants us to get married. She said it's her desire to get Mark and I married."

Sherry said, "She's so sweet. Joe, how can we repay them?"

Joe said, "Never say that again."

Sherry said, "I'm sorry."

Joe said, "Don't get me wrong; my point is, we cannot repay them." This he said and went chatting with Mr. Scott.

Sherry said, "You are absolutely right." And inwardly,*they love us and care for us so much but I don't know why my thoughts for Prastan always lingered in me. Is it that I got carried away by him because he's so cute? Is it that I got carried away because I had felt that he had done a lot for me and may be expecting a favor from me? Or is it that he's just a good man who wants to help people and doesn't look forward for anything? Or is it that I have this crazy ideas and imaginings that betray my own emotions? I am going to join the family now, and this is eating me inside. I don't want to marry Joe and still have this feeling within me. I don't want to marry him and then cheat on him. If I cheat on Jannet while I'm single I will break everyone's heart, and can walk away with it. And if I cheat on Joe after marriage I will break everyone's heart and cannot walk away with it. I must do something about this. In order to solve this problem I must confront Prastan. Girls lusted for him. Suppose I confronted him and he stretched out his hand for me. In this situation I have only one option. Accept his hand and forget Joe, break Jannet's heart and quit the job and look for another job. On the other hand if I accepted his hand,,could it be because he had done a lot for me? Or would it be that I loved him because he's so handsome? He helped many people; does that mean that all the female should have fallen for him as well? If not, then why should I fall for him because he has done so many favors for me?* Rubbing her chin with her right hand, *I think I solved one problem here. The truth here is that I fell for him because I loved him. I also knew that he didn't love me. I cannot compare myself with Jannet. She's the prettiest girl I have ever seen. I think he had loved me for who I am not for love's sake. So my point is again, if he stretched out his hand to me, it will be for the favors he has done for me. And if I grab his hand, considering the fact that he has helped so many people it wouldn't be for the favor, it will be because I loved him. On the other hand I cannot break Jannet's heart so I must forget this love thing I have within me. And on the other hand if he stretches out his hand to me in return for the favors, I will grab it, repay his favors and walk away from them for good. Let's see what will happen.*

Joe said, "Okay, let's hit the road." When they reached home they were all greeted and welcomed.

Jannet took her mom and dad at a corner and explain to them that Sherry is the only daughter for these people just like she. And that Joe wouldn't be comfortable living with in-laws. They will live in the house that we gave them so I want you guys to explain to Sherry's parents about this."

They replied, "You don't worry with that, dear; we will take care of that problem."

Jannet went in her room and then she called Mark and Joe to show them the beautiful ring that she had bought for Sherry in advance to see whether they would like it or not. Prastan went in the kitchen for a glass of ice cubes. Sherry then grabbed the golden opportunity and followed him behind. Prastan had noticed Sherry behind of him. He knew that she wanted to say something to him and was waiting to hear what it was all about. She said, "Prastan, I want to say something before we make any arrangement tonight." Jannet's room was beside the kitchen and so they can overhear when someone is talking in the kitchen

Prastan asked, "What is it, Sherry? What is bothering you?"

Jannet looked at Mark and Joe and the three of them looked at each other.

Not realizing that her voice could be heard. She said, *Let me get over with it.* And after hesitating for a fraction of a second she said softly, "The entire Allgreen people admire you and Jannet. They love you guys, respect you guys, and talk good things about you guys. I myself love you guys and respect you guys as well. You have done so many favors and good for people I don't think that they can repay you." She smiled at Prastan and then threw herself at him by stretching out her hands to him giving him the impression that she can and is willing to repay him for his favors in any manner. Prastan neglected to accept her hand and smiled. He knew that she could not say it in words to him because she might be heard but instead she had shown it in her action.

Prastan knew that they can be overheard and gave her the answer in a very technical and sophisticated way. When he spoke, it was firm and was nothing but the truth, however. He said, "Sherry, my parents were very poor, and I grew up in poverty. When my parents drowned I grew up all by myself and with the help of good neighbors I managed to survive. Then Mark and Joe came into my life, and I loved them very much. Then Jannet came into my life. I loved her very much and she loved me too, she went through all hardship and suffering with me and we promised to love each other until God decided to separate us. This also goes to Joe and Mark." Now, he was answering her question by getting to the point, "That is the reason why I am doing good because I came from nowhere and when I die I will take with me only the good things that I have done in this world. Jannet and I don't look for people to returns favors to us because we have done favors for them. God is helping us and shows us the way to prosperity, and we will continue to help people, to love people, and to respect people."

Jannet, Joe and Mark couldn't take it any longer; with

tears flowing down their cheeks, they came out the room and joined them in the kitchen.

Joe and Mark in one voice, "Sherry, they help many people and they don't looking forward for favors in return. They are godsend." Sherry grabbed Prastan with a tight hug and said, "You can say that again, Mark and Joe, they are godsend." She then released him and hugged Jannet, "Oh Jannet, you and Prastan are angels. We owe you all so much. We cannot repay you guys but we will pray for you guys." And inwardly, *Thank God I have gotten over it.*

Mark said, "Since we are on the same page now, and we are one little family, let's go and make some arrangements with the old folks."

Sherry asked, "Jannet, when we get old, will we get grumpy?"

Jannet laughed, "Why do you asked that question, Sherry."

Sherry answered, "Because my mom and dad are always picking on each other for no good reason."

Prastan added, "We all will be like that someday." This he said with a huge smile.

They went in the living room. By then Deecia and James had convinced Stella and Scott that Joe wouldn't be comfortable staying with in-laws.

Prastan said, "Well." This he said and clapped his hands. He then looked at Jannet, "Let's get them something to drink, Jannet."

Jannet said, "Sound good to me." She smiled. She then grabbed Sherry, "Let's go, girl; this moment called for some stimulation."

Jannet asked, "What would you like to have, dad?"

James said, "You know what?" This he said while glanced at Scott "Get me two drinks, one for Scott and one for me."

Jannet asked, "Anything special?"

James said, "Make that your choice."

Joe asked, "Need some help, girls?"

Sherry answered, "Of course we do." They went in the kitchen and returned with drinks for everyone. Prastan, Joe and Mark were drinking beers. James and Scott were drinking liquor, and the four ladies were drinking champagne.

Deecia said, "Oh, this tastes good." This she said looking at her glass.

Jannet asked, "How about another one? Hello, anyone listening."

Deecia said, "Why not. Come on Stella, let us celebrate this moment of joy, we are joining family now."

After the second round Jannet said, "Mr. and Mrs. Scott. Prastan and I thought it over and over many times. We have decided now to get Joe and Sherry married."

Scott said, "We are very happy, Jannet. Who wouldn't like to join a family with you. You guys have done so many good for us we will be unable to repay these favors."

Stella said, "So when you guys want to set the wedding for?"

Sherry glanced at Joe with a smile.

Jannet said, "How about the first Sunday next month?"

Scott glanced at Stella, "We never expect it so soon."

Sherry looked at Jannet and Prastan. Jannet smiled and said, "Don't you worry Sherry. We will take care of everything."

Mr. and Mrs. Scott were thinking where they would find the money to do the wedding so soon. And obviously everyone understood that.

Prastan said, "Mr. and Mrs. Scott, the only thing that we need from you guys is your okay and your blessing for them. We will take care of everything. You guys don't have to worry about anything. The wedding will be held at this house and from here the bride and groom will go straight to their own home. This is our desire."

Scott said, "Son, thank you so much. Honestly, we are not in a financial position right now. We have learned that angels are in heaven but we are seeing angels in front of us."

Jannet clapped her hands and said, "Okay, so this is confirmed. My brother, Joe will get married to Sherry on the first Sunday of next month."

Jannet gave Joe the ring she had bought for Sherry. Joe took the ring and placed it on her finger.

Everyone clapped their hands and in one voice they shouted, "Yeah, yeah."

They having a wonderful time among themselves, Stella said, "I'm so happy. I wish we could stay a little longer, but we must leave now. Sherry's father cannot stay up too late."

Sherry said, I'll see you guys tomorrow." This she said and gave everyone a hug."

On their way home Scott said, "Joe, I am giving you my only daughter. She is the only one we have. Please son, take good care of her."

Joe answered, "I promise, I will take good care of Sherry, and we will try to live a life like Prastan and Jannet. We will try to follow their footsteps."

Stella said, "I am very glad to hear that, son." They reached home.

Joe said, "I'll see you tomorrow, Sherry. I desperately need some sleep." This he said and gave her a hug. When he finally reached home everyone was already in bed.

The next day Jannet had informed everyone about the wedding, and hence she started to make preparations. Angie was so happy about the good news. She hugged Charles. Oh, Charles, isn't that so nice. Sherry is finally getting married to Joe."

Charles said, "I'm very much happy for them. They loved each other."

Angie said inwardly, *Now that she is going to get*

married. I don't have to worry about her trying to flirt with Prastan anymore. Yes, yes.

Peter said, "Guys, I have something to say."

Paul and Rick in one voice asked, "What is it Peter?"

Peter said, "Last week Prastan lent Charles and Angie money to buy their dream home. The first Sunday in next month Sherry and Joe will get married and will move over in the house that Prastan gave them."

Rick added, "That's true."

Paul said, "Make your point."

Peter said, "My point here, if I'm not wrong. When Mark gets married what will happen?"

Rick said, "I'm a bit lost here. What do you mean, Peter?"

Paul said, "Me too. I didn't get you point, Peter."

Peter said, "When Mark gets married I have a strong feeling that he will take over this house from Mr. and Mrs. James, hence, Mr. and Mrs. James will be staying permanently with Prastan and Jannet and when they do decide to sell their house they will sell it to someone close to them."

Paul said, "That make some kind of sense."

Rick added, "You are right. I have never thought of that."

Paul asked, "So what do you have in mind, Peter?"

Peter said, "After the wedding. I suggest that we should take a loan from Prastan and Jannet and buy our own house, just as Charles and Angie did."

Rick asked, "You think they will help us, Peter?"

Peter said, "The very first day we met we became friends, remember? They are very nice people, and I think that they love us too. They will help us. I don't think they will turn us down."

Rick said, "Okay, we will give it a shot."

Paul added, "Hey man, nothing but a try. It wouldn't hurt us to make a try."

Peter confirmed, "Okay, we settled at this."

Paul and Rick said, "Okay, let see what happen."

On Saturday morning the day before the wedding Prastan called Charles, "Hello, Charles."

Charles answered, "Hello, Prastan."

Prastan said, "Well, you know what, make sure Sunday morning you guys be over here early to help us do something."

Charles replied, "You count on that, Prastan."

Prastan said, "Oh one more thing. Don't forget Mike is coming over tomorrow morning and make sure you guys pick him first before coming over here."

Charles said, "Okay, Prastan."

Sunday morning the day of the wedding. It was slightly warm, calm, and pleasant, with blue skies and a few clouds floating slowly above here and there. The mansion was well decorated. Many cars parked on both sides on the street and in front of the house as well. Jannet and Prastan stood outside welcoming everyone. Bank manager Jim and Jessica, police inspector Roberts, custom inspector Tony and realtor Henry arrived. Peter, Paul, and Rick came in a few minutes later. Mr. and Mrs. Martin walked in slowly just behind them."

Martin said, "Hey Mark, would you please park my car somewhere."

Mark said, "No problem Mr. Martin. It's been a long time."

Martin said, "I know Mark, I know."

Charles, Angie, and Mike finally arrived.

Prastan said, "Well, look who we got here, Jannet. Glad to see you, Mike."

Jannet said, "Hello Mike, I glad you could make it." They welcomed him with a warm hug.

Mike said, "You guys really have a mansion; this place is very beautiful."

Angie said, "I told you dad, you are wasting your time over there. Prastan and Jannet lent us money and we bought our own house."

Mike said, "But you never told me this."

Charles said, "Actually, dad, she wanted to give you a surprise. You can stay with us, dad. Why don't we sell out everything we own over there and start a new life here?"

Mike said, "Maybe you are right, son."

Frankie and George had finally arrived. Dr. Nick came in a few minutes later.

The wedding went very well. Everyone was drinking, eating, and enjoying themselves. When the wedding finished the bride and groom drove away in their car to their own home.

Jannet clapped her hands "I'm so happy for my brother, Joe." She turned around and looked at Mark."

Mark said, "Oh, no, don't look at me like that." Everyone laughed.

Jessica mentioned, "I have a nice friend, Jannet. I think she is the perfect girl for him."

Prastan said, "Really, Jessica. Well, if you said she is perfect, I believe you."

Jannet urged, "Let me get to know her, Jessica."

Prastan urged, "Bring her over Saturday."

Jessica said, "Okay, I will."

On the following Monday at work Jessica showed Peter the picture of the girl that she had mentioned to Jannet and Prastan.

Peter said, "She is a pretty girl."

Jessica replied, "Actually, she's my cousin. I only hope things work out well." She then kissed the picture.

Peter said, "I didn't follow you. What do you mean?"

Jessica replied, "I only hope that they like each other."

Peter asked, "Who are you referring to?"

She smiled, "I am referring to Mark."

Peter said, "Mark, you mean our, Mark."

Jessica said, "Yes, our Mark."

Peter said, "I think Mark will like her; he'll go crazy for her." He then picked up the phone and called Rick and gave him the news. Rick shared the good news with everyone. Joe was extremely happy for his friend. Sherry picked up the phone and called Angie at the car dealer's office and shared the good news. Angie glanced at Charles and smiled. Charles was busy negotiating a price for a car with a customer. He whispered, "Must be something good." She then shared the good news with him. Charles picked up the phone and called Paul at the other office and shared the good news. Paul momentarily glanced at Mark and smiled. Mark noticed him and was very curious about his strange behavior and decided to pay him secret attention. Paul, however, was unable to hold it for too long and revealed it to him. Joe called his sister, Jannet at home and shared the spreading news.

Jannet said, "Don't tell me it circulated all over already."

Joe said, "You bet."

Jannet shared the news with Prastan and her mom and dad.

Friday morning Jannet had invited everyone over on Saturday night, and she reminded Jessica to bring the girl over. She also asked Sherry and Joe to make it early to help her with some preparations.

Saturday night everyone gathered together drinking, eating and having a wonderful time.

Prastan asked, "So what do you think about Allgreen, Mike?"

Mike replied, "It's beautiful, it's a perfect place to start a beautiful life."

Jannet urged, "So what are you waiting for?"

Sherry said, "Dad has decided to live with us. He's going back next week to sell his property as well as ours."

Prastan said, "Very good, Mike. You have made the perfect decision, and if you are bored and decide to work, I think Jannet will find the best job for you in this company."

Mike asked, "What job do you think I can do, Jannet?"

Jannet replied, "You can be our company driver."

Mike said, "That will be nice for me, that's perfect."

Jannet said, "Look who are coming, Jim and Jessica. And who's that girl with them, Prastan? Oh she's pretty"

Mark said, "I don't know; since when has my sister became so pretentive?" And he took a quick glanced at the girl and smiled inwardly in appreciation, and inwardly murmured, *she is pretty.* He then looked at Prastan.

Prastan said, "Don't look at me; I knew nothing about this; take me out of this." He placed both hands on his chest pretentively as well.

Mark said, "Yeah, right."

Jannet asked, "What are you talking about?"

Mark smiled, "I heard last week when you and Jessica were talking."

Jannet hugged him, "I got married, Joe got married,

and now it's your turn. Everyone as I said has their partner out there. You remember when I first met Prastan when Joe fell from the tree top."

Prastan said, "Because he was trying to be sneaky."

Joe said, "No, I did not"

Mark said, "I warned him to close his eyes and be quiet, but no, he wanted to be sneaky."

Joe said, "And so what?"

Mark said, " And so you fell down." Everyone laughed.

Deecia said, "I remembered that day you told me you went at a friend but instead you were under a tree." She smiled and then continued, "My sneaky daughter

Jannet said, "Stop it mom." She blushed and hugged Prastan.

Jessica introduced her cousin Dazy to everyone.

Dazy said, "He's the Mark?"

Jannet confirmed, "Yes, he is. He's my brother."

Dazy said, "Oh Jannet, I heard many good things about you and Prastan, about the company and about your parents." She turned at Jessica, "Indeed she is pretty." She then turned at Jannet, "Jannet you are the prettiest girl I have ever seen and your husband is so handsome and cute."

Jessica said, "I told you." She felt confident of herself.

Jannet asked, "So what do you think of him, Dazy?"

Dazy said, "Well, I don't know if he likes me; he's okay; I like him."

Jessica asked, "So what do you think, Mark?"

Mark said, "Yes, I like her."

Prastan and Jannet in one voice said, "Okay, we will take it from here."

Prastan said, "Okay guys, it seems everything worked out very well, so let us all celebrate happy moment. Let us all take this toast in the name of Mark and Dazy and wish them good luck and to speed up." Everyone toasted, "Yeah"

Mark asked, "And what do you mean by speed up?"

Prastan said, "Did I said tha?."

Mark said, "Yeah right, as if I knew you yesterday." Everyone laughed again.

During this auspicious occasion Peter had encouraged Paul and Rick for them to go and have a private talk with Prastan and Jannet regarding the discussion they had earlier. Peter called Prastan and Jannet to a corner along with Rick and Paul. Peter had spoken for everyone. Prastan and Jannet clapped them on their shoulders. Prastan said, "We will never forget you guys; when we needed help you guys were there for us and were our friends. And we will be friends forever and we will love each other forever, but to be honest with you guys, Jannet and I had this in mind." He hesitated for a few seconds "Okay, Jannet give them $6,000.00 each so that they can buy their own house and arrange for a work and pay plan with them." Peter, Paul, and Rick hugged Prastan and Jannet. Jannet asked for an excuse and went in her room and cut three checks. She returned and gave them the checks and wished them good luck. Prastan and Jannet considered the party a success.

On the following Monday Prastan called Henry his realtor friend, "Hello Henry."

Henry said, "Well, hello my dear friend, nice hearing from you. So what's up?"

Prastan said, "You tell me, man." He hesitated for a few seconds. "I need your help."

Henry urged, "Say it my friend."

Prastan said, "I want you to find three houses for me."

Henry said, "I have already sold you a mansion. What are you going to do with three houses now? I know that you have money and you can afford it. But are you nuts? Sorry to say that, my friend."

Prastan laughed, "It's not for me."

Henry asked, "For who then?"

Prastan said, "For Peter, Paul, and Rick. Do you remember them?"

Henry said, "Of course, I do. They are nice guys, but they have money? Sorry wrong question. How soon they need it?"

Prastan said, "As soon as you can find it."

Henry asked, "They were renting your in-laws' house. Am I right? Is there any problem?"

Prastan said, "Absolutely not. Mark will get married soon and we have decided to give him that house."

Henry said, "Now I get it now we are on the same page. Okay, my good friend, considered it done."

Prastan said, "See you later."

Friday morning Henry called Peter, Paul, and Rick and arranged to pick them up on Saturday morning to show them a few houses. On Saturday morning he picked them up. Peter sat in the front seat beside him and Paul and Rick sat in the rear seat.

Henry said, "So finally you guys have decided to buy your own house. That is very good. I am proud of you guys. So how much money you guys have decided to spend?"

Peter answered, "We have six thousand each and this six thousand must cover all closing costs."

Henry said, " Okay, so I know exactly what I am looking for."

Rick added, "That's right, we bite what we can chew."

Henry replied, "You are absolutely right, Rick. I saw many situations where people hang their hat too high and then having difficulty reaching it."

Paul said, "Well, Henry, we don't want something like that to happen to us."

Henry answered, "I agreed with you Paul, but you guys are good; it takes people with potential to save six thousand dollars within this short period of time."

Peter said, "We can't save that much, Henry. That is impossible. Prastan and Jannet lend us this money, and we will work and pay them with no interest."

Rick and Paul in one voice said, "Where we can find friends like them?"

Henry answered, "Of course, you can."

Peter asked, "You tell me where, Henry?"

Henry replied, "In heaven."

Rick said, "You can say that again, my dear friend."

Paul mentioned, "He also gave Charles six thousands to buy his house and work and pay as well."

Henry said, "Let us all considered ourselves lucky, probably, we are also godsend people."

Paul asked, "We are godsend people? Oh no! Godsend,people for what?"

Henry answered, "To have friends like Prastan and Jannet."

Peter laughed, "You can say that again, my friend."

Rick asked, "Henry, how much is your fee to find us a house?"

Henry replied, "If Prastan and Jannet are my friends and you guys are Prastan and Jannet friends then all of us are friends. What will it profit me to charge friends a fee? That money will finish one day. I don't want our friendship to finish one day; I want it to remain forever. So there is no such word as fee among us."

Rick said, "You are a good friend, Henry. All evil things and good things that men had done will live after them."

Henry asked, "Where did you learn that from?"

Peter answered, "We have learned so many good things from Prastan and Jannet."

Paul said, "We are trying to follow their footsteps as well."

Henry said, "So am I. I've learned a lot from them too. You see how many friends that guy has, and what kind of friends. We need people like him in this world. Let us continue to worship our friendship until our last day."

Within a week Henry found their dream home and with the help of everyone they were able to move over the following weekend.

On the following Monday Jannet called Jessica at the office and arranged a date for the wedding. She made it for the first week in the following month. Jessica discussed the date with Dazy's parents and later confirmed the date as a yes with Jannet. Everyone was now preparing for the upcoming wedding in the next few weeks.

Mike said, "I only hope I can sell my property before the wedding."

Angie said, "I don't think that that should be a problem, dad. I don't know if you can recall, dad, our neighbor—the guy across the street opposite us—told you that he was interested in a business like that. He also mentioned that any time you interested in selling the business you must give him the first opportunity. Do you remember, dad?"

Mike said, "Oh yes, yes, I can recalled that. That was a long time ago."

Charles sat in a chair in the living room and mentioned, "I knew that the housing market value fell dramatically, I will give you power of attorney—whatsoever price you can get for my house, don't hesitate to sell it; at least we can boost our payment for this house with the money"

Angie said, " That true. I had never thought of that."

Mike said, "Since I will be staying with you guys, you can use my money and reduce your debt. I don't need the money; I need the two of you. After the death of my wife, all my life I am working for my daughter. Who else do I have besides the two of you?"

Angie said, "Oh, dad." This she said and gave him a tight hug.

The following weekend Mike went over, and he was so fortunate; he sold both properties in the first week and returned back to Allgreen

The weekend prior to the wedding Jannet had made arrangement and gotten everyone to clean her mom's house. While cleaning, Jannet went in her room and called, "Dazy, Dazy."

Prastan laughed and said, "Oh no." and glanced at Mark and Joe.

Jannet said, "Shut up, Prastan."

Joe teased, "Girl, Dazy, this was my room."

Sherry said, "Shut up, Joe. That's a girl thing." And she punched him slightly on his right arm with her right fist.

Dazy asked, "So, this is your parent's house?"

Jannet replied, "Not anymore."

Dazy asked, "What do you mean, Jannet, not anymore?"

Mr. and Mrs. James said in one voice, "Because it belongs now to Mark and you."

Jannet said, "I have six brothers, Mark, Joe, Charles, Peter, Paul, and Rick and I am happy that everyone have their own house, their own car, they got their job and they will work, eat and live a happy life. Oh boy, I'm so happy for everyone." And after a moment of hesitation, she said, "Dazy, this was my room."

Prastan teased, "And on this wall, I used to—"

Jannet covered his mouth with her hand and said, "Oh shut up, Prastan." Everyone laughed

James said, "Well, since we have finished the cleaning, let's make a move."

Jessica said, "Dazy, you see what I was talking about. They have heart of gold."

Dazy added, "Indeed they do."

Jessica said, "Well, as from next week all the cleaning will be yours, sweetheart."

The wedding day had finally arrived.

The morning was pleasant, with clear blue skies and a few floating clouds here and there. The wind blew slightly. The bright sun rose slowly leaving the earth beneath and warmed the atmosphere with its sparkling glare.

Sherry, Angie, and Charles decorated inside the house with beautiful different colors of ribbons, balloons, flowers etc. Peter, Paul, and Rick placed tables, chairs, and benches here and there. Jannet and Jessica were in the master bedroom with Dazy fixing her hair and her wedding dress and, preparing her for the ceremony.

Jannet whispered, "Girl, you look pretty and charming. I think you'll give my brother a run for the moon."

Dazy smiled blushingly.

Prastan was in another room with Mark preparing him for his big day. He whispered, "Boy, you look good. I think you'll give her a run for the stars."

Mark said, "You're not serious."

Prastan said, "At this moment, I am dead serious."

Inspector Roberts came in. He waved his right hand to everyone. And with the respect for a police inspector, everyone waved back at him. He then asked, "Where can I find Prastan in this damn huge house." Prastan heard him and called, "I'm here in this room, Roberts."

Roberts said, "Too many rooms in this house. You probably have a tough time finding Jannet."

Prastan answered, "Not really, she find me."

Jannet shouted from the inside of another room "Yeah, right."

Roberts asked, "Is there anything I can help with, besides, handcuffing anyone."

Prastan laughed, "Well, since you insisted on helping. I need two persons to go and pick up the liquor and beer."

Roberts said, "Piece a cake if I can find someone to go with me." He looked around and noticed Bank Manager Jim doing nothing. He called, "Hey Jim, if you're in the middle of doing nothing, can you go with me to the liquor store?"

Jim answered with a smile, "Sure, isn't it too early to drink?"

Roberts said with a smile in his face, "I think that you hang out very often with Mark and Joe." And after they laughed together, he shouted, "What to buy, Prastan?"

Prastan said, "Enough beer and liquor. Just mention my name."

Jim smiled and asked, "How much is enough?"

Prastan shouted, "You guys do the math."

Jannet glanced at Jessica and said, "Police inspector is going to the liquor store. Oh boy, he will scare the hell out of those guys in the store."

Jessica said, "And my husband, he wouldn't drink today."

Jannet asked, "But why?"

Jessica said, "Because he will see all that liquor in the store and get drunk."

As they headed out the door Roberts said, "Hey Joe, if you're in the middle standing up doing nothing, you can go with us to the liquor store." Meanwhile, Jannet called Joe on his cell phone, "Joe, I don't think Roberts and Jim will know what to buy."

Joe said, "Okay I'll go with them." He then turned off

the phone and said, "Sure, let's go with the SUV, it's a lot of stuff you guys are talking about."

Roberts said, "You see what I mean, Jim, Joe is the right person for this mission."

Joe parked the SUV in front of the liquor store. Roberts came out and walked slowly towards the store followed by Jim. One employee glanced at the cashier, he said, "We're in trouble. We're not supposed to open this early; maybe he's going to give us a ticket. Damnit"

The cashier said, "I see no police car. Where the hell did he come from?"

His employee replied, "He came out from that SUV."

The cashier said, "Well, if he came out from the SUV, you don't have to worry.

That's Prastan's SUV, and that's Joe with them, so don't worry about anything."

Employee asked, "Who is Prastan?"

The cashier replied, "He's the owner of Sunshine Farm and all the car dealerships in Allgreen."

The employee said, "Oh, that guy, people talk good about him. And I heard he's a very simple person. If all rich people would have taken his footsteps this world would have been better place."

Inspector said, "Hello gentlemen, and don't be scared. I'm with Joe, and I'm a friend of Prastan."

The cashier replied, "Morning sir. Hello Joe, how are you this morning. How is Mark?"

Joe mentioned, "Mark is getting married today."

The cashier said, "That's so sweet. Help yourself, Joe and give everyone my regards."

Joe said, "You bet, I'll do that."

They filled the SUV with beer and liquor.

Joe said, "I'll see you guys later."

The cashier smiled and said, "You take care, Joe, take care guys."

On their way home Jim mentioned, "I think we bought too much liquor and beer."

Joe said, "Even if so, it doesn't matter anyway. Every weekend we hang out together, so, we will make good use of it."

Roberts said, "You're right. I think I have to check you guys out more often."

Jim said, "I will also put a thought on that."

When they reached home Peter, Paul, Rick, and Charles help unload the beers and liquor and placed it all near the pool. Shortly after the ceremony had commenced, the priest announced, "And now I pronounce you as husband and wife. You may now kiss the bride." Everyone shouted at the top of their voices and clapped hands. Joe kissed Sherry.

Sherry asked, "What's the matter with you. He told Mark to kiss the bride not Joe to kiss, Sherry. Damn you," wiping her lips.

Jannet said, "Give him a break, girl, my brother seems overjoyed today," and once again everyone started to laugh, everyone drinking, eating, and enjoying themselves. Mark and Dazy went and hugged Prastan and Jannet and said, "Thank you guys for everything."

Jannet had noticed in Mark eyes and foretold that something was bothering him. She asked, "What is it, Mark? Spit it out."

Mark asked, "Do we have to go now?"

Prastan said, "No, you stay here—drink eat and enjoy yourselves, and when you feel like going, then you go."

Roberts said, "And you don't have to worry about drinking. Today is your day; I'll follow you home."

Prastan added, "As a matter of fact, we will follow you home." They continued the celebration until dark.

Jannet said, "Okay, it's time for us to follow you home, brother."

Prastan and Jannet are indeed a godsend couple on the surface of planet earth. Their businesses are growing and all their employees are happy. They worked very honest and faithful for them.

Though Sherry had promised herself to avoid the burning love she had in her for Prastan, she was still unsure of her promise and admired him now and again.

Though Angie had promised herself to forget the love that she had in her for Prastan, deep inside she still loved him and would not hesitate to grab any opportunity that came along.

Mark and Joe, though they are now living separately, they still spent most of the weekend with Prastan and Jannet.

Peter, Paul, Rick, Angie, and Charles visited now and again.

CHAPTER FIVE

ONE morning Jannet woke up from her bed with a slight headache. She placed her hands on her head.

Prastan asked, "Is everything okay, Jannet?"

She replied, "Yeah."

Prastan asked, "Do you have a headache"

She replied, "Yeah, but it's very slight."

Prastan asked curiously, "Have you slept well?"

Though Jannet had slept well, to avoid Prastan from asking her many questions, she said, "No. I did not."

Prastan said, "Well, that's the problem. If you don't sleep well, you may have a headache. I have to go to the farm's office this morning."

Jannet asked, "Why?"

Prastan said, "Joe and I will visit the farm. I haven't visit the farm for a long time. At least Frankie and George will be glad to see me visit, and at the same time, they may show me some of their progress they may have made."

Jannet wanted to visit Doctor Nick for the headache she had and had no intention to go with Prastan at the farm. She knew that if she asked Prastan to go with him, he would definitely deny her because of the headache. She said, "Oh yes, I would like to see Frankie and George's progress."

Prastan said, "Excuse me. You'd better stay home and

rest that headache you're having; maybe some other day when you feel better."

Jannet smiled inwardly and said, "Thank you." She then lied, "But, I want to go with you."

Prastan said, "Sorry, sweetheart."

After having breakfast together Prastan went to the office. Jannet made her visit to Doctor Nick's office. She approached the young receptionist at her desk. The receptionist thought, "My God, she's so pretty." She then asked, "How may I help you?"

Jannet said, "Hi, good morning. I am here to see Doctor Nick."

The receptionist asked, "Do you have an appointment?"

Jannet said, "No, but would you tell him that Jannet is here to see him."

She then went and formed the line at the back.

The receptionist said, "Sure, I will." She went in the doctor's room and said, "Excuse me Doctor, someone by the name of Jannet is here to see you."

Doctor said, "Ask her to fill out the form."

The receptionist said, "Okay." As she turned around she murmured, "She's so pretty."

Doctor said, "Excuse me, you said, pretty?"

The receptionist said, "Like an angel."

Doctor said, "That is our Jannet, bring her in."

The receptionist asked, "You know her?"

Doctor said, "She's the owner of Sunshine Farm and

all the car dealerships in Allgreen. You should have seen her husband, girls still crushing on him."

The receptionist murmured, "Must be real charming." She walked out of the room and said, "Jannet, Doctor said you may go in."

Jannet went in the room slowly, "Morning, Nick."

Nick said, "Well, nice to see you, Jannet. How is Prastan?

She said, "He's okay. He's going to the farm this morning."

Nick asked, "And how are the boys, I mean, Mark and Joe?"

She said, "They are doing just fine, you know as usual, they never change."

Nick asked, "Well, how may I help you this morning, Jannet?

After a deep breath, she said, "I woke up this morning with a headache."

Nick asked, "Ever happened before?"

Jannet said, "No, it's the first time."

Nick said, "Okay, we'll figure it out."

Doctor ran a few tests on her and finally came out with a wonderful result. He said, "You don't have to worry, Jannet, you are perfect, but I have a wonderful news for you."

Jannet asked, "What is it, Nick?"

Nick said, "Congratulation, Jannet, you're three months pregnant."

She was so happy and excited, she said, "Believe me, Nick, he'll go crazy but don't tell him. I want this secret to be confidential among mom, dad, you, and I. Next week we will celebrate our wedding's anniversary at the beach, and we will invite all employees. I hope to see you there."

Nick asked, "Will you announce it openly?"

Jannet said, "No, I will tell him, and I will ask him not to tell anyone about it, because, news spreads very fast." They laughed.

Nick said, "You can count on it, Jannet, I will be there, and I won't let this secret out."

Jannet said, "Okay, see you then."

She returned home smiling. Her mom and dad noticed her and momentarily glanced at each other.

Jannet said, "Mom, dad, I have something to tell you all."

Her mom said, "Come sit here, dear; come sit here next to me. Now, tell me everything." She was expecting to hear some stories from her.

Jannet asked, "Everything like what, mom?"

Mom said, "I mean, everything you have to say or anything you wanted to say."

Jannet said, "Oh." After a moment of hesitation, she continued, "Mom, dad, next week Saturday will be our wedding anniversary."

Dad said, "That's the good news, damn, I was expecting to hear something else."

Jannet asked, "Something else like what, dad?"

Dad said, "You know." Fanning his right hand, he then continued, "Like something else; like some other story."

Jannet clapped her hands, she said, "Mom, dad, I will tell you all a secret, and I want you all to promise me not to tell."

Dad said, "Now you're getting to the point."

Jannet asked, "What point?"

Mom said, "Oh give her a break. Go ahead, dear, don't listen to him. He's nosy."

Dad said, "No, I'm not. Go ahead sweetheart, I'll zip my lips."

Jannet said, "This morning I woke up with a slight headache."

Dad said, "That's it, that's the secret, a slight headache."

Mom said, "Would you please be quiet for a moment? She wants to say something."

Jannet said, "This morning when I woke up with this slight headache, I went and saw Nick. And guess what?"

Mom asked, "What?"

Dad said, "He gave you a prescription to get headache pills."

Jannet said, "No."

Mom asked, "Then what, dear?" She knew exactly what she was getting at but pretended not to.

Jannet said, "Oh mom, oh dad, I'm pregnant."

Her mom hugged her and said, "Oh dear, I am so happy for you I can't wait to see my grandchild."

Dad said, "Me too, I can't wait to hold and play with my grandchild."

Mom said, "Should be around three."

Jannet asked, "How do you know, mom?"

Mom said, "We gave you life, dear. When you were a baby and couldn't speak, we looked at you and knew exactly what you wanted."

Jannet said, "We don't know whether it's a boy or a girl."

Dad said, "It doesn't matter once we have a grandchild."

Jannet said, "Well, only four of us knew, and let it be a secret. Saturday we will be celebrating our wedding anniversary at the beach. I want to give Prastan a surprise. I will tell him at the beach when the moment is appropriate. By the way, where is he? He didn't return from the farm yet." She looked around and called, "Prastan, Prastan."

Deecia glanced at James, "They are born for each other. He's only out of her sight for a moment, and she's searching for him."

James said, "God blessed our children. What more can we asked for?"

Jannet stamped her feet and said, "Oh no."

Deecia once again glanced at James and said, "You see that, she missed him."

James asked, "What's the matter, Jannet? Come sit near me."

Jannet went near him.

James said, "Don't lie to me, dear. You missed him."

She blushed and said "I missed him, dad."

James said, "I knew dear, but come on; it's only two hours, and you missed him."

She rested her head on her dad's lap and said, "We are part of each other, and he's within me."

Deecia said, "We knew that, dear. And that's all we are asking God for."

Momentarily Prastan reached home sweaty, hot, and tired. Jannet noticed his tiredness and quickly fetched him a glass of orange juice. She said, "Prastan, you are tired."

He took a sip and said, "Well it seems like Joe and Sherry are doing just fine. Frankie and George are doing a wonderful job as well. The farm is in excellent condition."

Jannet said, "That is good news."

He took another sip and said, "We are making money, and our employees are working very hard and honest for us, as they had promised us. We will increase their paycheck; we will give them a ten percent increase starting next week. What do you think, Jannet?"

Jannet said, "Anything you say, Prastan." She hugged him and said, "Prastan, Saturday will be our wedding's anniversary. Let us celebrate it at the beach. What do you think?"

Prastan said, "Anything you say, Jannet. If it's good for you, it's good for me."

Jannet said, "You can give them the good news at the beach."

Prastan said, "You are wrong, Jannet." After a few seconds he continued, "Let me rephrase what you have just said: 'We will give them the good news.' I think that sounds better."

James said, "That means you have to invite all employees. Am I right?"

Prastan said, "Yes, you are right, and to be honest with you all, I see no difference between them and us; we are all human beings. In the eyes of the Lord he sees us as one. We all have to go back to him one day, and we have to explain to him everything that we have done on earth. At one time in life we were in their shoes; we are prosperous all because of them; they will feel happy celebrating with us; they will feel like they are part of the family, and they will work like the company belong to them."

Jannet hugged him, "Oh, Prastan."

James and Deecia in one voice said, "We are proud of you my son; keep up the good work."

After a moment of relaxation, Jannet called Joe at his office. Joe picked up the phone. "Hello, Jannet. How are you?"

Jannet answered, "I am fine, Joe."

Joe asked, "So what's new? How is everyone?"

Jannet answered, "Everyone is okay, Joe. We will be throwing a party this Saturday at Allgreen's beach; it's our wedding's anniversary. Have you forgotton?"

Sherry stopped her task and was focusing on Joe's conversation.

Joe said, "Come on Jannet, it's impossible for Mark and me to forget your anniversary."

Sherry covered her mouth with both hands and whispered, "It's their anniversary."

Jannet said, "I want you to invite everyone."

Joe asked, "Everyone like who, Jannet?"

Jannet said, "I mean everyone receiving a paycheck from us."

Joe said, "I got you, and that is Saturday at our beach."

Jannet laughed and said, "Yes, Joe.." After the conversation she went and sat beside Prastan. Prastan tapped her with his left hand on her right lap. She smiled at him and asked, "What? What Prastan?"

Prastan said, "When will you inform the rest?"

Jannet said, "I don't have to do that."

Prastan looked at her and leaned back, and before he could say a word the phone rang.

Jannet said, "You see what I mean?"

Prastan glanced at her and then picked up the phone, "Hello."

"Hi Prastan, it's me Angie. What time will it be?"

Prastan said, "Around 10:00 A.M., but we will be there earlier to prepare."

Angie said, "Okay, we will come and help out with the preparation."

A few minutes later, Jessica and Dazy called respectively and offered to help out with the preparation as well.

Prastan glanced at Jannet and smiled, "You're right. You don't have to do that."

Jannet and Prastan woke up early on Saturday morning. After a shower, they went in the kitchen and were surprised to see that mom and dad had already prepared breakfast for everyone. Prastan and Jannet took their cups of coffee and went by the pool. They drew the curtain and slid open the door. They were greeted with their second surprise for the morning when they saw everyone such as Mark, Dazy, Joe, Sherry, Charles, Angie, Mike, Peter, Paul, Rick, and Jessica. And everyone in one voice shouted, "Happy anniversary."

In spite of a few floating clouds above, the morning seemed pleasant and favorable. It was quiet except of the singing of birds.

Prastan said, "Well, let's rock and roll. What you guys waiting for?" They gathered all necessities and drove to the beach.

Charles and Angie set up the grill, Peter, Paul, and Rick set up the canopy; Mark, Dazy, Joe, and Sherry set up a few chairs and tables while Mike set up the beach bar.

Prastan stood all by himself as he gazed the river and far across to the horizon. He recalled his past when he was twelve years old; when his parents got carried away by the huge and dynamic wave; when he ran back and forth on the shore shouting for help and no one was there to save his parents from drowning. He also recalled when he walked out of Jannet's life and had to cross this river; he remembered that Peter, Paul, and Rick had rescued him; not forgetting Mike, who gave him a job to survive. He remembered he knotted his fate and left it in the hands of the Lord. And the great Lord showed him his miracle. Today, everyone the Lord inspired to help him was around him. His tears flowed down his cheeks while he uttered a few words to the Lord.

Mark and Joe went near Jannet; the three of them looked at him and shook their heads. They approached him from behind; the rest of the crew had noticed and followed as well. They knew what he was thinking and all stood behind him while he was uttering thanks to the great Lord, he said, "Oh Lord; I want to thank you for everything; thank you for the mercy you have shown me; without you, I am just a corpse; oh Lord; I had knotted my fate and left it in your hands. Please inspire me what to do Lord; the same way in which you inspired everyone to help me and came into my life. Lord, I want nothing in this beautiful world except to help people. Lord, I knew one day I would come to you. I don't want to answer any questions." When he turned around he saw everyone behind him. Jannet dried his tears and said, "Truly, he's out there and he's looking at us from all directions." She cheered him up with a kiss. "Come on, it's our wedding's anniversary."

In less than an hour all employees had arrived; including Mr. And Mrs. Martin, Dr. Nick, Inspector Roberts, Jim and, of course, Tony.

James said, "Prastan, I suggested that you guys should give the employees the good news before the party begins. In this way they will be happy since they have never expected an increase in salary."

Jannet said, "Dad has a point, Prastan."

Prastan said, "Okay, let's do it." He called everyone's attention. Everybody gathered together. He continued, "My dear loving people. Today is a very special day for us; I mean, for all of us. Today, I am going to share this exciting moment with you all; I am going to share our wedding's anniversary with you all. I am going to give everyone an increase in their paycheck starting next week."

Everyone shouted, "Yeah, yeah."

Jannet said, "We will give you guys a ten percent increase in your paycheck."

Everyone shouted almost on top of their voices, "Thank you Prastan, thank you Jannet."

Prastan continued, "And I am going to share with you guys as well, exactly, what is in my heart."

Everyone braced back and couldn't take their eyes off

of him. He continued, "My dear loving people, I came from nowhere, but I'm positively sure I knew exactly where I would be going" This he said and pointed his right hand up. "God took away my parents from me when I was twelve, but he gave me my loving Jannet, my loving in-laws, my loving friends, and all of you. I want to share my love with you all. I want to share my life. Let us not forget that we won't be here forever; we came and we have to go some day. You are the people who own my company; without you, we have no company. Don't let this company down; you all depend on this company for your daily bread, and to survive, likewise us. Just close your eyes and imagine that you are out of a job; what will happen to your family?"

Everyone murmured, "That's true, that's true."

Jannet hugged him. She shouted, "Let's celebrate our anniversary, lets the party begin."

Everyone was enjoying themselves—drinking, eating, laughing, and having lots of fun.

It was almost noon when Jannet had decided to break her silence to Prastan regarding her pregnancy. They held each other tightly on each other's arms, she walked him a little distance away from everyone. At the same time most of the employees were looking at them admiring a wonderful couple.

Since everybody was busy, Sherry took the opportunity

and was admiring Prastan and Jannet and imagining herself in Prastan's arms.

Angie said, "Charles."

Charles asked, "What, Angie?"

Angie said, "Look at Prastan and Jannet; they look so cute. Would you like to go for a stroll as well?"

Charles said, "Sounds good to me; it will help digest my food."

While walking Angie momentary saw herself in Prastan's arms.

Angie and Sherry though they had love and respect for Prastan and Jannet, they were uncertain whether they could live up to their promises and see themselves as Jannet. Jannet knew that Angie and Sherry no matter what, they will continue admiring him. She promised herself to be careful, and to avoid something like this to ever occur.

Prastan asked, "What's the matter, Jannet? Is everything okay?"

Jannet said, "Yes, I have a little surprise for you."

Prastan was anxious to know about the surprise. "What is it, Jannet?"

Dr. Nick, James, and Deeica were looking at them since they were the only one who knew about the secret. They wanted to see how Prastan would react and how excited he would be. Jannet sat on the ground facing the wide river and with her right hand parted her hair in the middle. *Prasjan* was anchored in the river at about a three-foot depth of water in the event anyone would like to take a ride.

Inspector Roberts, bank manager Jim, immigration officer Tony, and realtor Henry joined Dr. Nick, Deecia, and James. Everyone was looking at Prastan and Jannet and wondered why they went a little distance away from everyone. Deecia had no choice but to explain to them that her daughter was pregnant and she was going to break her silence to her husband. Everyone in one voice said, "That is so wonderful. Let's see how Prastan is going to react."

Jannet said, "Look how beautiful she looks."

Prastan asked, "What are you talking about, Jannet?"

Jannet said, "*Prasjan*. At least Peter, Paul, and Rick named the boat after our name Prastan and Jannet."

Prastan said, "Is this the surprise, *Prasjan*? That what you brought me over here to tell me how beautiful *Prasjan* looks. My God, can't you come up with something better than this?"

Jannet said, "Okay, sit, sit here, just in front of me."

Prastan said, "Okay, whatever you said, my Lord."

Jannet said, "I'm not your Lord. I'm your beloved wife. And the Lord made us for each other, and no human can separate us; *only God can separate us.*"

Prastan said, "Jannet, tell me something that I don't know." This he said while on his knees facing her with his lips close to hers.

Jannet said, "Okay, close your eyes," she commanded. With his eyes closed he was wondering about the surprise. She kissed him on his lips and then whispered, "I'm pregnant."

Prastan said, "Really Jannet.." He opened his eyes.

Jannet said, "Yes, Prastan, I'm pregnant." He kissed her and then hugged her.

Prastan asked, "When did you learn this?"

Jannet said, "Do you remember a week ago I had a headache?"

Prastan said, "Yeah, I can recalled that morning when I was going to the farm and you wanted to go with me but you had this headache."

Jannet said, "I only pretended that I wanted to go with you, but actually, I wanted to go and see Dr. Nick because I had a feeling that I was pregnant, but I wasn't sure."

Prastan said, "Damnit, Nick never told me about it."

Jannet said, "It's a secret, Prastan. We have kept it a secret from you. I wanted to give you a surprise, a big surprise."

Prastan said, "So, let us find a name for our baby."

Jannet said, "Okay, lets say if it's a girl, I'll name her, Ekisha."

Prastan said, "Nice name—where did you get that from? I like it, but if it's a boy I'll name him Neil."

Jannet said, "Okay, sounds good." They kissed and

hugged each other again. Prastan stood up pointed his right hand at her and said, "Ekisha." And then turned his right hand on his chest and said, "Neil." He moved backward towards the river looking at her and repeated the name, "Ekisha, Neil; Ekisha, Neil; Ekisha, Neil."

Jannet smiled and laughed at his excitement and whispered, "You are a wonderful husband, Prastan. I love you dearly. You're my life."

Prastan turned around and ran towards the river and never looked back.

Jannet shouted, "Where are you going, Prastan?"

Everyone had noticed Prastan and questioned themselves, "Where is he going?"

Jannet walked slowly towards the river. Mark and Joe quickly approached Jannet and asked her, "What's the matter with him?"

Jannet explained to them that he was excited and the reason for his excitement. Mark and Joe hugged Jannet and said, "Congratulations to both of you." And in one voice, "We can't blame him for his excitement. We are excited ourselves."

Prastan ran in the water and jumped in *Prasjan*. He started it and speed into the deep.

Jannet shouted, "Prastan, come back here; come back here."

Everyone approached Jannet and at the same time all eyes were at Prastan. Moments after, the boat rode over a floating tree and flew up in the air. Prastan wasn't quick enough to hold onto the boat tightly, so he flew off the boat. When he landed in the water his head hit on a branch of the second floating tree. He managed to hold on to the branch. He repeated the name once again "Ekisha, Neil; Ekisha, Neil." then a few seconds later he became unconscious. The water current was strong and pulled him away into the deep. Everyone wanted to know what caused that accident and were crying. They rushed towards the river, but he was too deep in the water; they couldn't reach him. Peter, Paul, and Rick who were once fishermen and were very good swimmers as well swam to the boat but couldn't find him. Tony the dock captain, Mark, and Joe ran to the dock. They jumped in a boat and speed towards the scene. Peter, Paul, and Rick went in *Prasjan* and the two boats were searching for him. By this time Prastan was away into the deep.

Jannet fell down; she became unconscious. Sherry, Angie, Jessica, Dazy, and her parents held on to her. Dr. Nick and her parents then rushed her to the hospital. Inspector Roberts called for a helicopter and joined the search along with George and Frankie. Sherry, Angie, Jessica, Dazy, Jim, and Charles called the party over and were cleaning up.

The search went on until it became dark. The only thing they could see was the light across the river on the other land. Mark and Joe cried bitterly, they said, "Oh Lord, please don't do this; many mouths depended on him for a piece of bread. He's a good man. We all belong to you Lord, but it's too early for you to take him away; everyone needs him. Please, Lord. Take us instead." They raised their heads and looked up at the stars and moon and shouted on top of their voices, "Prastan."

Inspector Roberts had considered the safety for everyone. He had no other choice and called the search off. Everyone cried bitterly for Prastan. They prayed for him to survive.

THE END

TO BE CONTINUED